To Greg Rees, my brilliant dealmaker editor

**I**

A convoy of five jeeps cuts across the desert at blinding speed – a series of five bullets. The vehicles stir the eroded soil and a cloud of dust lifts and lingers, irritating the eyes and nostrils of the men inside. Haji is well used to desert sand, but some of the fighters – youngsters brought up in Europe's wetlands – don't have a clue. They haven't learnt to cover their mouths, so their throats are dry, their voices gravelly and they grind sand between their teeth. They drink gallons of water from plastic bottles recovered from humanitarian relief drops, most of which never reach their intended recipients. The truth of the matter is that the intended recipients are either dead or have long evacuated this area. There is no point letting water go to waste. Water has the value of pure gold in these parts – you don't say no to it when it falls from the sky free of charge. The youngsters waste it; Haji doesn't. It would be a sacrilege. Saving water is in his blood. Besides, the more you drink, the more you need. Haji is like a camel – he can go without water for days. He is ready for when there is no water, and that time will come because this is desert.

The whites of the young men's eyes and teeth flash in their sun-ripened faces as they laugh and make plans for their destiny. They're excited to make war – they see it as an opportunity to earn glory. For Haji, war is an everyday necessity, like water is for them. In war there is no retirement, only death. You live war – you die war. No exceptions. Haji watches the blossoming youth, his hooded eyes narrowed as if he is dazzled by them. Their beards are black, his is laced with dusty grey – the colour of the desert sand. He has sand embedded in the pores of his skin. Back home, in Afghanistan, his brothers used to say Haji was made of sand, for he could disappear into it without a trace. He is even better at it now that he is sixty years of age, grey and musty – an invisible old man.

He tries to catch up on some sleep while his young comrades boast and joke, and issue bloody threats to Assad and the West as the convoy heads for the Iraqi border. What border, Ismail asks cockily, there are no borders. Show me the border, he shouts and waves his machine gun. The boy is twenty-five at the most, and he sounds the same as those British soldiers that Haji has come across in Helmand Province. Others call him *Geordie-Is,* and that is supposed to account for his accent. Something to do with where he comes from, not that it makes any difference here except when Geordie-Is gets to appear in a video to send a message – loud and clear – to the Infidels. He loves that. He can talk for Asia, and he takes credit for everything. He's their PR man. Haji prefers to do his job and disappear into the sand. Loud talk isn't his way, but to everyone his own...

He is dozing off, his chin bouncing on his chest as the jeep jerks and turns on the windy dirt road. His young comrades' voices blend with the hum of the engine. Some of them follow Haji's lead, go quiet and nod off. Like water, sleep is a rare commodity so you're well advised to get it whenever you can.

Without a warning, Haji is thrown off the vehicle and the day turns to night in the thick black capsule of smoke and dust. He didn't hear it coming – he didn't sense it. It was one of those surreptitious drones that hit one of the jeeps in the convoy. The vehicle caught fire, which spread to the others, piled up on top of one another. Haji should consider himself lucky to have been catapulted out of the jeep and to remain alive; others have been crushed inside or torn to shreds on impact. A few bodies have been tossed up in the air and are scattered around. Haji knows they're dead because they lie limp, awkward and bloodied, and aren't wailing in pain, which they would be doing if they were alive.

He can't see much in the black smoke but he hears something – a plaintive voice of a boy, pleading for help, in English. It must belong to Geordie-Is. Haji strains his eyes to discover the young man suspended between the burning jeep and the sandy floor at a strange angle, as if his body is pouring out of the vehicle, flaccid and covered in blood. The extremities are just charred stumps, but Geordie-Is is alive. Haji pulls himself up to his feet, but his left foot can't take his weight – it must be broken or the ankle is twisted. Haji can only limp slowly towards Geordie-Is, which again is lucky because the jeep's petrol tank explodes. A heatwave hits Haji in the face, and he flies back…

His brain leaps back too – back in time, back to the freezing December night of 1979. Haji doesn't want to go there but he has no say in the matter – his brain is fractured and does its own thing. It throws up unwanted memories, and they fit in with the chaos of exploding petrol tanks and flying body parts.

Chaos. Confusion. Betrayal. Annihilation.

President Amin assures them the Soviets are here to help. Only a few hours ago they came for lunch, ate his food, accepted his hospitality. They are his guests. Yes, they have rolled in with heavy artillery and tanks, but the barrels of their tanks are pointed at the rebels – the enemies of the State. Haji believes the President's every word. He has every reason to. The Russians are friends – comrades; they can be trusted. Haji knows that – he's married to one of them. She is the light of his every day. Svetlana.

It is the revolt that has forced the President to hole up in this fortress and bring the Soviets to keep guard. The Shia elderly are stirring trouble, mobilising Mujahedin to take up arms. They stand no chance: Tajbek is a fortress manned with well-trained personnel and the Soviet army guarding it on the outside. The revolt will subside. Sooner rather than later, Haji hopes. He'd rather be with Svetlana.

The night is damned cold. He's manning a machine gun, but his fingers are numb and would struggle with pulling the trigger. It won't come to it. It will all blow over. He cups his hands and exhales warm air at them. The moisture in his breath turns into white mist. All is quiet until a mine goes off in the distance. They have mined the access road to the palace - the enemy is on the move. They wouldn't dare unless they have a death wish. An outburst of gun shots contradicts him. It is a full blown offensive. His duty is to protect the President.

Chaos. Confusion. Betrayal. Annihilation.

Fighting outside. Shots fired. Series of shots. Explosions. It could be the mines. It could be the tanks firing.

The Mujahedin must have overcome the first line of

defences. Sharp, staccato sounds grow in volume. Screams – starting abruptly and stopping even more suddenly. Footsteps, heavy boots, shots. Afghani soldiers from below are retreating to where Haji is stationed. And further beyond – they are running away.

Chaos. Confusion. Betrayal. Annihilation.

Haji hesitates. He can't use his machine gun because of the retreating soldiers. He would be killing his own. He waits until the last of them – or so he hopes – stumbles by. He sees beams of white light crossing on the stairwell below, and he hears voices. His finger tightens on the trigger. His comrades on both sides are equally ready in position to receive the rebels with a firewall.

There are fewer shots now and more voices. He is beginning to recognise them. They aren't Mujahedin – they are Russians! He can tell by the swearing. The curses that fly around in Russian are of the highest order. Haji exhales and loosens his finger from the trigger of his machine gun. The Russians are coming. They must have dealt with the rebels. He is almost smiling when he finally sees the first helmet with a red star wobble over the entrance. The Russian points his gun and shoots, aiming neatly at the man to Haji's right. Haji drops to the floor and watches as the Soviets pour in, swearing and cursing in Russian to tell their own from the Afghans whom they are killing indiscriminately.

Chaos. Confusion. Betrayal. Annihilation.

Haji knows he is doomed. All of the other men from the Presidential Guard are dead without one shot being fired from their side. He picks up an abandoned gun from the floor and joins the Soviets, shooting into the darkness, storming room after room, swearing heavily in Russian as

well as they do. But his unruly tears argue with his actions –
Haji is weeping for his fallen comrades as he tramples over
their bodies. He must get out of this graveyard before it
swallows him.

**II**

The Winterbournes' flat is a miniature African dollhouse. It is brimming with artefacts: a leopard skin serves as a rug, primitive art made of straw and bamboo sticks adorns the walls, carvings of triumphant elephants with raised trunks are lined up on the windowsill, a native Zulu spear has been propped against a narrow, long shield, and photographs – dozens of framed photographs - occupy every inch of available space. The photographs belong to a different place and a different era, somewhere far away from Bath - somewhere in the heartland of Zimbabwe. There stands a colonial-style farmhouse wrapped in wide verandas, sprawled comfortably in splendid isolation from the civilised world, basking in the hot African sun. And there are its occupants, a family of four: a father leaning on a rifle, a mother raising a toast with a glass of what looks like cloudy lemonade, a barefoot teenage daughter in a straw hat, and a ruddy-faced son grinning proudly next to his Yamaha motorcycle. Only two of those four are in the room: the father and the mother, and they are hardly recognisable. Time, and something else – something with more bite to it than time – has taken its toll on them. The father, Harald, has lost his rifle, most of his hair, and the brazen spark in his eye. The mother, Pippa, looks a shadow of her former self,

7

bereft of her curves, the glass of sugary lemonade missing from her hand, the tinge of copper-red washed away from her hair.

'Read it to me, Harry,' Pippa implores her husband, the sheet of paper shaking in her hand. She is sunken in her chair, curled up and hunched; only her trembling hand – with the letter – dares to reach out of her cocoon.

'You read it, Pippa. We've read it together at least ten times now.' It isn't a complaint. Harald wouldn't dream of being short with her, but she knows the letter by heart. She knows what it says – she just can't believe it.

'Read it again, will you? Maybe we missed something. I want to hear it. Sometimes you see what you want to see, not what's really there. It's different when someone else reads it to you, and you just listen. I'll close my eyes and just listen.'

Harald sighs, but only imperceptibly. He doesn't want her to feel silly. Truth is, he too wants to read the letter over and over again to reassure himself that his mind isn't deceiving him. When they read the letter for the first time, their minds froze, like a fuse in a defective circuit, protecting it against a sudden surge of electric current. They read the letter and looked at each other, numb and disbelieving. Only when they read it again did Pippa clap her hands and Harald take her in his arms, even managing to lift her from the floor – despite his bad back – and sweep her through the air. She was as light as a feather.

'Let me down!' she laughed. 'You'll break your back, you daft oaf!' They sat down, put their two grey heads together, and read the letter, first silently, each at a different speed, he waiting for her to finish before they read it again, out loud.

'Are you sure it's from Will?' she asked.

'Who else?' he said. 'It's his name at the bottom.' Her face crumpled in supplication.

'It's not a prank, then? Tell me!'

He shook his head. 'No, it isn't.'

Her eyes are closed, her face thrust up as if she has poised herself for sunbathing. The skin on her face is smooth. When was the last time he kissed her? 'Are you reading it yet?' she wants to know, without opening her eyes.

'I am.' He puts his glasses on, smoothes the lined paper out on the table, and inhales.

'*Dear Ma and Dad*,' Harald can hear Will say those two primary words, *Ma* and *Dad* – like the primary colours from which all other colours can be made - as he used to say them before his voice broke, a sweet, chiming voice. Harald's voice on the other hand is weak and shaky; it falters.

'Go on, Harry,' Pippa urges him.

'*I got your address from Auntie Rose in Port Elizabeth. Don't blame her for not telling you we were in touch – I made her promise. I wanted to contact you directly when I was ready. Sorry it's been a while. I had to deal with it my way. I can't say I've been successful – not entirely, but let's not talk about that. Maybe one day. I know we'll have to.*

*Auntie Rose tells me you're both well, living in a nice part of England. She tells me you took us there when we were young, but in all honesty I can't say I remember any of it. I would like to remember but I may have been too young, so it's all gone. There are plenty of things I'd rather not remember, but I do. It's never the way you'd like it to be, at least not for me.*

9

*I live in Sydney, as you may have gathered from my address on the envelope. At first I moved a lot from place to place, never settling down – I guess I didn't want to get used to anything or anybody. I found work in hotels, started at the bottom. I'm now Front Office Manager – would you ever think that that's where I would wind up? Wearing a suit and a name tag? Not me. I always thought I'd run a tobacco farm. Remember?*

*Anyhow, drop me a line if you like. Love -'*

'*Your son, Will,*' Pippa says the last line of the letter together with Harald. They are smiling at each other, tentatively and silently, because they don't want to snap out of this moment.

Ahmed takes off his soaked hoodie and hangs it on the hook by the front door. His trousers are wet too – it isn't just the rain, but also the wind that rages in near-horizontal blasts, chucking water at him by the bucket-load. It wasn't such a good idea to cycle to lectures this morning. Malik took a day off and stayed at home.

'Bloody weather,' Ahmed murmurs under his breath. Their basement flat is damp, cold, and crawling with woodlice. The central heating is on but it's no defence against the wind blowing through the gaps in the flimsy windows. They aren't double-glazed because the building is listed, so everything has to be the way it was two hundred years ago when the damned thing was first built.

'Tea?' Ahmed shouts towards the lounge where Malik is crouched in front of the computer screen. Without waiting for Malik's response, which he knows isn't forthcoming any time soon, Ahmed puts the kettle on and drops teabags into the mugs. Both mugs are dirty but so is every other dish and utensil in the kitchen – Malik hasn't done any washing up, though it is his day. They have to have a chat about this, Ahmed makes a mental note, the place is a pigsty. Once the note is made, he puts it out of his mind. Ahmed shies away from confrontations with Malik – they inevitably lead to more obstinate derelictions of duty on Malik's part.

Armed with the two teas, Ahmed heads for the lounge.

'Thanks, matey,' Malik cups his hands around the hot mug. 'I think I'm coming down with something nasty,' he informs Ahmed in his thick Geordie accent. He doesn't look his best, that much is obvious. Dark rings under his eyes have deepened of late and the beard he's been cultivating in the last nine months makes his face look rough and hollow. He yawns and stretches his neck. 'This bloody damp will be the end of me.' Another yawn. Ahmed has to bite his tongue – no use pointing out to Malik that all those long nights in front of the computer without seeing the light of day would run anyone into the ground. Malik is not a baby. He knows what's bad for him and he chooses to go with it anyway.

'Bumped into Pippa and Harry on the doorstep just as I was coming in. They were going out to celebrate.'

'In this weather?'

'I know. They don't go out when the sun's shining, but there they were, umbrella in hand, heading for Terry's tearooms,' Ahmed chuckles. 'I told Harry to forget the umbrella – it's blowing gales. Told them it wasn't a good idea to go out in this weather, but there was no stopping the pair of them. Off they went!'

'What's the celebration all about?'

'They got a letter from their son in Australia.'

'I thought both their kids were dead.'

'So did I, but it wasn't my place to remind them of that. We must've misunderstood. You don't see their kids visit them, but that doesn't mean they're dead.'

'It's not that. I'm sure Harry mentioned once... the urn on the mantelpiece – isn't that where they keep their kids' ashes?'

'That's the soil from their farm.'

'Both, I think - the ashes and the soil.'

'Wasn't it all ashes in the end?' One thing Ahmed is sure of is that Harry and Pippa's tobacco farm was burned to the ground. Sixteen years ago, because that's when they say they came to Britain.

'Maybe. Poor sods. I can't help feeling sorry for them – they're like the walking dead...'

'Well, you don't have to, not anymore. They're different people now - joy to the world and all that lark... Invited us for Sunday lunch!'

'Cool! We'll have to get a bottle of wine, or something.'

'Pippa likes her flowers -'

Malik cuts him short, putting his finger to his lips to shut him up and waving his hand to signal him to sit down. He turns up the volume on the so far mute television set. They are both gawping at a photograph of a young Asian man posing in front of a black flag, producing a V-sign and a wide smile. Behind the image, Fiona Bruce's deep and considerate voice informs them that the man, Ismail Najafi, a British national, is believed to have been killed in a targeted drone strike by the Americans. He fled to fight in Syria over a year ago. His identity has been established via a complex

12

and painstaking voice recognition and facial reconstruction process. The man's most gruesome ISIS propaganda videos featuring decapitations and torture have been used in that process. His family in Newcastle are devastated. They had been calling upon him to give up fighting and return home, but their pleas fell on deaf ears. They are not ready to give interviews and have asked for their privacy to be respected, but issued a statement begging for the cycle of violence to end now – their son's death is not to be avenged…

Malik interrupts the broadcast. 'I know him. I know that bloke… Ismail Najafi,' he exclaims, 'we went to school together. Same class. We played football together, can you believe it!'

'Bloody hell!'

'He's a nice guy.'

'Was.'

'You never know – maybe the bastards missed.'

Pippa loves the flowers. She has arranged them in a cut glass vase in the middle of the dining table. Through the glass you can see the stalks with a rash of tiny air bubbles on them. The roast beef melts in Ahmed's mouth. It reminds him of home and of Mum's cooking. She had added the Sunday roast to her Iranian cuisine recipe book long before Ahmed was born. He has never known Sundays without the Sunday roast.

Malik is complimenting Pippa on the fluffiness of the Yorkshire puddings and the tenderness of the beef, not to mention the crispness of the veg – who would've guessed Malik was such a food connoisseur? 'I needed this,' he points at his near empty plate, 'You saved my life, you know?'

Pippa shakes her head and smiles, flattered. 'That's a bit of an exaggeration.'

'No,' Malik waves his knife at her to demonstrate the strength of his conviction. 'I'm not exaggerating. Trust me, you're a lifesaver.'

'If you say so.'

'I do!' Malik gobbles up the last forkful and wipes his mouth with a napkin, which he then crumples into a ball and throws onto his plate. 'I hear we're celebrating something here, Ahmed tells me.'

Harry gets up and fetches an envelope from the mantelpiece. He holds it reverently like a winning lottery ticket, and passes it to Malik. 'Our son wrote to us. We haven't heard from him in sixteen years.'

Malik takes the envelope and gazes at it, uncertain what to do with it. 'I'm glad for you,' he says. 'Really glad.'

'Go on, open it. You can read it if you like. No secrets there.'

'Well…'

'Read it to us, please,' Pippa asks. She is such a dear old lady you can't say no to her, so Malik reads out the letter. Pippa watches his lips as he reads, her own lips silently forming the words Malik says out loud. Within the first few words she falls out of synch with Malik, racing ahead of him – she has obviously learned the letter by heart. When he finishes reading the letter, Malik puts it back in the envelope and passes it to Harry.

'Great news - to find out he's alive after all those years of you thinking he was dead! Must've come as a shock… I mean, a shock in the best possible way…' Ahmed cringes,

Malik has put his foot in it.

'Oh, no!' Pippa exclaims, but she's smiling so she can't be too upset. 'We never thought he was... Will isn't dead – he just wouldn't speak to us. For years, he wouldn't.'

'That's a bit radical, isn't it?'

'He had his reasons,' Harry says. He isn't smiling. His gaze has travelled away, towards the window.

'What reason on this earth -'

'Grief,' Pippa tells him. Now she too is upset. The smile has vanished. She has reached for Harry's hand. He lets her fingers curl into his and tears his eyes from the window to return her affection. To give her strength. She inhales deeply and says, 'Will had a sister, Cathy. Two years older than him. They were very close. When you live in the middle of nowhere, on a farm, miles from the nearest town, you don't meet many people your own age to socialise with. Those two had only each other to play with since they were little. Cathy of course, being older, would always mother Will – more than I would; I was too busy with the farm! And she was the apple of his eye. Will adored her so he couldn't... She died when she was twenty. He couldn't -'

Pippa doesn't know how to complete the sentence – her lips try to form some sound, but she shakes her head and stifles that sound with her hand.

'I'm sorry, we shouldn't be prying,' Ahmed says.

'No, don't worry. We'd have to talk about it some time, some day,' Harry tells him. 'About Cathy's death.'

'Especially now that Will's got in touch. If he can face it, so should we.' Pippa squeezes her husband's hand and nods to him reassuringly.

'Had she – Cathy – been ill?'

15

'Oh no, she was as fit as a fiddle! No, no long illness to prepare us for it. It was sudden, you see – riots and mob rule, unrest throughout the whole country. Mugabe had promised land to everyone, but it was taking time. Too much time for some... And there were hard times, people got tired of waiting. War veterans – they called themselves *war veterans*, but most of them were too young to remember the war, let alone... They went about land redistribution their own way. It was a mob of more than thirty that marched on our farm. We barricaded ourselves inside - as well as we could – and tried to call for help. I couldn't hold them off for long on my own. Most of our farm workers had fled – can't blame them. I knew the police would turn a blind eye to the goings-on so I was calling around the neighbours, but they were no better off than us – trapped inside their own houses or on the run if they had been lucky enough to see it coming... Still, there was hope: I was armed, I could fend them off for a while until help arrived or until they got bored and moved on... as long as we were all together -'

Harry has to stop. He reaches for a glass of water. His hand is shaking as he carries it to his lips – he puts it back down without taking a drop. 'It was then we realised Cathy wasn't with us in the house. Pippa shouted to look for her, but someone – can't remember who... was it Sunny? – someone said they saw Cathy running into the tobacco field. She was probably terrified when she saw the veterans coming – she must've thought she could hide... She knew that field inside out. We thought: *ok, she's safe. They don't know she's there. As long as she stays there quiet as a mouse.* Then at dusk, as they got fed up with screaming and camping outside the house, they torched everything – set the fields on fire, too, with Cathy there… We found her the next morning… We had looked through the night after they'd left, we called her name, hoping that maybe… We found her with the first light, right there, not that far from the house. She hadn't even tried to run. Too afraid to move, too afraid to make a sound…' Harry wipes off a stray tear. 'We gathered the soil mixed with her ashes from where she sat – she had been sitting, you see, curled up, with her knees to her chin, and that's how she died. We kept the soil – that's all we've got left of her. Will went mad with grief.'

'But it wasn't your fault – what happened,' Malik says what Ahmed is thinking. 'Why wouldn't he speak to you all those years? You weren't responsible -'

'But we were, weren't we, Harry?' Pippa is looking at Harry – it's a hard, demanding stare. They aren't holding hands anymore.

Harry nods. 'We were. I could've sold the farm, taken the compensation that was on offer, pittance as it was, and kept my family safe, and Cathy alive. I could've – should've done it, but I couldn't bring myself to let go of the farm. It was all we knew, it was our home, our livelihood. I was arrogant thinking this whole land redistribution malarkey would go away. It didn't. Will never forgave me for that. I never forgave myself – I never will.'

Pippa's small hand is back squeezing his. She says, 'But he has forgiven you, hasn't he? He wrote to us. Shall we read his letter again? Will's letter.'

17

# III

Awaiting her turn, Gillian is sitting on the edge of her bed, feet dangling. She is gazing at Fritz, who is gazing back at her – his expression a mirror reflection of hers: sheer despair. His torn ear twitches as the noise in the bathroom intensifies; it isn't just the gurgle of running water or the hiss of the toilet tank, it is also the hum of conversation. So Charlie has now joined Tara in the bathroom, and the wait stretches indefinitely under Gillian and Fritz's very noses. Fritz sits up on the bed and begins to groom himself with minute attention to detail. He keeps doing the same patch on his hind leg for a couple of minutes, then moves on to clean behind his ears. With her fingers Gillian brushes her unruly locks. She wishes she could do more by way of personal hygiene this morning; she wishes she could do without a bathroom and lick herself clean like Fritz. She wishes she were a cat: free to do her own thing in her own house, to walk about naked, snack on gherkins, and not stumble across items of men's underwear in the crevices of her sofa. Well, on second thoughts, she wouldn't mind that last bit if those items belonged to her man, not to Charlie Outhwaite.

Fritz completes his morning ablutions and expels a well-pronounced yodel, which translates into *I want my breakfast*. He glares at her and adds a brisk, *Now*. Gillian rubs her face (the closest she can come to washing it), throws her dressing gown over her pyjamas (she has dug out the only pair of pyjamas in her possession – the one she keeps for when she needs to go to hospital), and takes herself – and Fritz – downstairs to the kitchen. She passes by the closed bathroom door where someone flushes the loo while a deep male voice asks for the towel. Are Tara and Charlie this intimate with each other? He's been virtually living with them through the whole of the summer holiday, moving in as soon as Deon had left. It has been almost half a year since Gillian and Fritz had their house to themselves.

Under the stairs is Corky's makeshift bed, with Corky in it. The dog jerks his head upward and eyes Fritz warily, watching his every fluid step; Fritz, on the other hand, gives Corky a positively freezing cold shoulder. Gillian is glad that six months into their cohabitation they have finally agreed on the pecking order in their mixed-species pack. She can hear Corky rise from his bed and follow them to the kitchen, his soft paws padding on the stone tiles.

She is relieved to have at least her kitchen to herself. She dishes out two smelly varieties of wet pet food, one dishful for the cat, another for the dog, both looking and smelling exactly the same. She puts the kettle on for herself and proceeds to scramble the last three eggs in the fridge. Not very hospitable of her, but Gillian has never claimed to be an exemplary hostess. In fact, she is anything but. People, especially long-faced young men casually shedding items of their underwear all over her house and sleeping in her daughter's bedroom, get on her nerves. Gillian is a bundle of nerves, taut as a violin string. She goes through the house every evening, restoring ornaments to their rightful places, straightening coasters on the coffee table, ordering shoes on the shoe rack, picking up empty mugs from bizarre locations – who on earth would take their coffee to the toilet?

She relishes her private moment, eating scrambled eggs on toast, three slices – one for each egg. Above her head, creaking floorboards on the landing announce that the bathroom has been vacated at last. She burns her lips on her hot black tea while, at the same time, trying to chew the last bite of her toast. It is now or never: it's her only chance to repossess the bathroom. She lets the animals out in the garden – Fritz first, Corky right behind him – and tiptoes upstairs, hoping to make it through this morning unseen and unheard. She is already late. Detective Chief Superintendent – following his recent promotion - Scarfe has called a staff meeting at ten: some training on rolling out the Prevent programme in local schools, ready for the start of the new academic year. Not quite the top of Gillian's priorities, but definitely top of Scarfe's.

Just as Gillian pushes the bathroom door open, Tara's towel-wrapped head pops out from her bedroom. 'Oh, there you are! Be home by seven – we've got a surprise for you! And a dinner, too!'

The briefing has turned out to be a whole-day affair. Gillian is bored stiff. Listening isn't her strongest quality, unless it is she who asks questions and demands answers. She listens when she has a reason to. In any other circumstances, she drifts away into her own – very busy – world, which needs to be continually *inventorised*, as she calls her mental note-taking. The homeless colony in Sexton's Wood has grown in size and the landowner – Philip Weston-Jones, who insists on being referred to as Sir Philip - has threatened to take the law into his own hands. They are *trespassing* and it is his learned opinion that they should be prosecuted. He nailed a sign to that effect next to a well-trodden footpath that leads into the wood through a grazing paddock. So far the sign has been consistently ignored. At the end of his tether, Sir Philip has demanded *police intervention to protect his property rights*. It sounds good but it won't do without an eviction order. And even with the order, things aren't as straightforward as they seem. The homeless fraternity is an elusive bunch. Trying to fish them out from the wood, one by one, is near impossible. They squeeze through the cracks and blend with the background, offering neither resistance nor cooperation, and the next day they're all back to rebuild their underground dwellings. *Rabbit holes*, Webber calls them, which is a surprisingly accurate term, if politically incorrect. Their occupants disappear into one hole only to re-appear from another one, and walk away undetected. That brings back a childhood memory of Bugs Bunny and Porky Pig – a memory Gillian has to smile at.

'Anything funny I said?' Scarface is addressing Gillian, his expression on the lines of *We are not amused.*

'No! No, sir! It was... I was just,' Gillian stammers, 'I was squinting to read the... the... what's on the board.'

'You may want to have your eyes checked,' Webber whispers into her ear, his expression that of Prince Philip about to commit another unforgiveable blunder. Which he does. 'First thing that goes at your age is the eyesight, I'm told.'

Erin guffaws. Gillian fixes her with an unforgiving stare.

What's so funny about being forty... OK, forty-three? Erin is only six years younger, and so is Webber. They're not that far behind. Anyway, you're only as old as you feel. It's a feeble reassurance, considering that lately Gillian has been feeling drained and de-motivated, contemplating retirement from the Force. She needs a case – a decent manslaughter at the very least, though a nice juicy murder would go a long way in revitalising her outlook on life. Chasing homeless buggers around Sexton's Wood doesn't come close despite the fresh air and panoramic views over Wensbury Plains.

'This may be a good time to break for tea,' the guest speaker throws Gillian a lifeline. 'Shall we reassemble in, say...' he checks his watch, 'fifteen minutes? At two forty-five.'

The three of them, Gillian, Erin, and Mark Webber, are gathered around the buffet table, sipping tea from dainty cups and munching on flapjacks – a far cry from their regular diet. It's all for the benefit of their guest, one Eduard Gosling from MI5, who is standing at the far end of the room, chatting to Scarfe. The Chief Super is positively elevated by association. His sycophantic laughter thunders through the room – Gosling must've told him a joke. Webber nods towards them and mimics Scarface's earlier remark with remarkable accuracy. 'Anything funny I said?'

Erin chortles, again.

'Leave off, will you, Webber?'

He salutes. 'Yes, ma'am!'

They each pick up another piece of flapjack and proceed to chew thoughtfully. Erin peers at her watch. 'Two forty,' she informs them, torturous resignation etched into her face. 'We should be going back.'

'What is the purpose of this… this *Prevent* thing? How is it relevant to us?' Webber complains. 'It's not like we are awash with Muslim fundamentalists here in the Shires, is it now?'

'You never know, DS Webber. Like they say – better safe than sorry,' Gillian shares the words of wisdom though deep down she has to agree with him. In Sexton's Canning people murder each other for perfectly logical reasons. Crime makes sense here: take the landowner hunting down homeless trespassers with a shotgun.

'I'll need something stronger than a cup of tea when this day's up. I've been watching paint dry for way too long, God help me,' Webber moans as they regroup back into the conference room.

'Drinks at the Bull's Eye?' Erin suggests.

Gillian nods approvingly, 'We'll reconvene there at six.'

It's seven thirty - give or take - when Gillian rolls in home from the pub: early by her standards, but Webber had to be home to put his girls to bed (*Kate still isn't with it*, as he puts it with a pained look on his face, so Gillian doesn't ask any questions). It's pouring down and, as she had to walk home, she is soaked to the bone and her usually fluffy coiffure resembles a wet mop, fresh out of a bucket. Rainwater has somehow managed to get under her collar - she can feel it trickling between her shoulder blades. She pats her pockets for the key. Corky barks from the garden. Has Tara forgotten to take the beast out of the rain? He must be missing Sean, especially when it's raining and no one seems to give a toss about his personal… his canine welfare. Tara takes after Gillian in the forgetfulness department. Like mother, like daughter, Gillian muses proudly, still searching for the key to the front door in the deep recesses of her spacious pockets. The door swings open and a stream of light pours out of the house. The skinny silhouette of her forgetful daughter is standing in the doorway. Before Gillian has a chance to remind her of the poor dog, Tara hisses through her teeth, 'You forgot, didn't you? I asked you to be home by seven – once in your life! I didn't ask you for a new car or a loan – just to be home by seven!'

'I am -'

'No, you're not! It's… seven thirty-six! Get in! You've missed the starter.'

Is that a problem? Is that what the fuss is all about? Gillian is just about to inform Tara that she isn't hungry – she's had a steak and kidney pie with mash and veg at the Bull's Eye – when she changes her mind. In the dining room the table is laid for ten – laid quite elaborately with her best china and silver cutlery, not to mention her nan's silver candlesticks – and the people sitting at it gaze at her most cordially (at least, some of them do – Tara is looking away).

'Well… hello… everyone…' Gillian's smile turns awkwardly lopsided. She takes a seat. She is baffled to see the assembly of people at the table. Seeing Charlie there, even Tara's friend Sasha with her boyfriend Rhys, isn't that perplexing, but Sasha's parents? They, in their turn, appear equally bewildered. It isn't like Sasha's mother to sit demurely at a table, quiet as a mouse, but here Grace sits – quiet as a mouse, her jovial Caribbean temperament in the grip of utter stupefaction. Nathaniel Garland, Sasha's father, looks bland and inscrutable, seriously out of his comfort zone, but then again that is his usual look: a man who

24

swallowed a broomstick. Nathaniel isn't one for large gatherings. He is shy and withdrawn as a rule, for which fact his wife Grace normally makes up for tenfold. Not tonight. Tonight even Grace doesn't know how to interpret this occasion. Her large dark eyes blink in earnest, her fingers are tugging at a napkin.

Gillian's eyes travel to the couple at the far end of the table. She instantly knows who they may be. 'Mr and Mrs Outhwaite?' she ventures an educated guess. It doesn't take a genius to work out the red-headed man with a long face, both physically and metaphorically, is Charlie's close blood relation. The woman looks nothing like her son – assuming she is Charlie's mother. She sports a smooth complexion, wide jawline and deep chestnut-coloured hair, but that's just *Nice 'n' Easy*. Her face is bland and open, her eyes pale – too bland and too pale for her dark hair. She is wearing a scarf wrapped in multiple layers around her neck, swallowing it whole, so that it seems that her face sprouts straight out of her torso.

'Call me Theresa,' she waves from her distant seat. 'You must be Tara's mum. We've heard a lot about you.'

Gillian manages a faint smile and looks pointedly at her daughter.

'They didn't hear it from me,' Tara shrugs, a spark of mischief in her eye. 'Talk to Charlie.'

'We've heard lots of good things, too,' Charlie's father attempts to save the day with this lame diplomacy. Charlie grins stupidly.

'Gill, is that right?' Theresa wants to know. Gillian hates this abridged version of her name, but she nods. 'Yes, Gill... Gillian, but you can call me - Well, call me Gillian, actually.'

'Jerry, Jerry Outhwaite. Nice to meet you at long last.' The forlorn, unsmiling expression on the man's face contradicts his words.

'You too. Glad you could make it...' Since nobody means what they say, Gillian lies, too. What she really wants is for all these people to go away. It's one thing to have Charlie in unlawful occupation of her house – quite another to throw his entire family into the mix. This borders on an invasion!

'And this is Rhys's mum – Lorna.' Tara points vaguely towards a slim blonde woman lurking over Rhys's shoulder. What she is doing here is beyond Gillian's powers of deduction. She smiles at her nevertheless, and the woman – Lorna – smiles back, looking painfully uncomfortable. She must be wondering herself what the hell she's doing here in this woman's house, sitting at her table with a bunch of total strangers. The gathering of disconcerted individuals was beginning to resemble one of those assemblies of suspects in an Agatha Christie novel, just as Hercule Poirot is about to unmask the real killer. Gillian puts on a brave face and takes her seat. She knows she is innocent and yet she is anxious. What the hell is going on?

An all-pervading silence follows after the initial ritual of greetings and salutations. The *suspects* eye each other warily, each pondering the others' potential sins. Polite smiles are quivering on their lips. Gillian has no other wish than for all these people to go away. Something brushes by her leg under the table. She looks down. It's Fritz. He doesn't seem to have any answers either – he remains silent. Not a single yodel. Poor thing, must be in shock.

26

'We may as well get on with the main course,' Tara says, glaring resentfully at her mother. 'It isn't quite how we planned it, but we can't overcook the fish. Everything else will have to wait.'

'White wine for you, Gillian?' Charlie attempts to disarm the animosity hanging in the air. Gillian thanks him most profusely, even though she doesn't drink white wine, not even with fish, and even though she has been at the red for the first part of the evening and is bound to end up with a nasty hangover tomorrow morning for all that mixing.

The food is served by Sasha and Tara. Gillian tucks in. How does steak and kidney pie go with sea bass? She should find out soon enough…

'This fish is delicious,' Grace enthuses. 'I'm not a fish person, but this is… it's *epic*!' The word sits oddly on her lips, not quite age-appropriate, like a pair of jeans two sizes too small. 'I didn't know you girls could cook! I bet it was Tara!'

'We made it together, Mum. Charlie brought the recipe.'

'It's my gran's recipe,' Charlie says. 'When I told her the occasion she said only the best would do. Best cook in the world, my gran!'

'So what *is* the occasion?' Gillian is glad Grace asked the question. It proves that Gillian isn't the only one at the table who hasn't got a clue what's going on.

'Our engagement!' Sasha says. 'Double-engagement: me and Rhys, Tara and Charlie. We're having a surprise engagement party, ta-da!' She throws her arms up in the air and assumes a gold-medallist's pose.

'Bloody hell, you can't possibly mean it!' It isn't the most appropriate reaction to the announcement, but it is too

27

late when Gillian realises that – she's already said it.

'That's my mum for you!' Tara declares, her left eyebrow elevated with sarcasm.

'Congratulations are in order?' Theresa looks like she's bitten into a lemon. Jerry is still looking morose – no change there. Grace starts to cry and asks her husband if he has a handkerchief. He doesn't. Lorna has temporarily vanished behind her son. Has she fallen off her chair? It is at this point that Fritz gives out a harrowing yodel and shoots from under the table. Someone must have stepped on him.

'Is the cat all right?' asks Nathaniel Garland.

'You're too young,' Gillian persists with her hostilities. 'You don't know what you're doing. You have uni and… All of you need to think it through -'

'Mum,' Tara has fixed her with a stern gaze, 'just stop there. Don't say another word.'

# IV

The vessel is called *Afzal3*. It's a small fishing boat cracked open by rust. In places the rust has cut through metal like acid and created burned out holes of various shapes and sizes. The bigger of them have been patched up with whatever unlikely materials could be found prior to their departure. The salty Mediterranean water has been seeping through those holes since the day the boat left the Libyan coast. Every morning the *passengers* wake up to more and more water. At the start of the voyage it was just the wet floor under their feet, now the level has risen to above their ankles. It is even higher at the stern and, because of that, the boat's tail is sinking and dragging them down. The boat is losing speed.

People from the back are pushing towards the bow. If the boat was packed to the brim at the start of this voyage, it was nothing compared to the conditions now. Standing room only. You can sit if you pull your knees high up to your chin. The stench of human sweat and excrement is suffocating. People are moaning, but feebly – they have no strength left to make noise. Even babies have stopped crying. They just whimper. Nothing brings relief. There is nothing on-board to offer hope. Hope lies beyond the horizon. They are trying to get there fast, before water runs out. But since they are slowed down by the weighty stern, water rations have been cut to less than a bare minimum. Haji can live on that – he is a desert camel after all – but others are dying. The Italian shore must come soon, but so far there is nothing in sight but the empty, flat horizon. It is like they are already dead.

Haji is staring out into the sea. With the night approaching, the sea has lost its colour. It is just a darkening grey, like a rapidly fading monochrome photograph. The merciless sun has dipped behind the horizon, taking the heat with it. It may be colder but that doesn't help with the thirst. He can feel Boy's eyes on him: large, round eyes of a child. As the boy is losing weight, his eyes seem to be growing. He is about six or seven, the oldest child in that family. Haji doesn't know where they're from or where exactly they're going – you don't ask questions you wouldn't like to be answering yourself. They are North Africans and are heading for Europe. Some things go without saying. There are five of them: the parents and three children, Boy and his two younger siblings. One, about four, is a girl. She is slumped in her father's lap, her head flopped onto his chest. Her eyes are closed, her mouth gaping open, her bloated lips cracked and drained of colour. She's been sleeping a lot without waking. Maybe it is a blessing, maybe it's some kind of a coma. The other child is just a baby. It is nestling in a shawl tied around the mother – you can only see the top of its head, the black twirls of hair. She – the mother – hasn't fed it in the last twenty-four hours. Her milk must've dried up. She's asleep too. The whole family are hunched and curled into each other, their heads dropped to their chests. Only Boy stays wide awake; those large, round eyes fixed on Haji. He must be finding Haji fascinating. With his wide

Asiatic cheekbones, his comparatively light skin and heavily hooded eyes, Haji is a curiosity. He definitely isn't the typical African man Boy is accustomed to.

The sun is gone; darkness is upon them. It has shrouded their misery and muffled those few plaintive cries some people still have the strength to utter. Haji returns Boy's attention, nods to him and points to the sky above them. It is punctured with stars, many distant stars, calm and indifferent, but beautiful. Haji hopes Boy will see their beauty. He does – he has lifted his head and is gazing at the sky. So is Haji. Stars bring peace upon him.

On the night the Russians took Tajbek there were no stars. He saw no stars. Most of his comrades from the Presidential Guard were dead. As he was running alongside the Russian soldiers, the air blue with curses, he tripped over many bodies. Once, he fell – his face levelled momentarily with Ismail's face. His eyes were open but unseeing. A bullet hole was stamped on his head – right in the middle. It had taken a skilful marksman to make that hole. Haji got to his feet and ran, then, as he got to the gate, he started crawling. Each time he heard voices he would freeze and play dead. He crawled and didn't dare to get up to his feet for so long that the fabric on his sleeves and trouser legs wore off and his knees and elbows bled. When he finally made it to the *microrayon*, he stood and looked up, and saw no stars.

Svetlana hadn't fled with the other Russians – she was waiting for him to come home. She ran into his arms and kissed him all over, gibbering so fast in Russian that he couldn't make it out. His blood – and perhaps the blood of his dead comrades – stained her dress and her skin. 'I didn't believe you were dead, Haji... I didn't believe them,' she whispered, her hot breath on his frozen face. He can feel the warmth of her breath on his face to this day. He can feel her plump lips melting his. He can feel her lips on his eyelids and in his hair.

'We must go! Take only the basics, and we must run,' he told her, and he didn't have to explain any further. She knew too: they would be after him, he survived the mutiny, he was a witness. They couldn't afford to leave any witnesses behind. He was a marked man.

She washed and dressed his scuffed knees and elbows, put him in civilian clothes: a shirt and a long Afghan robe, a headdress the tying of which he had to help her with – her hands were shaking, and she was weeping like an old woman. She then covered her short fair hair with a veil, and they left under cover of night, heading for Haji's *kishlak* in the easternmost part of the Pandsher Valley...

There is shouting on the boat. Commotion. Men and women, encouraged by each other, stronger *en masse*, pushed against the wall, are demanding water. Haji doesn't know what started the riot. It could've been that more people had pushed up from the stern, escaping the flooding. They were being squashed and have grown desperate. Despair breeds defiance.

Two of the smugglers come down to deal with the situation, both armed. They brandish their weapons in a display of might. Haji sighs. They are deluding themselves if they think they have the monopoly on killing. Despite their guns and their theatrics, Haji reads fear in their faces. People are screaming, waving their fists.

'No water! No water left!' The older one of the smugglers presents his empty hands in a gesture of helplessness. He turns and points towards the dark horizon. 'Italia! Wait! Italia close! Europa!' The sun rising in front of him hits the metal of his automatic pistol. It shines in Haji's eyes. People aren't listening or they don't believe the smuggler's assurances. The shouting intensifies and, when that happens, children begin to cry. It's mayhem. Some passengers have risen to their feet and are approaching their minders, fearless and furious. Demanding water. Pleading for water. The younger of the two smugglers loses his footing and slips. He is angry for his humiliation and to cover up for it he grabs a shabby man closest to him and pushes him down towards the stern. The shabby man falls to his knees, splashing water around him. Another person is thrust on top of him. And another one. The smuggler is throwing people across the deck into the flooded stern. 'You want water?' he yells, his voice high with irritation. 'You got water - down there!' He kicks another person – it's a woman. Her companion hurls himself at the assailant, but the older smuggler reaches for his pistol and shoots the man.

Silence.

Dead silence. And then the widowed woman starts wailing and scrambles towards her husband's body. Others join her and the boat begins to sink.

It was inevitable.

Large bubbles, swollen with air, boil over – the stern submerges within seconds. Everyone presses to the bow, but it's no good. The bow is going to go, too. Someone, the skipper, rushes out of the cabin and sends a flare into the sky. It explodes, red illuminations in the grey morning sky.

People are jumping off the boat before its mass drags them into the depths. The family of five – Haji's neighbours – are in disarray. The father and Boy have dived in, the father with the four-year-old girl in his arms. The mother and the baby just fell into the sea, and gave in to it without a fight. They went down like a smashed block of concrete. Boy is splashing haplessly, screaming, choking on water. Haji realises Boy cannot swim. He dives in and searches for him in the whirlpool of sinking bodies; his fingers meet Boy's arm, and they claw at it. He pushes him up towards the light of the rising sun.

It is a matter of seconds for the boat to vanish from sight and a matter of half an hour before the sea swarming with people becomes calm and still. Haji and Boy are treading water, waiting for a miracle. Haji isn't one to let go and he is right not to – he hears a distant buzz of a helicopter. He recognises it instantly. He knows the slashing of the air with the rotating blades. He points to Boy, 'Rescue,' he says. 'Wave arms!'

They both wave them, and they shout.

The helicopter pauses over their heads. Water ripples around them, unsettling Boy. Haji has to grab hold of him again. A harness on a rope is being lowered from the helicopter and when it hits the surface it is dragged along it, close enough for Haji to get hold of it. He fastens it under Boy's arms and watches him being lifted to safety. Then he dives between the waves, and swims away. The land – Italy – cannot be too far. He knows helicopters can't fly far and he can see the outline of the coast. And even if he doesn't make it to the shore, he'd rather die free than be captured.

# V

It is Oscar's purgatory. He can't escape it and he no longer tries. He has to cover the distance again, do the excruciating five-hour advance up Mount Langdon. He will be doing it until the Judgment Day, and then - who knows? Will that be the end of it? He is praying for it to end, like he did on that day.

That day, as they embarked on the ascent, he thought he'd rather be up there on the summit, face to face with the enemy, in hand-to-hand combat – get the job done and go home to Heather. It was the plants underfoot that made him think of his young wife back home. Wet heather and gorse.

He has to do it again; he knows there is no escaping it. Huge white boulders provide little shelter from the punishing wind. It is cutting horizontally and drives freezing rain into his face, and into the faces of his men. The temperature has fallen below minus 35. The visibility is limited not only because it is night-time but also because of the weather conditions. That is a big problem: they are sitting ducks. The Argentines could be hiding behind those boulders. They could be in gaps and crags, waiting for him and his men. He is straining his eyes to look into those crags and to spy out the enemy. His heart is pounding with the effort, and with the sheer fucking fear of the invisible bastards hiding somewhere there. And they are there, waiting, holding their nerve. Lieutenant Oscar Arthur Holt is holding his nerve, too. But his heart is pounding in his ribcage like a fucking four-pound sledgehammer. No-one can hear it because of the blistering naval bombardment from HMS *Avenger*. It is to soften up the Argentines, but in the end it isn't just the Argentines who go weak in their knees. Everyone does, including Oscar. The shellfire is fucking relentless. Missiles are whistling over their heads, aiming for the crags up high, hitting hard rocks and ricocheting at random angles. He should know his men are safe but knowing is not the same as believing. Under the heavy artillery barrage the whole mountain erupts in flames, and he is taking his men directly into that inferno.

He doesn't want to go there – he knows what awaits him and that he must avoid it at any cost, he's been there so many fucking times, over and over again the same upward path into the heart of Purgatory, but his legs do their job of taking him there. Despite the cold wind and lashing rain. Despite the exhausting trek. Despite the bombs and the fires. Despite the horror that awaits him there.

When his paras are too close for comfort to the Argentine positions, the artillery offensive stops. The silence that follows is deafening. After listening to the barrage of shellfire, you can't hear a thing. And you can't see a thing – the night takes over. The night becomes a friend – it offers cover. He looks at the men around him: hunched, some weighed down by the heavy night-vision or radio equipment, treading stealthily in silence. Upwards. Sergeant Butler and Corporal Walsh have attached bayonets to their rifles. He can see their faces only because they are the two men closest to him. They are already drained of blood, white as ghosts. Already. He wants to tell them to stop and retreat. He knows what awaits up there, and he doesn't want to go any further. But this is his purgatory. He isn't really in charge. He is only pretending to be to keep the morale up.

It is too torturous to keep your mind on what lies ahead. Oscar shuts his mind down. Not a single thought crosses his head. They're going up: he and his men. Whatever is up there, they have to confront it and overcome it. You need a clear head. The emptiness pervades every fibre of his body. The silence. The vacuum of thinning air. The darkness.

It isn't too late to go back.

An explosion rips the night to shreds: one of his men trod on a mine. And now it *is* too late for him.

The Argentines crawl out from the holes in the mountain – a hail of machine gun fire hammers the paras' heads; flares go up towards them, exposing their positions, opening the night into a premature dawn. Oscar is dodging bullets, running for the nearest shelter - a cavity in the bare slope - but it is soft and flattens under his weight. It's heather and gorse. The earth around him is ploughed with bullets. They turn it over. It splatters in his face, into his mouth. He can't breathe. His throat is full of soil. It's suffocating him -

He wakes. The breathing is still laboured and wheezy. His face is wet with sweat. Mechanically, he wipes it off: the sweat and the wet soil. He sits up, brings his breathing under control. The light of the bedside lamp – sudden and red – startles him. He recoils. A scream escapes him.

'Go to sleep, Oscar, for God's sake,' Heather mutters from her side of the bed. He searches for her face, just to assure himself that *this* isn't a dream. She is holding on to the duvet, most of which he has pulled away from her as he jumped up. Her eyes are closed – she's trying to hold on to her sleep as much as she is holding on to the duvet. The red light of the lamp is kind to her face. It is soft and smooth. Her platinum blonde hair is swept away from her face and has made a halo around it. The diamond in her ring reflects the light and sparkles. Oscar is fully awake – thank God! – for he knows the dazzle comes from a ring, not the enemy's flare.

'Sorry, my love. A bad dream.' He is looking at her, feeding on her domesticity and feminine vulnerability. He's breathing evenly.

'Turn the light off. I've got work tomorrow. Go to sleep, Oscar.'

Reluctantly, he switches off the lamp. Darkness will bring back the nightmare, he fears. He lies on his back, eyes wide opened. He doesn't want to go back to sleep. He got away with it lightly tonight. He woke just at the right time, before -

The bunker is well camouflaged. It's really just a cave fortified with sandbags, a sharp escarpment overhanging it and offering cast-iron overhead and rear protection to the gunner inside. The bastard is hard at work. Bright yellow sparks shoot out of his machine gun without a break. Three paras are down, the rest cowering behind boulders, unable to carry on with the charge. Check mate. The bastard sniper has a one hundred-and-eighty-degree visual over the whole of the southern slope where he has Oscar's men pinned down. Oscar has to make a decision. He can't sit here and wait for ever. He tasks Walsh and Butler with taking the bunker. They'll attack it from both east and west simultaneously whilst Oscar and the rest of the company engage the gunner head-on with constant fire. 'I've got you covered!' he hears himself shout over the noise of the battle, spit flying out of his mouth. Walsh can't control the shaking of his lower lip. His eyes are in the grip of panic. Butler is in charge. He nods. He too wants this job done quickly and efficiently. He too wants to go home, but he's more experienced than the twenty-year-old Walsh to know that the only way home is through that fucking bunker. 'Sir!' he confirms their orders.

An insanity of relentless fire follows. Butler and Walsh take off and soon Oscar loses visual contact with them. If he can't see them, neither can the sniper. He must be busy crouching behind the sandbags, covering his arse. Bullets punch those sandbags and crash into the escarpment like a hailstorm. As soon as two hunched silhouettes materialise near the bunker, Oscar gives a signal to his men to lower the line of fire. He watches in slow motion as Walsh tosses a grenade into the mouth of the bunker and Butler charges in, his bayonet first.

He doesn't make it. His body is pushed up and back, a series of bullets animating it like a puppet on strings. He falls. Walsh stabs the mouth of the bunker. Oscar screams and gets to his feet, and runs – runs blindly at the fucking gunner; the paras follow. Not a single shot is fired at them. Butler's down. 'Sergeant Butler! Richard!' Oscar is pulling up his torso, but it resists him, heavy as lead. 'Get up, Butler! This is in order!'

'He's dead, sir,' Walsh informs him, his lower lip stiff. 'He got 'im…' He is pointing to the body of the Argentine gunner, a small dark man who's staring back at Oscar with wide-open, dead eyes. Screaming, Oscar shoots at those eyes; empties a whole magazine. Walsh is pulling at his sleeve. 'Stop, sir! He's dead!'

His wild cry wakes Heather. 'Oscar, wake up!' Her grip is on his arm, her fingers digging into it. Thank God, he's awake! A dream that happened thirty years ago. A fucking dream.

'Sorry, I'm sorry…'

'You've been screaming. Again.'

He swings his legs off the bed. 'I'll go and get some water. Do you want anything, Heather?'

'I just want to sleep.'

Katie hasn't changed in the last thirty years. Only her hair grew out of its deep chestnut brown and is now wired with grey. It is still thick and long, and he still wishes he could stroke it and bury his face in it. Her face is a constant – the same high cheekbones and deep set eyes, velvety skin, untouched by time. It froze that day all those years ago when he stood on her doorstep, telling her how sorry he was – and she just listened, numb and still. Pain sculpted her face in cold marble that day. Even today, years later, when she opens the door to him and conjures up a smile, it fails to reach her eyes. 'Look who's here, Tommy,' she announces Oscar's arrival to her grandson. To Oscar she says, 'We didn't expect you today. It's a nice surprise. Come in, please…'

'If that's OK?' He is always timid with her, despite all those years of his urgent, impromptu visits and despite their closeness.

'Of course it's OK. Tommy loves your company. We both do.'

'Hi, Oscar!' Tommy acknowledges him with a passing glance from above his tablet. He's sprawled on the floor in the living room, knees up, his back propped against the side of the sofa. He's had a haircut; his blond tresses sheared off, he suddenly looks older. Oscar would normally tousle his hair, but today there's nothing to tousle; it's a short crop. Oscar sits on the sofa and looks over Tommy's shoulder at the tablet. 'What's the game?'

'Just playing,' Tommy shrugs his shoulders. 'It's boring.'

'Then why play it?'

'I've got nothing else to do.'

'You could try doing your homework,' Katie suggests.

'I told you, Nan – I haven't got any.'

'Teachers don't like too much marking. Oh well… You could read a book.'

'Now, there's a thought!' Oscar gives Tommy a friendly punch.

'I have a better one,' Tommy puts away his tablet, 'but it depends on you…'

'Shoot!'

'You know how you promised to take me camping? And fishing? And that we'd sleep overnight in a tent, make a campfire and cook what we caught…'

Oscar searches Katie's face for any clues as to how to respond. Tommy gets there first, 'Nan, please! You said, when I was two digits you'd let me, remember?'

'You're not two digits yet -'

'I will be! In six weeks' time – forty-two days and six

and a half hours, to be precise! Well – you promised…'

'I don't know…'

'Please… I've never been camping, or anything! I just have a boring life! That's all I have!'

Anxiety creeps into her eyes. They dart between Tommy and Oscar. He can tell she wishes he had never made any stupid promises to the boy; he shouldn't have come today. But Tommy is unrelenting and she'll have to say yes. They all know that. 'Nothing bad will happen! Oscar will be there to protect me, won't you, Oscar?'

'With my life!' What else is he supposed to say?

'You see?'

'All right, then… You can go, for a day – camping, fishing, but no sleepovers. The nights are too cold this time of year. You'll be back by six.'

'By midnight!' Tommy grins.

'By ten o'clock sharp, and that's final!'

'When? When are we going?'

'I'll make plans – will let you know as soon as I have the all-clear from Mrs Holt.'

Tommy jumps to his feet, his face lit with excitement. He's holding his tablet, a tangled earphone cable hanging down. 'I'm telling Robert! He won't believe it. He said Nan would never let me, because I don't have a dad. That'll prove he's a liar!' He sprints out of the living room, his feet punching the stairs as he heads for his bedroom. Katie winces when he mentions the word *dad*. Oscar pretends he hasn't noticed that. He says, 'Don't worry, I'll take care of him.'

'I know you will. Thanks. I have to let him do these things, if only to prove Robert a liar.' She smiles. It is her usual surface smile, one that doesn't spread to her eyes. Oscar wishes she'd stop pretending with him. She is quick to offer him tea and promptly scuttles away to the kitchen, leaving him alone in her living room, facing the photographs on the mantelpiece: Tommy, Izzie when she was a schoolgirl, and Richard in his uniform, medals shining on his chest...

Hiding behind her cup, she tells him, 'I thought I saw her, two days ago.'

'Her?' He is putting his mandatory two teaspoons of sugar into his cup.

'Izzie.'

Oscar puts away the teaspoon without stirring the sugar into his tea. He tries to see through her cup, see what her face is saying. She hasn't spoken of Izzie in years, since Izzie walked away, leaving behind Tommy and Katie on their own, disjointed, like a broken string of beads. 'This young woman I saw – she looked just like Izzie: the same long hair, same deep brown colour... She had it picked up, you know – twisted into a hairclip, just like Izzie used to... I followed her, called her name. *Izzie! Izzie, stop! Isabella, it's your mother!* I yelled like a total maniac. The woman didn't answer. It wasn't her name, obviously. Though the way she walked, the way she pointed her toes as she walked... Izzie would do that, she did ballet, remember?'

Oscar nods. He remembers. He remembers that day when he sat with Katie at the kitchen table, sewing sequins onto Izzie's costume. They had made a butterfly shape. Izzie loved it. When she put it on, she did resemble a butterfly.

'I ran after her, angry that she wouldn't stop, that she was ignoring me, was trying to get away from me... Selfish girl!'

43

Katie jolts him out of his reverie. 'I wasn't going to let her, not again. I would demand answers. She'd give me answers. She'd tell me why the hell she let me think, all those years, let me think she was-' Her voice breaks off, crumbles away. She puts down her cup – almost drops it on the saucer; it falls with a clank; some tea splatters. 'Oh, look at this mess!' She dashes out and comes back with a cloth, starts dabbing the spilled tea. 'It's going to leave stains!' she laments, her hands jittery. Oscar quietens them with his hand – places it gently over them. They stop. 'It wasn't Izzie, was it?'

'I grabbed her shoulder, she turned. I gave her a fright, poor girl. Of course, it wasn't Izzie. She looked like that ten years ago. What would she look like now?' She gazes at him. There is a plea in her eyes and they slowly well up. A sob escapes her. Oscar takes her in his arms and buries his face in her hair.

'Now, now,' he says soothingly. 'We don't know anything for sure.'

'You went to see her, didn't you?' Heather knows. She always does – she can see it in his eyes, smell it on him. Whichever way she knows, doesn't matter - she doesn't like it. She is looking at him, resentful. Something stabs in his gut. She has no reason to be angry. She has no right to deny him those moments. He needs them, and he has a duty of care, it's simple. 'You think you owe her something, don't you? Well, you go on thinking what you like, but *I* don't owe her anything! I don't see why I have to put up with this… this…'

'Calm down, for God's sake! I just popped over to see how she – how they were doing. It's not a sin. As it happened, she needed a friend, someone to talk to.'

'And you were on hand, naturally,' she snorts – a woman scorned. 'I wish you had as much time for me as you do for her.'

'I have a lifetime for you, Heather. You're my wife. I love you, don't forget that!'

'If you say so.' She escapes with her eyes. Why doesn't she believe him? She is his wife – he's made *her* his wife. Why can't she accept that? He can't win with Heather. She will have to come to the right conclusions in her own time. Oscar slumps in his chair, picks up the remote and puts on the News. It's a habit of a lifetime, he does it automatically, even if, more and more frequently these days, he doesn't really watch it. What matters is just the knowledge that the world goes round and round quietly in the background. After a fashion – the debris of what once must have been a fishing boat floating off the Italian coast tells a different story. Oscar knows the narrative to this tragedy. He heard it before. Too many times for comfort.

'I'll just fade into the background then, shall I?' Heather mutters under her breath as she settles on the sofa, legs curled up as is her longstanding tradition. Oscar wishes he could give her a good smacking, or a great big hug, but, wisely, he chooses neither, just shakes his head, smiles ruefully and says, 'Silly old girl you are, Heather! How can I not love you?'

# VI

It looks like an upturn. Yvonne's upper body has been
slightly elevated in her bed so that, as she puts it, she can
watch the action instead of the ceiling. There isn't much
action on the ward – in the main, people just die. 'That's
what we come here to do,' Yvonne informs Wanda
philosophically.

Wanda puffs up her pillow and takes her pulse. She has
difficulty finding it in the first place. 'That's what I mean –
I'm as good as dead,' Yvonne points out.

'Just be still, for goodness' sake!'

'I'm as still as can be. I'm not going anywhere.'

'Good. It's looking good, Yvonne. You just carry on –
regardless!' Wanda learned this phrase a few days after she
started working at the hospice, and she has been using it
liberally ever since. Yvonne finds it amusing. She even
chuckles. That is a good sign! She has been wasting away
since she arrived four months ago: losing weight, losing
muscle tissue, and most tragically, losing the will to live.

'Stop fussing around – you're making me giddy!'
Yvonne is a right troublemaker, but Wanda knows better
than to take her antics seriously. She is pumping up the
armband to check her blood pressure. 'What good is that
going to do?' Yvonne sighs. There is a slight tremble to her

voice – the pain must be nibbling away at the edges. She's already on the highest possible dose of morphine – any more of it, any more frequently dispensed, would simply kill her. She has to wait for her next fix. Wait and bear it. She purses her lips, and suddenly she looks tired and defeated. 'Sit with me awhile,' she says weakly. 'Tell me... things.'

Wanda settles on the side of the bed. Yes, she is a busy woman: rounds to do, several more patients to check upon, but company is the best medicine you can offer to a terminal cancer patient. Everything else fails sooner or later. Wanda knows this from experience; she has been working in the hospice for three years now, since she arrived in the country. She has seen most of her patients die, and they told her they didn't want to die alone. She takes out Paulina's photo, shows it to Yvonne. 'I got it yesterday, from my mother,' she looks tenderly at the image of her smiling child showing off a big gap in her teeth. 'It was Paulina's seventh's birthday last week. She had a party, all her friends came with presents. She was showing us what she got on Skype, then she ran off...'

'Of course she did. She was busy having a party.'

'It didn't feel good when she ran off like that. She wasn't even looking at us – not really. I could tell her heart wasn't in it.'

'Like I said, she was having a party. That's where her heart was.'

'I miss her.'

Yvonne puts the photo in her hand. 'Then you should go and be with her!'

'Do you think?' Wanda wants to hear it. She let Andrzej convince her to come here – *to build their future* - but it is

47

the present time that is slipping away from her that she is more concerned about. Money isn't everything. They can buy a smaller flat. Wanda wants someone to tell her that, someone wiser, like Yvonne.

'I do think that. You must go and watch your daughter play, lose the rest of her milk teeth and grow up, become a woman. Her childhood, you know, it won't wait for you – it will pass. Life passes – it's in its nature to pass, to slip through our fingers.' She winces. The pain. Wanda wishes she could ease it for her, but according to Yvonne's chart she won't be due for another painkiller for a couple of hours yet. 'I wish mine just got on, and be done with me...'

'You mustn't say that, Yvonne. You're looking better today.'

'Ha!'

'There's always hope.'

'Even you don't believe that. I'm dying and I just want to die quicker!'

'Don't say that -'

'I can say what I like. I've had a good life, and I'm done with it. My children are grown-ups. They have their own families. They don't need me hanging around their necks -' She grinds her teeth and shuts her eyes. 'Go! You've got things to do...'

Wanda lowers the back of Yvonne's bed, watches her head flop backwards, and caresses her hand which is curled with pain into a tight-knuckled fist. She strokes a wisp of her hair from her forehead before leaving.

She is startled to run into Yvonne's son as she steps out into the corridor. He is standing there, just outside the door, large and smart in his black suit jacket. He says, 'I've been eavesdropping… She doesn't talk to me, not like she does to you. She wants to die, doesn't she?'

'She just needs to rest.'

'I'm talking about what she wants, not needs!' He is towering over her, an intimidating man. Wanda tries to push by him, but he blocks her exit. 'Resting doesn't come into it. I can't bear to watch her suffer. She's my mother. She wants to die. How much longer does she have to suffer,' his voice trails off.

'You'll have to speak to her doctor. I'm only a nurse.'

'You can help her.'

'I am doing my best -'

'I don't mean that.' His glare is intense and unhealthy. Wanda is frightened of him. There should be a panic button somewhere around, next to the fire extinguisher. 'You can help her *die*. That's what she wants. She wants the pain to stop. I can pay -'

'I don't want your money. You are insulting me.'

'Surely you can see she's suffering. It's just basic human kindness. It's within your power to -'

'No, it isn't. I'm a Catholic, not a killer,' Wanda is walking away, and the man lets her.

She is sitting in front of a blank television set. It is off, but she can still hear the TV from the neighbours' flat. They listen to it loud, all hours of the day and night. It never goes silent. Most of the time Wanda is too tired to care, or even to notice the noise level. In a way it is comforting to know that somewhere in the background the hustle and bustle of everyday life goes on – *carries on regardless*. Wanda smiles at the thought of that phrase, a phrase that sums up

Englishness.

Andrzej won't be home until well after nine tonight. And when he gets here, he'll grab something quick and easy to eat and go to sleep. He has another mid-day shift tomorrow. He needs to be well rested. Driving trains isn't a walk in the park. You have to be alert at all times – you never know when someone decides to cross the rail tracks in front of you, and get his foot stuck between the sleepers. Andrzej has seen it all. But he hardly sees his wife. Sometimes, depending on their respective shifts, they miss each other altogether. Sometimes they pass each other in the doorway – two ships in the night. They exchange small pecks on the cheek and proceed in their opposite directions. It is rare that they both have a day to spend together at their leisure. It is that constant race against the clock – making money, *building their future*, saving for the flat in Krakow. And flats in Krakow don't come cheap. But Wanda has already decided – it will have to be a smaller flat. Or a different – cheaper – city. They are going home. And with the Brexit vote, they may have to go home anyway. It should make it easier to convince Andrzej that this isn't his home, that he shouldn't grow too attached to it. Yes, he has been here for ten years – most of his working life. He is used to things here, but he will just have to make the effort to say goodbye to it and to find his way back home. He has missed out on so much: Paulina's birth, most of her seven birthdays, his best friend's wedding and, most recently, his own father's funeral. Always too busy to take time off, no matter what the occasion. It seems his life here has swallowed him whole.

She can hear his heavy steps on the landing, then the key turns in the door.

'I'm home!' he shouts cheerily from the doorway. *No, you're not!* Wanda grinds her teeth. She hears him take off his boots and hang his rustling waterproof jacket on the peg in the hallway. He comes into the lounge – a peck on the cheek. 'I'm starved,' he says for hello.

'I'm homesick. I want to go home.' She ignores his needs.

Andrzej sighs. 'We've been here before, haven't we? We need another two-three years, that's all. Then we'll go, cross my heart and hope to die!'

'You've been saying that since I came here. Remember, I only came here to take you home? And I'm still here, three damned years later! I want to go now – tomorrow,' she digs her heels in.

Another sigh. 'You know you're being irrational.'

'I don't care. We must go home. Sit down. For God's sake, stop hovering over me! Just sit down!'

He slumps next to her on the couch. 'OK, I'm sitting down.'

'I had an eye-opening chat with one of our patients. Yvonne, her name. She has days left, a couple of weeks if she's lucky. She wants to go, really… It's heart-breaking I can't do anything for her…'

He pats the back of her hand, 'I know how these things unsettle you. You can get a job somewhere else. They need nurses all over the show. Apply in a normal hospital, they'll have you like a shot, with your experience…'

'No, no, it's not about the hospice or Yvonne dying. It's about me – I'm dying, inside… Yvonne sees these things. You've got that clarity of mind before you die.' She can see a tiny, almost imperceptible smirk quiver on his lips.

Andrzej is such a cynic! He hates superstitions. The dying woman's intuition is just hocus-pocus as far as Andrzej is concerned. Wanda has to refocus him, 'Don't say anything – just listen. We talked, Yvonne and I. I showed her Paulina's photo. She said I – we – should be with our child, watch over her, be there for her. We're wasting our lives here while her childhood flies by... I can't take it. It's wrong to be away from your own child. Out of choice!'

'OK. We'll bring Paulina here.'

He tries to give her a hug, but she pushes him away. 'No, we won't. We aren't bringing her here now that things are so uncertain. Absolutely no way! We're going home.'

His expression is grim and hard. He knows how to put on that face. His eyes can be soft and twinkling at times, but at a drop of a hat, they can harden into lumps of pale blue ice. 'No, we're not. We've agreed and we're going to stick to our agreement. Another two-three years and we'll have enough cash raised for the flat. We'll buy it outright, no credits, no debts. That's the best we can do for Paulina.'

'The best we can do for her is to be with her, like real parents!'

'I don't want her to watch me sit there, at your mother's, unemployed, without hope, like I used to.'

'Things have changed in the last ten years! You'll find a job. They need train drivers. They need nurses. It's a different world!'

'No,' he says quietly, but his tone is more powerful than if he were shouting. 'Two-three years...'

Wanda can't hold back her tears. 'I can't carry on like this! You don't care about Paulina! You don't know her. She hardly recognises you. You've destroyed our family. There's

52

nothing left between us and our child, nothing! I can't do this!'

He gets to his feet, 'No – it's me! I can't do what you're asking me! Not yet...'

'I'll leave you... If you don't come home with me, I'll leave you. I swear I will!'

He gives her another hard, unfeeling look, and leaves. She can hear him slam the door behind him, his steps receding on the staircase, and then all she can hear is the neighbours' TV.

Andrzej is on his third vodka. He drinks it neat, like they do in Poland. Nowadays, it'd be a pint for him – he has integrated well, hasn't he? But not today. Today, he is drinking alone and he is drinking neat vodka. It is his usual pub, the *George & Dragon*, just around the corner from the housing estate where he and Wanda live. He doesn't come here often, and never alone, but today is different. He has to think.

The bar is full of drunken people and drunken voices. The usual Friday night piss-up. Andrzej sits on his own, on a high stool at the bar. It's easy this way to order another vodka without having to get up.

He is shit scared.

It's not like him to be scared – a black belt in karate, a Junior European champion, fourteen years ago. He used to be fearless until reality had its way with him. Real life, it turned out, isn't about winning small battles. Real life is an uphill struggle. A war that goes on. In Poland, he was losing that war. He might have been, once upon a time, a Junior European champion in karate, but he had no real life skills and no work. No prospects. Not until he came here and trained to be a train driver. He has vindicated himself over the last ten years. He has proved himself. He is a breadwinner and yes – damn it! – he is a good father to Paulina. She has everything she will ever need, and more! He loves her more than anything. And he loves Wanda, damn it! He just shows it differently...

'Another one?' the barman asks.

Andrzej nods and searches his pockets for cash. He finds a note, gives it to the barman. He receives his change and his fourth vodka.

He can't lose them, Wanda and Paulina. What would be the point of proving himself if he lost them? The whole idea was to provide for them and buy a flat in Krakow, the city both he and Wanda fell in love with on their honeymoon. He promised her they would make their home there. And when that was secured, he would start his own karate school. He had it all mapped out and everything was going to plan. He can still do it, he's on track. But not without Wanda and Paulina. He may as well cut out his own heart. He downs the vodka and slams the glass on the bar, upside down. He's done drinking. Done thinking.

Andrzej staggers home on unsteady legs. The rain has stopped temporarily, but the wind is whipping him mercilessly and tries to knock him off his feet. He stumbles into a couple of puddles. With his senses numbed by the alcohol he can feel neither the water in his shoes nor the water trickling under his collar and down his spine. He reaches his block of flats, climbs up the stairs and stabs the key into the keyhole of his front door. He succeeds opening it, tumbles in, kicks off his wet shoes and hurries to the lounge. Wanda is still sitting on the coach, in the same place, the same position, in front of a blank TV screen. Her face is swollen with crying and her eyes are vivid red. They look at him, sad but determined. He will be damned if he loses her. He mumbles, 'Yeah, okay, we're going home...'

'We are?'

'I said, we are.'

She jumps off the couch and runs to him and squeezes his cheeks between her hands, and plants a kiss on his lips. He grabs her, returns her kiss. His lips and his hands are kissing her face, her hair, her whole body. She is pulling off his wet clothes; he is pulling off hers. He is so thirsty for her! The hangover of almost losing her has drained him dry. And now he will have his fill making love to his wife.

# VII

The *George & Dragon* isn't Gillian's regular watering hole. Situated on what people call the 'Allotments Estate' on the northern outskirts of Sexton's where allotments used to be, it isn't anywhere near Gillian's usual hunting spots. It's too far to walk, which isn't any good if you want to have a few drinks and can't drive. Coming here was Charlie's idea – his idea of bonding with his future mother-in-law. He picked her up at the station and drove her here.

Doubled up, they run across the car park in the unforgiving weather, the wet wind lashing at them and tugging at their clothes. Inside, the pub is pleasant enough, but character-less. It used to be a mill once upon a time, and after that it had sat abandoned and derelict for decades until the Allotments Estate was built. It was restored rather hurriedly and castrated of all its original features which would no longer serve any purpose. Gillian doesn't like it and she doesn't like its clientele – predominantly males in their twenties and thirties watching sports on a large flat-screen TV, shouting and swearing. Charlie naturally fits in.

They find a table. That isn't difficult as hardly anyone bothers to sit down in this establishment. They're all standing and moving around a lot.

'What'd you like?' Charlie asks.

'Can you afford a glass of red?'

He smiles and nods, taking himself and the flame of his strawberry-blond hair to the bar. That is the busiest part of the building. The patrons are all crowded around it, guarding their instant access to their next drinks. Charlie squeezes into the crowd. Gillian waits and gazes at the bunch of drunken young stallions without much interest. They simply aren't in her demographic bracket and couldn't possibly offer her anything she hasn't already seen or done. Even though she is starved of a man. How long was it since she had sex? Not since Sean. Ever since Sean she has been dwelling in a sexual desert. She blames Charlie Outhwaite for that. She couldn't bring home another man as long as that little twat remains co-habiting under her roof with her daughter. And now, to make it even more impossible, he is marrying her!

Where is he with those drinks? How long does it take to get a bloody drink? Charlie seems to be missing in action.

Gillian inspects the bar area packed to the brim. In the corner, a man in his mid-thirties, with a full, round face and a short crop of fair hair, is drinking alone – small shots of vodka or tequila, one after another. He is clearly intent on getting smashed.

'Here you go!' Charlie appears, bearing drinks. He places Gillian's glass on a placemat – very tidy, very unlike him. The multiple mug rings all over her beech kitchen table testify to his habitual disregard for property.

'Thanks.'

'Glad you could make it. I know how busy you are.'

'Alright. So what do you want? Spill it out.' Gillian isn't one for long preambles.

Charlie groans. 'I don't want anything… Just for us to get

57

along. You know – have a drink from time to time. Talk…'

'So you do want something.'

'Well, no. Like I said -'

'You want us to get along, right?'

'Well, yes.'

'OK.' Gillian drinks half of her glass of wine, and looks, pensive, at the table. She nods, 'I see.'

'So we are friends?'

'I wouldn't take it that far.'

'You don't like me, then?'

She finishes the rest of her wine. 'My turn?' She points to his still full glass.

'No, thank you, I'm driving. I can get you another one though.'

'Thanks.'

Reluctantly, Charlie gets up from his seat and wanders to the bar. He must've realised by now that this conversation will be nowhere near as easy as he had hoped. Gillian waits and watches the lone drinker at the bar put his glass upside down on the counter, get up, and stagger towards the door. He's had enough. Gillian has had enough, too. No, she doesn't like Charlie Outhwaite. Since that day at the airport, nearly two years ago, when he walked away from Tara, leaving her sitting alone on top of her luggage, crying. Gillian will never forget his hand caressing his girlfriend's back, the kiss the girl planted on his cheek and his face when he turned around to glance back and away again, and shatter Tara's last hope. No, it's not her job to like him. But she will watch him, every step of the way. If she can help it, she'll not let him hurt her daughter. Of course, the key phrase here is *if she can help it*. If. Because how could she stop him?

What could she do? Sweet fuck all.

'You must know I'd never hurt Tara.' Charlie places the second glass of wine in front of her. 'I love her.'

'I'm glad to hear that.'

'You must believe me. Things happened in the past that will never happen again. I was confused. Stupid! I was stupid. I didn't know what I wanted... I didn't know how to tell Heidi about Tara – Heidi was my girlfriend since we were sixteen... I, I... I couldn't bring myself to tell her. But I was wrong. I should've... There was no excuse. I'm not looking for excuses. But that's behind us. We're moving on and it seems to me that you are not.'

Does he expect her to tell him not to beat himself up over the past? She doesn't say any such thing. She drinks her wine and nods vaguely.

'I know you're against our marriage -'

'You're both a bit too young, don't you think?'

'No, I don't. I've no doubts.'

'Good. Tara doesn't have any either, but then she's a very impressionable girl.'

'Look, Gillian, can we just forget about the past? Have you made no mistakes? Just cut me some slack here...Tara and I – we're in love. We want nothing more than to be together. Give us a chance, will you? I... I...' He is stammering. 'I won't let anything bad happen to her.'

'Neither will I.' She means this to sound like a warning.

'We just need your blessing. Tara needs it -'

Gillian's mobile rings. It's work. She picks it up, 'DI Marsh.'

'We've a suspicious death,' Webber tells her, 'a seventy-eight-year-old woman in a residential home.'

'What makes it suspicious? People die in residential homes all the time.'

'They found her in her bed with her mouth taped. Otherwise they wouldn't think much of it.'

'Which residential home?'

'*Golden Autumn Retreat*, in Bishops Well.'

'Okay, I'm on my way.' She looks at Charlie's nearly full beer glass. 'Can you give me a lift to Bishops Well? It's not far from here.'

'Gertrude Hornby, seventy-eight. Advanced stages of Alzheimer's. She hasn't been recognising her own daughter in the last few months. No hoper, they tell me.' Gillian and Mark are looking at the body of an elderly lady, lying in bed, with the duvet drawn affectionately to her chest and tucked under her arms, her hands bound together on her stomach, her head resting on a smooth, well- puffed- up pillow. It seems that someone, who cared very much for her, has put her to sleep, turned off the lights and tiptoed out of her room. The only thing out of sync with this idea is the brown adhesive tape stuck across her lips. Packaging tape.

Gillian's first instinct would be that it was another case of mercy killing – a family member putting their loved out of their misery, but that tape doesn't make any sense. 'Why tape her mouth?'

'Beats me.' Webber tells her.

'How exactly did she die?' Gillian asks Dr Almond. He is new and they aren't yet on a first name basis; in fact, she doesn't even know his first name. He only started collaborating with Sexton's CID this summer. The most distinctive if not distinguishing feature about him is his huge walrus moustache and equally enormous sideburns, which had given Gillian an almighty fright when she first encountered Almond. He looks like a reincarnation of Kaiser Wilhelm.

He takes off his face mask, but this time she is prepared for the voluminous facial hair that springs from under it. 'It looks like she's been smothered, but I can't be definite until after the full post-mortem examination.'

Gillian doesn't care for the full post-mortem. 'So the packing tape did the job, you reckon?'

'No. The tape over her mouth alone would not have done the job, as you've put it so daintily. It's only decorative as far as I can tell, and it was probably added later.'

'What makes you say that?'

'Even if her mouth was covered with the tape, she'd still be able to breathe through her nose. The tape doesn't restrict nasal passages. My view is she was smothered in the more traditional way – a pillow over the face. But, like I said, I'd need to carry out -'

'A pillow? You think this pillow may have been used,' Gillian points to the pillow under the woman's head, 'to kill her and then replaced neatly in bed?'

'Maybe. As I said -'

'What time?'

'As I said -'

'Approximately, what time?'

'Between four-thirty and five, maybe earlier. It's very warm in here so the cooling of the body would've occurred at a slower rate.'

'OK.' That's the best Gillian can do to thank him. She turns to DS Webber., 'We need CCTV recordings between

61

four and six.'

'I've already asked. Two CCTV cameras: one at the front, one at the back door. The duty manager is getting the tapes ready for us. She's also mentioned that Mrs Hornby had only one visitor today – her daughter.'

'What time?'

'She didn't say. We can check entries in the Visitors book. It's kept at reception.'

'Let's do that.'

Wearing the usual protective overalls, latex gloves and paper shoes, they leave the room and head to the reception office. They traverse a long corridor with doors on both sides leading to individual residents' rooms. One such door opens right in front of them and a small, skinny woman peers out, probably intrigued by the voices and commotion in her neighbour's room. She takes one look at Gillian and Mark Webber, clutches her chest and emits the most harrowing shrill shriek known to man. She staggers backwards and is caught by Webber before collapsing to the floor.

'Don't touch me! Don't touch me!' she is slapping him about as he tries to escort her back to her room and explain that she has nothing to fear – they are police officers.

A carer is running towards them, shouting, 'It's all right, Mrs Fallon! Calm down! It's only the police.' The carer takes over from Webber, who is by now well traumatised, and leads the old lady back to her room. Turning towards Webber, she says angrily, 'You scared the living daylights out of her with all that alien getup! Lucky she didn't have a heart attack. She's got a weak heart, don't you, Mrs Fallon?'

Mrs Fallon whimpers.

Gillian smirks as Webber takes himself out of his overalls.

The carer fixes Gillian with an equally scolding glare, 'You too, if you don't mind!' and shuts the door.

Suitably chastised, they find their way to the reception on tiptoe. The duty manager, one Mrs Robson, is there, ready with the CCTV tape. She is a chubby woman in her mid-fifties, dressed professionally in too small a suit jacket and high heels that make her little feet in contrast with her swollen ankles look like Miss Piggy's trotters.

Gillian introduces herself to Mrs Robson, who is already acquainted with DS Webber. She checks Gillian's warrant card carefully as if she has reason to doubt Gillian's word and her rank. She says, 'This is terribly upsetting for all the staff, and the residents will be beside themselves with grief when they find out in the morning. Mrs Hornby was well loved by all. Of course, this whole... *business*... has nothing to do with any of us.'

'Can we take a look at your Visitors book?'

'Poor Mrs Hornby has been nothing but a breath of fresh air since she joined us two years ago. She used to be a teacher at our local primary school. She taught me and then my daughter, bless her... And even when she retired, until her mind started going, she'd been working for all sorts of charities – mainly children's charities... She loved children, our Mrs Hornby. Everyone here knows... I mean *knew* her as a wonderful person. Kind. Loving.'

'Yes, great. We're not looking for a character reference,' Gillian reminds her. 'Could we have that Visitors book, please?'

Mrs Robson wipes her nose and points her to the book,

'Yes, of course. Feel free to have a look. We keep very detailed records: arrival and departure times, signed personally by every visitor.'

Webber reads the entries. 'Right, Cherie Hornby, that's the daughter?'

'Yes, Cherie – Mrs Hornby's only child. She visits… *visited*… every day, regular like a clock. Doted on her mother, especially after Mrs Hornby's condition deteriorated. In the last six months,' Mrs Robson sighs, 'it has been painful watching her go downhill so quickly… Poor Cherie! I saw her leave in tears many times. But what can you do? Nothing! There's no cure…'

'She arrived at four twelve and left at four twenty… That was a very short visit, wouldn't you say? Is that normal?'

'No, of course it isn't *normal!*' Mrs Robson appears highly irritated by the question. 'Cherie would stay for an hour, or more – *normally*. But today, it was particularly tough for her. She left in tears. Very upset. I remember clearly because I asked if there was anything I could do and she said no, unless I could make her poor mother remember who she was. She said Mrs Hornby was very agitated and asked her why she was going through her belongings. She accused her of stealing from her. Cherie was beside herself…'

Gillian and Mark exchange a brief, knowing glance, and he thanks Mrs Robson for her assistance. Armed with the CCTV tape and the Visitors book, they head for Mark's car.

'Has Cherie Hornby been informed?' Gillian asks.

'Yes, Family Liaison have gone to see her.'

'We'll leave it until tomorrow,' Gillian decides to be tactful and considerate of the woman's loss. But not for long. 'Tomorrow morning we'll have to bring her in.'

'Yeah,' Webber agrees. 'If you look at the way the victim was tucked away in bed -'

'Lovingly, is the word. It looks like the daughter, definitely.'

'But I can't figure out the tape. What's with the tape over her mouth?'

'Maybe she just didn't know how to go about it – about smothering her effectively. Maybe it wasn't as quick as she thought it'd be. Maybe she feared the woman was still alive and she wanted to finish the job. It could've been a final touch. Clumsy, unnecessary, but how was she to know? It isn't every day that people euthanize their parents – she just didn't know how to do it.'

'A bit gory for a loving daughter, though. As much as I can understand mercy killing, especially with the distress of watching your loved one turn into this raving stranger accusing you of stealing… You want to end their suffering. Make it quick. But that tape…' Webber grimaces.

'Yes, it's odd. It was applied post-mortem. Plus, it implies premeditation – someone has brought that tape into the victim's room. Why? What were they hoping to achieve with that? What are we dealing with?'

They are sitting in the car. Webber starts the engine. 'So what's it going to be – are we visiting the daughter or should I drop you home?'

'An inexperienced, emotional killer – a spur of the moment killing, perhaps assisted suicide – or a well-thought-through murder?' Gillian is thinking aloud. Inventorising contradictory raw data. 'What if the mother had a lucid moment and asked her daughter for help? Maybe the mother had the tape at the ready... Did they find the packing tape at the scene?'

'No.'

'Yes.'

Mark Webber looks at her., 'Yes to what?'

'To dropping me home. We'll have more detail tomorrow from the forensics and the pathologist. The daughter can wait. She isn't going anywhere.'

They drive in silence. Gillian doesn't like this case. She doesn't like assisted suicide cases altogether. Who is she to tread over people's family lives and their pain of watching their loved ones suffer the indignity or agony of terminal illness? She prefers to sweep those cases under the carpet whenever she can, whenever inconclusive evidence permits. But this case is different. It's that damned packing tape.

It is nearly midnight when Webber drops her at her doorstep and speeds off home to his ailing family. Gillian knows things have taken a turn for the worse with Kate. Webber doesn't say much about it, but he did say the other day that his mother had come to stay with them to look after the girls when he is at work. So that says it all. Gillian doesn't want to pry. He will talk to her when he's ready; if he's ever ready. She tiptoes inside her dark house. Tara and Charlie must be already in bed, asleep or doing things people sometimes do in the dark, things she doesn't want to contemplate. At least she doesn't have to face Charlie Outhwaite and fend off his attempts at family bonding. She feels a bit guilty about dragging him away from his pint, though. She should make it up to him. Maybe take him for a drink to reciprocate for his efforts.

66

She kicks off her shoes and tells Corky to be quiet when he starts yelping in delight at seeing her. At least someone does. She pats the dog on the head. 'Good boy, Corky. Do you miss your master? Do you miss Sean?'

The dog's ears twitch at the sound of his owner's name. It'll be a while before he sees him again. Sean has been sentenced to life imprisonment. He will have to serve a minimum term of sixteen years, which isn't surprising considering that the use of explosives was involved. A long time for a man, an even longer one for his dog.

Gillian has been contemplating visiting Sean in prison. Now that his sentence has been passed there is nothing in the rule book to stop her. She just can't find the time. Work is one thing, but with the wedding now – will she ever be able to do what she wants? Right now she wants a cup of tea, but can't be bothered. She is too knackered to put the kettle on. She drags herself upstairs. Before going into her bedroom and collapsing in bed, she has this strong need to see her daughter, make sure she is all right. She listens by Tara's door for any sound of activity. There is none. She pushes the door open. It wasn't properly on the latch so it gives way without any resistance. The feeble light from the landing streams into the room. Tara is sleeping with her mouth open, her head resting on Charlie's chest. His arm is wrapped around her and his face is slightly obscured by her hair splashed across it. They are two matching pieces of the puzzle, joined together. They look happy. Made for each other. Gillian may have to accept it. She smiles, shuts the door carefully so as to not wake them, and shuffles to her room. She must remember to take Charlie for that drink.

# VIII

The house is on a hill overlooking the olive grove. Haji has just walked through without being seen by anyone except an old donkey who gave him an impassive glance and went back to grazing. The olive trees are swelling with fruit: big, juicy olives, tasting like heaven. Anything would taste like heaven when you haven't had a scrap to eat in days. But the olives have hardly touched the sides. Haji needs a decent meal, and some rest. He feels giddy and disoriented; his feet are raw. The smugglers had made everybody take their shoes off, which was all the same on the boat, but climbing rocky cliffs barefoot and walking along dirt roads has proved very trying. Haji has bleeding cuts to show for it. With the dirt getting into the cuts, he fears he may end up with an infection that will put him out of action for days. He must find a place to wash his feet and get some sleep before he continues on his journey. The farmhouse looks promising. It is isolated. From what he can gather, there are only two inhabitants: an old man and his wife.

He has watched the house for a couple of hours: the comings and goings. The woman came out once to feed chickens. The man sat on a bench under the window for hours, smoking and dozing off from time to time. When his wife popped out, he talked to her animatedly. It seemed like

68

he was lambasting her for something, but she wasn't having it, giving back as much as she took, if not more. They both spoke fast and loud, waving their arms and wagging their fingers. It amused Haji to watch them. Then the woman went back inside and the man chuckled to himself before collapsing into a contented silence on the bench.

A postman came and went, delivering no post. He propped his bicycle against the wall and sat next to the farmer. They had a cigarette and stared at the horizon for a while. The farmer's wife popped out again, and they all started talking over each other, loud and agitated, arms flying, like they were having an argument. By then, Haji had realised this was how the Italians spoke: fast and furiously. But it wasn't a row.

When the postman is well out of sight, Haji musters the courage to approach the farmer. He seems like a decent man. His ruddy face is moulded with wrinkles, olive-brown, earthy. He cocks his head when he sees Haji, gets up from his bench and makes a few steps forward towards him.

Haji waves his arm and smiles – he comes in peace. He tries not to hobble too much so that he looks fit and strong, so that the farmer is happy to give him work. 'Hello,' Haji says in English, hoping the farmer gets the gist, 'I'm looking for work. Any work? I can work hard.'

The farmer frowns, eyeing Haji's face, crumpled clothes, and bare feet with suspicion. He is clearly taken aback by Haji's request and by the foreign language he is hearing, but he understands. He says, 'No, no! No work! You go!' He is waving Haji away.

'I can pick olives,' Haji suggests, pointing towards the olive grove. He is nodding encouragement to the farmer, and smiling. Smiling is good. There is never too much smiling.

'No work! No work!' the farmer repeats, backing into his house. There is fear in his eyes. Haji has seen and smelled fear so often in his life that no one could ever hide it from him. The farmer won't be persuaded to give Haji work and shelter – he is scared of him. He is now talking in Italian, gesturing to him angrily and frowning. Haji doesn't have to know Italian to understand the message – the man wants him gone.

'OK, I go! OK, no problem!' Haji assures the man and turns his back to him. He starts walking, this time limping away slowly to show the man that he is weak, that he poses no threat. He can feel the man's eyes boring into his back. Then he hears the door slam, and he knows the man has gone inside. Haji turns and runs back to the house, bleeding feet notwithstanding. He has no time to spare. Even as he approaches the house, he can see inside it through an open window. The farmer is on the phone. His wife is next to him, cupping her hands with anxiety, bending her fingers. Haji knows they're calling the police.

He kicks the door in and strides up to the couple. He takes the man out first, cutting his throat in one swift move as he takes hold of his chin and lifts it to expose his jugular vein. The knife slices the skin with ease. The woman shrills. It is the same noise that other woman made on the boat when her husband was shot dead by the smuggler. The same noise all women make in the face of death. It's a harrowing sound. It stabs Haji in the gut. The farmer's body becomes heavy in Haji's embrace. The moment a person dies, their body weighs a ton. Haji drops it. It hits the floor with a thud. The woman's cry dies on her lips with that thud. She glances at

Haji and runs.

It's no good for her to run. She won't make it without her husband. An old woman without her man, she is doomed. In a way, Haji will be putting her out of her misery. But even if he weren't feeling sorry for her, he would still have to kill her. He can't afford to let her go free. The first thing she would do would be to call the authorities and alert them to Haji's presence. He is an illegal alien.

He follows her into the darker, cooler interior of her stone farmhouse and catches up with her in a windowless corner. She has nowhere to run so she slumps to her knees and cries, and pleads with him. She wants to live even though her husband is dead and she won't make it without him. The instinct of survival is a blinding force. Haji puts his finger to his lips and tells her to shush, her whinnying getting on his nerves. She nods keenly and tries her best to be quiet, now reduced to only just a whimper. He leans over her, steadies her head by holding it by the hair, and cuts across her throat. And she becomes as heavy as her husband. Haji leaves her convoluted body on the floor in a puddle of her still pulsating and still bright red blood.

Now that the farmer and his wife are reunited, Haji takes over their house. He has until tomorrow noon when the postman is likely to come along as he did today, and find them both dead. Stepping gingerly over the dead farmer's body, Haji raids the kitchen and has a feast of bread, cheese and Parma ham. He stays away from marinated olives. He drinks cold milk from the fridge. When he is full, he scours the house for a medical box. There is bound to be one on a farm. And there is: bandages, an antiseptic spray, a box of aspirin tablets, plasters. Good. He can tend to his wounded feet, but he will do it after he has a wash.

He has a long, warm bath. The heat opens up the cuts on his feet and they bleed into the bathwater, rendering it pink. Haji washes himself thoroughly. He borrows the farmer's razor to shave after cutting his beard and hair. His reflection in the mirror looks unfamiliar: scarred and sallow. If it wasn't for his heavily hooded eyes, he wouldn't recognise the man staring at him from the mirror. His feet are still bleeding as he negotiates the stairs back to the kitchen, leaving bloody footprints on the stone steps. He slumps in a chair, sprays the antiseptic on the soles of his feet, and bandages them, including his ankles. He finds that doing that helps with his left ankle, the one that suffered badly in that blast on the Syrian-Iraqi border five months ago.

He has found nice Western clothes in the wardrobe upstairs. They belonged to the farmer and he won't have any need for them any longer. The farmer wasn't big and neither is Haji. He is made of wire and bone. And, of course, sand. The clothes are well-fitting. He will take a spare set on his forward journey. He will blend with the background, looking just like all the other men in Italy. They are olive-skinned and dark-eyed, just like him.

Downstairs, in one of the rooms, a TV set is playing softly. Haji has been subconsciously aware of the hum of the television all along. Now, he sits on a settee facing the TV set, puts his weary feet up and looks at the screen. At first, his eyes are vacant, then he scowls and leans forward to see better. His eyesight isn't what it used to be and he has to squint, but he is sure: he is looking at Boy! He would recognise those large, hungry eyes anywhere, any time! Boy is being tended to in a hospital bed while a journalist is talking to him with the help of a black interpreter. It's in Italian and Haji doesn't know what is being said, but he is so glad to see Boy alive and well. Even though the child is crying. Children often cry.

It has been a long and precarious journey north. Traversing Italy by train and in the back of many unsuspecting lorries, Haji has seen many wonders along the way, but the city of Venice is the greatest curiosity yet. It's built on water. Such an abundance of water! Haji is fascinated. Every few metres he crosses another arching bridge and looks down on another canal, full of green water lapping against mossy banks. Seagulls rest on mooring poles. Tenements spring out of water, it seems, and some people have to travel in boats to get to their front doors. What a curiosity!

With the money he found at the farmhouse, Haji bought a writing pad and a pencil. It has been decades since he held a pencil in his hand. At first it feels awkward and his fingers are too stiff to get a decent grip, but soon it all comes back to him. With his rucksack by his side, he sits on some steps that are part submerged in water and sketches the piazza on the other side of the canal: the terrace of narrow townhouses with colourful shutters and the vibrant greenery spilling out of hanging baskets. White sheets are flapping on a washing line stretched between two first-floor balconies over a narrow alley. In his mind's eye, or nose rather, Haji can smell the freshness of the wash day. If only he could convey that somehow in his sketch…

He always liked drawing and painting, not that he had any formal training in fine arts. He didn't even know he was any good at it, not until he had travelled to Moscow to study.

And it wasn't fine arts, it was chemistry. Still, away from Kabul and the suffocating tribal mentality dictating that being a man he had to act like one, not like a feeble-minded woman, Haji discovered the finer things in life, like drawing and poetry, and the wonders of the exotic Orthodox architecture. In Moscow he found parks, museums, and places superfluous to man's everyday needs, and yet, he soon discovered, indispensable. No one minded if from time to time he took himself out of lectures to walk the streets, marvelling and absorbing the magic of the city. He was free to spend hours sketching little street scenes and corners that captured his attention. Soon he introduced colour to his pencil sketches. Unlike sun-bleached Kabul, Moscow was buzzing with colours: strong, definite primary colours. Its beating heart was suitably red: Red Square. It was pulsating with life which was pumped into the arteries of wide roads that led away from it and into the greater body of the Russian capital. Through his drawings he grew into the fabric of the city and became its citizen, body and soul. He became a Muscovite.

Just like today, in Venice, Haji would wear Western clothes. He had long hair and sideburns. He fitted in and thought he couldn't be any happier, until Svetlana breezed into his life and showed him the true meaning of happiness.

'I like the colours,' she said, 'So vivid! I bet that's what it looked like when it was built all those years ago.' She was standing behind the bench upon which he was sitting, deep in work. He was using watercolours to add final touches to his rendition of the magnificent Pokrovsky Cathedral. He was gratified that someone noticed he had taken poetic licence with the colours of the domes and carved porches.

And he was exulted to discover that that someone was Svetlana.

He stared at her for a while, lost for words. She wasn't just any old girl – she was an apparition. Perhaps it was in the way the sunlight bounced off her gold-plated hair; perhaps it was the breeze that tugged at her summery dress and pressed it against her slender body, revealing her perfect shape. Perhaps it was the softness of her tiny hand when she offered it to him and said, 'I'm Svetlana.'

She was so small he thought he could hold her on his palm, but it was she who took hold of him, and claimed him. She laughed, 'Do you have a name?'

'Haji. Haji,' he stammered.

'Are you an artist, Haji-Haji? I love beautiful things and your watercolour is beautiful.'

'You can have it!'

'Oh, I couldn't possibly!' She protested, but he could see it in her eyes that she wanted it. He whipped the painting from the easel and thrust it at her, a bit too hard.

'Sorry.'

She didn't acknowledge his apology – she was holding the watercolour with her small hands, her eyes feasting on it; Haji's eyes feasting on her.

'Can I draw your portrait?' He dared to ask only because he was afraid he would never see this girl again, that, being an apparition, she would vanish like a puff of smoke and be gone; the memory of her would slowly fade away and one day he would wake up and be unable to recall her face. He was a stupid young man to have thought that. Svetlana was unforgettable. But he struck lucky – she agreed. That day, he sketched his first portrait of Svetlana as she was laughing, a

75

little uncertain, a little nervous, her head thrown back slightly, her upper lip full and sinuous, and a streak of her blonde hair crossing her cheek.

Haji pulls out a waterproof pouch from under his shirt. It hangs on his neck and contains things most precious to him, things he could never replace. One of them is Svetlana's portrait – the first one he drew of her. He holds it gently in his hand, not to damage it. It is very fragile – it's nearly forty years old. He feasts his eyes on it all over again, like he did that first day they met.

They went for a walk in Izmailovsky Forest. It was bursting with new life and all those woodland sounds and colours, and with light seeping through the canopies of trees. Soon they were holding hands, and two years later they married and she came to live with him in Afghanistan. His Russian bride – his life in colour.

Haji replaces Svetlana's portrait in the pouch and slides it under his shirt. He returns to his drawing. A middle-aged couple are standing behind him, casting their shadows over his sketch. In a strong American twang, the woman says, 'Look here, Doug, awesome drawing! I wish I could draw like that!'

Haji turns to face them. He has to shade his eyes against the sun. Their features are indistinct, their bodies corpulent. He tears the page with the sketch out of the pad and hands it to the woman, 'You can have it.'

'Oh, I couldn't possibly!' she exclaims, but takes the drawing. The man called Doug thanks Haji and wishes him a good day. Haji closes his eyes and lets the sun kiss his eyelids, like Svetlana used to.

# IX

So now Ahmed knows what's going on with Malik. He is training to be a train driver! Discipline has returned to his life. No more late nights languishing in front of the computer screen and scouring social media. No more moaning and groaning about the weather and the world's seven plagues. No more beard. Yes, the long cultivated beard is gone from Malik's face and once again he resembles your average human being. It is the face that brings Ahmed's old friend back from the dead: youthful, soft, and round-eyed – a face you can trust when you're lost and want directions in the street. That beard of his used to be a deterrent. It would put anyone off. It put Malik's girlfriend off, though he would never admit that. He won't talk about it either. He talks about other things. 'The world needs train drivers, doesn't it?' Malik tells Ahmed, laughing. 'Look at all them striking on Southern Rail! Someone has to do the job. It may as well be me.'

'If you say so.' Ahmed tries to shrug it off. But he's uncomfortable. Malik's motives are unclear. Why is he doing this – this bizarre work experience project? He has now put his studies on hold and stopped attending lectures altogether. He says he's taking a sabbatical, which would be OK. If it made sense. It's not like Malik needs money to pay his way through college. His family are wealthy. So far they've been paying for everything. He didn't even have to take any student loans. So why? 'Did you tell your folks?'

Malik fixes him with a hard glare. 'Why would I? It's nobody's business but mine.'

'Shouldn't they know you left uni?'

'I didn't leave, did I? I'm taking a break. Just stay out of it, yeah?'

'They have the right to know.'

'For fuck's sake, Ahmed, you're like a fucking broken record. Get a life! Just stay out of mine.' He slams the door behind him.

Ahmed leaves a few minutes later, the usual time he does so every morning. He catches the 8:53 bus from just outside the building. As he climbs up the stairs from the flat to the street level, he finds that Pippa is waiting for him. She is standing at the top of the steps, pressing a white envelope to her chest. Her eyes are burning with excitement. Despite the chill she is wearing only her flimsy blouse, which may be enough in her well-heated flat but offers no resistance to the biting cold outside. Her legs are bare, though she has slippers on.

'I've just missed Malik,' she tells Ahmed. 'I saw him from the window, shouted after him to wait, but he was gone. Must be late for school, I thought.'

'Yeah, I guess.'

'You don't go together, like you used to?'

'No. Different places, different directions, I'm afraid. But how are you doing? You all right?'

'Oh, we're fine! We're better than fine!' she gushes.

'We're walking on air!'

'Good. I'm glad to hear that.'

She is gazing at him, expectant and delighted, hoping he'll ask more questions – the usual, neighbourly chit-chat. But Ahmed is already late for the bus. 'I'll see you later, Pippa. Send my regards to Harry, won't you?'

'Oh yes, of course. He's upstairs. A bit of a cold. God knows how he got it. I call it *man flu*. He considers himself bed-ridden,' she chuckles.

'Malik wasn't feeling too good last week. Maybe Harry has caught his bug.'

'Ah!'

'Well, I'd better be going.'

'Yes, of course! I'll see you later!' She turns, her little smile friendly and warm. She has this knack of warming up his heart every time he sees her. Little old ladies have this effect on Ahmed.

'Oh dear!' She rushes back, 'Oh dear, dear! What a fool I am! I forgot why I came here in the first place... The letter,' she presents the white envelope she has been clutching close to her chest. 'We wrote to Will, you see?'

'Great!' Ahmed is definitely late, his hope of catching the 8:53 now gone. He may as well stay and listen. He'll walk and give the library a miss. It's not the end of the world. The walk should do him some good.

'It took us several attempts,' Pippa shakes her head, bemused. 'Would you imagine writing to your own son being such a mission impossible? Well, it was! It was a torture! We didn't want to get a word wrong... It's so important – our first contact! Dear me, I'm still shaking just to think about it.'

Ahmed doesn't know what to say so he smiles and nods.

'In the end, after much deliberation, we decided to invite him to come and visit us. An open-ended invitation, you see, not to put him under any pressure whatsoever. Harry thought we had to make it clear that we didn't expect him to come – we just hoped... You see, I'd rather if Will knew how much, how much I really want to -' her voice crumbles.

'How much you want to see him?' Ahmed finishes the sentence for her.

She nods. 'Would you mind awfully sending this letter off for us? Harry being bedridden...'

'Yeah, no problem.' He takes the letter and glances at it. It bears an address in Australia, written in a beautiful hand.

'We put a first-class stamp. He should get it soon,' Pippa beams. 'Thank you, Ahmed. Very kind of you.'

'Don't mention it.' He puts the letter in his backpack. Of course, now he will have to swerve by the Post Office to pay for the postage to Australia. The first class stamp won't take the letter beyond Dover, but Pippa doesn't need to know all that technical detail. 'I'll send it on my way to uni. Consider it done.'

The nearest Post Office he can think of is in the Co-op on a fairly new estate, just two streets away. It will be a diversion from his route, but that's the least he can do for an old lady in a flimsy blouse and a pair of slippers, an old lady who is a good friend. It is the other friend of his that Ahmed fears he can do nothing for. He suspects there is something sinister brewing under the surface of Malik's transformation. There is an ulterior motive behind that whole absurd idea of Malik becoming a bloody train driver, and that motive doesn't bare scrutiny. What reason on this earth would

Malik have to abandon his degree, a decent engineering degree, in the name of learning to drive a train? One thing springs to mind. Should Ahmed be calling the police?

He might be wrong. Malik is his friend. Malik is not the type.

They'll have to talk first. Tonight.

The estate is bustling with life. Every parking space is taken, cars glued to the kerb and double-parked in the middle of the road. The morning school run. Mums are walking their children to the school gate, pushing prams, chatting, letting the children run free, cross the road and climb the playground apparatus on the school grounds. A couple of girls are hanging upside down on parallel bars, their skirts wrapped around their heads. A boy has climbed up to the top of the monkey bars and refuses to come down. A line of children has formed beneath; some are shouting at him to get down – it's somebody else's turn. Malik smiles at the memories of his school playground in Worcester. He was that boy on top of the climbing pole, claiming supremacy over the world.

'What you staring at?' A hostile male voice brings him back to earth. A big man, bald and scruffily dressed, has rounded upon Ahmed. He has a little girl with him, holding her small hand in his big paw. The girl is also gazing at Ahmed with a round-eyed and round-mouthed curiosity.

'Nothing,' Ahmed mumbles and starts walking away. He has obviously aroused some suspicion: a man without a child hanging around a school. People are paranoid these days.

'Pervert!' the man shouts after him.

A few pairs of eyes burn into Ahmed's back.

'What you doin' here? Get out! Go back home! We voted

you out!' Every word is a lash. Ahmed picks up pace. He is running. He doesn't want to run but his legs aren't responding to his will. He is running away, like a beaten dog.

He seeks shelter in the Co-op. He slows down and starts catching his breath. His heart is pounding. He tries to calm down, look normal and act as if nothing is amiss. He feels like everybody's eyes are on him, but when he dares to look he finds customers minding their business – the business of shopping, something one ordinarily does when in a shop. But to Ahmed it seems like they are only pretending not to notice him, not to know. Deep down they're willing him out; they're willing him to go back home. And they don't mean Worcester. There is a conspiracy of hostile silence around him. They're watching him.

He joins the queue for the Post Office counter. He is convinced that the woman in front of him has shifted slightly forward when he stood behind her. Has he stood too close to her? Has he invaded her space? Does she resent his physical closeness?

The woman reaches the front of the queue and heads to the next available teller. A light displaying number 2 flashes and Ahmed follows the arrow. He buys the extra postage for Pippa's letter, pays cash, tells the teller he doesn't need a receipt. He doesn't even notice that the teller is a gorgeous young Asian woman, and that she is smiling at him. She likes him, but Ahmed doesn't know that. He thanks her without looking up, and leaves.

He hasn't gone to lectures today. Nor did he bother with the library. He has spent the day loitering aimlessly about town.

It feels like he is hung-over. His temples are throbbing and he is thirsty as hell, but he can't bring himself to do anything about it. He is just walking. A weak thought has crossed his mind that he should report this to the police, but he banishes that thought faster than it can take any tangible form. He wouldn't be able to take the humiliation of making the complaint. And how would he explain being there in the first place, watching the kids play? He keeps walking.

The first touches of Christmas have sprung up in shop window displays. They are erecting stalls for the Christmas market. Buskers are performing on street corners, their clashing tunes sparring in mid-air, taking a stab here and there with a higher note, louder bass, faster beat. The streets are rippling with shoppers for the best part of the day; then it all starts dying out towards the evening when the shops close. Wandering the emptying streets feels less safe. Sometimes Ahmed is forced to meet somebody's eye. It's discomforting. The crowd moves from the shopping precinct and into the pubs. Young men chat outside pubs with young women dressed in pink fairy dresses and bunny ears. Hen and stag nights mingle. Cigarette smoke wraps itself around them. A homeless man with his best friend,, aa black Staffordshire terrier with a greying snout, , has made himself comfortable by the entrance to a posh French restaurant. A waiter from the restaurant is asking the man to move on but the man is having none of it. He tells the waiter to go and fuck himself.

Ahmed's feet are killing him. He goes home.

'You look shit!' Malik greets him. 'Where have you been?'

'Nowhere... I posted a letter for Pippa.' Ahmed doesn't

want to talk. He'd much rather Malik wasn't home so he could just throw himself in bed and sleep.

'What – you been posting a letter all day long? Don't give me that shit! What's with you?'

Ahmed shrugs. He doesn't want to talk about it, and he doesn't even want to say that he doesn't want to talk about it.

'All right, suit yourself. I'm hungry. Going to Tariq's. You coming, or what?'

'Don't know...' Ahmed realises that he hasn't had anything to eat all day. He is starved, and still bloody thirsty, but he has just dragged himself off the streets to come home. If he could help it, he'd rather leave the streets behind him. But he knows that the fridge is empty, or if there is anything there it is well past its expiry date.

'Come on, then! Don't keep me waiting. I fancy a shish kebab.'

They're eating their kebabs outside the joint, sitting on the stone wall of the neighbouring car park. At least Malik has shut up – his mouth is full. It's dark now so he can't see Ahmed's face, which is a blessing. They are hunched on the wall; the cold wind is trying to dislodge them from it. A loud bunch of revellers stagger into Tariq's, their drunken voices and the women's short skirts and high heels testifying to their party mood. They crowd around the counter, ordering their takeaways. The fluorescent light inside the establishment indecently touches the girls' half-naked bodies. It's a cold night. It must be the alcohol and adrenaline that keeps these women warm. The party bursts into laughter. Malik's body stiffens. Ahmed can sense it. They are sitting close to each other, their arms touching. He can sense Malik's discomfort. And he can hear Malik speak, 'Fucking white slut. Look at that filth!'

Ahmed looks, and he recognises one of the girls. Cara, Malik's once-upon-a-time girlfriend. He was head-over-heels in love with her. About a year ago. Then they broke up, suddenly and without an explanation. Malik came home, drunk as a skunk, and said he was through with her. And then he never spoke of Cara, and Ahmed never asked.

Cara kisses the man on whose arm she is hanging. It is only a peck on the cheek. She lowers her head onto his shoulder, her long blonde hair spilling onto his back. The man takes off his jacket and throws it over her shoulders. He kisses her on top of her head.

'White slut,' Malik grumbles. He chucks his half-eaten kebab in a bin. He misses – pieces of meat and salad roll out of the paper wrapper.

'You finished with her a year ago. She can see who she likes.'

'She was seeing who she liked a year ago too,' Malik informs him. 'The bitch told me I wasn't good enough for her. Apparently I'm not the type you take home to meet your parents. Why do you think that is, Ahmed? You have all the answers.' There is raw hurt in Malik's eyes, like it has never gone away. Ahmed knows that kind of hurt, so he tells Malik about this morning on the estate. And he instantly feels better, because Malik understands him better than anyone. They are best friends, again.

# X

Cherie Hornby is bewildered. Her eyes zigzag between DI Marsh and DS Webber. They are red and swollen. The poor woman must have been through a sleepless and tearful night after the Family Liaison officers visited her yesterday with the worst possible news. Assuming it was news to her that her mother had been murdered. It may not have been news at all. Gillian hasn't made up her mind yet.

Miss Hornby is a spinster. A short woman with good posture and a spiky, tight hairstyle, something a paramilitary feminist would be proud of. Most certainly, soft and gentle femininity isn't her forte, and that makes one think she is capable of killing. But the bloodshot eyes and the demeanour of a hapless babe in the woods tell a different story. If she killed her mother, she definitely hadn't planned it. Manslaughter is a distinct possibility, however.

'Would you like a cup of coffee?' Gillian tries to put the woman at ease.

'No. No, thank you.' She flinches as if Gillian had offered her a cup of poison. 'I don't know why I've been arrested…'

'This isn't an arrest. This is a voluntary interview. You're simply helping us with our inquiries into your mother's death.'

A thin gasp escapes her when she hears the last two words, *mother* and *death,* uttered alongside each other in the same sentence.

'We need to clarify a few things to fill gaps in our timeline,' DS Webber informs her in his usual highly efficient manner. 'You may have been the last person to see your mother alive, apart from her killer, of course. You may be an important witness. We need to know what you remember while it's all fresh in your mind.'

'Are you sure?'

'Sure of what, Miss Hornby?'

'T... that Mum was... that she didn't die of natural causes?'

'Pretty sure. The evidence points to a third party involvement in her death. Conclusively.'

'How did she die?'

'She was smothered.'

Another desperate gasp. And then, 'Who would've done such a thing! To a hopeless woman! And why?' Her swollen eyes search Gillian's face.

'Precisely. We need answers,' Gillian says. 'Let us go back to your last visit to see your mother – yesterday, at...'Gillian checks the file, 'at four-twelve pm. Is that correct?'

'Probably. I always visit Mum at about the same time – four o'clock.'

'And you left her at about four -twenty? Ten minutes... not even ten minutes...'

'She upset me. She really did! I shouldn't have got upset - - she doesn't know what she's saying, but I couldn't help it.'

'So you were upset with her? What about?'

Miss Hornby sighs, interlocks her fingers and presses her forehead into them. 'I wasn't upset with her... I was just – upset! With myself, if anyone. She said her hankies had been going missing. She doesn't even use handkerchiefs any more. She uses disposable tissues... I told her that, and she went berserk. Cried and shouted, said I had stolen all her hankies. A thief and a liar, she shouted. Ordered me to leave, never come back. She wanted a different nurse, a nicer nurse. I was a thief; she was going to make a complaint about me! I'd lose my job! That'd be my come-uppance for thieving from old ladies. I should be ashamed of myself.... On and on! It was utter drivel and I shouldn't have taken it personally, but you... You can't sometimes. I left. I ran out! Of course, I would be back today and she would've forgotten all about the damned hankies! If I hadn't left her on her own...' She looks genuinely crestfallen, but appearances can be deceiving. Everything is relative in the murder business, Gillian reminds herself: the woman could be distraught that her mother is dead and yet she could still have killed her. It's quite a common thing in assisted suicide. Except with all the emotions flying high, this looks less like assisted suicide and more like a spur-of-the-moment manslaughter. If it wasn't for the packing tape. Of which Gillian and Webber choose not to speak to Miss Hornby.

'So you ran out of your mother's room – upset?'

'Yes, but I wasn't angry with her.'

'No, you were just upset. Very upset?'

'Yes...' she glances at DI Marsh without comprehension.

'I'm asking how upset you were because you still remembered to sign out... you know, the Visitors book... If

I were very upset I would've most likely forgotten...'

'What are you saying?' The woman is visibly shaken by the implied accusation. Who wouldn't be? 'It's a force of habit. I always sign in and out. Mrs Robson is very particular about it. They all are.'

'So you signed out. Did you speak to anyone?'

'I don't know. I can't remember,' she looks at Webber, imploring him to believe her since DI Marsh seems so mistrusting. 'You wouldn't remember if you were upset and just wanted to get the hell out of there, have a good cry at home without anyone seeing...'

'But you did speak to Mrs Robson, she told us,' Gillian is a pitbull.

'Maybe I did...'

'OK, let's leave that aside. When you left your mother's room, did you see anyone outside - - in the corridor, the reception area? Anyone you didn't recognise? Anyone behaving oddly?'

'A killer, you mean? Someone who could've killed my mother? Because I didn't! That thought has never crossed my mind! She was an innocent old lady. She wasn't suffering, wasn't in pain – just... just forgetful... Why would I want to kill her? Why would anyone?'

'Someone has, Miss Hornby, so please help us here. Think back: did you see anyone?'

She shakes her head. 'It's a daze... I can't... I saw a nurse, I think... I think Mrs Fallon opened her door and asked me if everything was OK... Or maybe it was a different day. There were people, carers, residents... I'm getting the days confused. I can't think!' She buries her face in her hands and slides them up and down. She looks up at the interviewing officers, 'This is insane. I can't remember anything. My mother's just died!'

Webber looks at Gillian intently. His eyes are saying the poor woman has had enough. Sometimes Gillian has to be reminded of such things. She is not good at letting go. She nods, 'Thank you, Miss Hornby. We'll be in touch. You're free to go for now.'

The woman gazes at her, uncomprehending.

'We are very sorry for your loss,' Webber puts it so much better. 'I'll have someone take you home.'

Scarface wants to see her in his office about *a delicate matter*. Gillian could bet it is something to do with Miss Hornby from Bishops Well, Scarface's home turf. He treads ever so carefully around his little bumpkin-pals, so very carefully that Gillian herself has become proficient at tip-toeing. She could become a ballerina and do a good job of it. Now, Miss Hornby. She probably takes tea with the Scarfes every Tuesday. It will be a minefield of side-stepping sensibilities. Perhaps for the better. Perhaps Gillian will receive Detective Superintendent Scarfe's rubber-stamp blessing to dispose of this probable assisted suicide as quickly and as discreetly as possible.

She would be glad to, but for the packing tape stuck over the victim's lips. That tape can't be swept under the carpet. Gillian readies herself for a battle of wills as she knocks on Scarface's door.

'DI Marsh, here you are, at last!' He hardly raises his eyes from above the paperwork on his desk. 'I need you to pay a visit to the squatter colony in Sexton's Wood. You do have a minute, don't you? If not, you will have to make time. It's of paramount importance.'

Gillian was right. Philip Weston-Jones is the self-anointed laird of Bishops Well. He is also Scarfe's longstanding comrade and crony-at-large. His interests are supreme to everything else. Let's face it, the man has connections and rarely hesitates to call in favours. So it's nothing to do with the mercy killing. Unless he wants her to mercifully execute the homeless occupying Sexton's Wood, who, as everyone at the station knows, are making a nuisance of themselves to Sir Philip. He wants them sorted.

'Actually, sir, I'm in the middle of a murder investigation – Gertrude Hornby. You may recall…'

'This won't take long.' Scarfe is short with her, as usual. 'It's all about community links, DI Marsh. Local residents need to feel assured we're here to look after their safety, day and night. There has been another case of criminal damage on the Weston Estate – the usual suspects, as you may imagine… We can't let it slide. They are becoming bolder and more daring with every new day… We need to be seen to take this blatant vandalism seriously. I promised Sir Philip my senior officers would handle this matter from now on. You *are* my most senior officer, as it happens.' He eyes her as if doubting his own description of her.

'Sir!'

'Good! Let's get on with it! Keep me abreast of your progress. In writing, please.'

'However, the murder investigation…' Gillian shifts from one foot to another.

'Oh, yes!' Scarface points his finger at her, 'and go gently on Cherie Hornby, for God's sake! She couldn't harm a fly.'

91

Yep! Scarface has covered all bases. Gillian is dispatched away from his office and into the greener pastures of the Weston Estate to take Philip Weston-Jones's statement (which could easily be done by a constable, but it won't be) and then to Sexton's Wood to box the squatters' ears. Of course, she can't go by herself, and therefore another officer's time will have to be wasted on this errand. It's a sensitive mission – only senior officers! She will be damned if she drags Webber with her. Anyway, he would have to get his shoes muddy in the woods and he wouldn't like that. He is better off carrying on with the Hornby case. Gillian pats Erin on the back as she passes by her desk, 'DC Macfadyen, you're coming with me. Weston Estate, then Sexton's Wood. Bring your wellies.'

Webber is peering from above his computer, glad it isn't him. He winks at Erin, 'Hope you know how to curtsey, Macfadyen! His Lordship likes them meek.'

'Cut that shit out, Webber.' Gillian is annoyed as it is. She doesn't need any more aggravation. 'Speak to Riley – see if he can shed any light on that packing tape. Where it came from, anything specific about it… Chase up Almond on the post-mortem, too. I want it on my desk today.'

'Yes, boss.'

'Oh, and go back to the residential home, get Mrs Robson to watch the CCTV coverage with you. See if she can identify everybody on it. Miss Hornby said she saw a few people in the corridor. I want to know who they were.'

'Yes, boss.'

'Right! We're off for tea and scones.'

Sir Philip doesn't have the time to receive them and Master

James is away, the sour-faced butler informs them as he leads them through the marble-tiled hall, but Master Joshua will. It is he who runs the estate and deals with domestic matters, such as the break-ins and theft of stock. He and Dave, the glorified manager who is the cook's son. The butler pauses to assess both Gillian and Erin with a critical eye. 'Which one of you is the detective?'

'We both are,' Erin takes out her warrant card for the second time. 'DC Macfadyen, and this is DI Marsh,' she gestures towards Gillian.

'Is that so?' the butler looks doubtful. He must be at least seventy and, like most of his generation, does not believe in political correctness. 'They make women police inspectors these days? Young women, at that…' His final comment is his mitigation, Gillian smiles under her breath. He gives her the evil eye. They are in the reception room: large windows, high ceilings, and wonky period furniture huddled around the open fireplace, which is cold and dead as a dodo. The room is draughty and cold. 'Take a seat. Master Joshua will be with you shortly.' The butler points vaguely to the floor and departs.

'What a bloody circus!' Gillian mutters. 'I wonder how long we'll be kept waiting for his bloody highness.'

'I already feel like I've done it – whatever it is! Like I'm in the headmaster's office, waiting for my lashes,' Erin grins. 'Guilty as charged!'

Contrary to their expectations, they don't have to wait long. Assured footsteps resonate on the marble flooring outside and a man in his mid-thirties makes a grand entrance: a big, indulgent smile on his full lips and a quiver of his eyebrow on his smooth forehead. Wearing breeches, riding boots and a tweed jacket, he is a living throwback to Mr Wickham of *Pride and Prejudice*. 'I hope Gerard offered you a drink?' he gushes and proceeds to pour himself a glass of some spirit from a crystal decanter. 'Brandy?'

'We're on police business, sir,' Gillian informs him drily. She doesn't like him, or his manner. 'DI Marsh and that's DC Macfadyen.' He eyes them in an openly lecherous way, his wet eyes lingering on Erin's bosom and then on Gillian's legs. Gillian feels like a horse for sale – is the bastard going to look her in the mouth next? 'There has been a complaint made about vandalism on the estate, I understand?'

'Oh yes, that! Father is inconsolable! It's the hobos from the Wood. Broke in last night and helped themselves to supplies. Davey will be able to tell you precisely what was taken, but they are becoming bolder and now we aren't talking a couple of eggs and a bag of flour – they take the livestock! The other day they nicked a damned sheep from the grazing paddocks on the Brambly Meadow. It's beyond a joke!' He downs his brandy in a cavalier fashion and pours himself another one. He waves the glass towards them, 'You're sure you don't want to join me? I don't like drinking by myself.'

'No, thank you, sir.' Gillian wishes she could slap him. He isn't handsome but is very sure of himself. He has a wide behind and narrow shoulders but is tall enough for that not to make him look chubby, just ungainly. 'How do you know it's the squatters from Sexton's Wood? Do you perhaps have CCTV cameras at the estate, anything we could view to identify the intruders?'

'No, of course not, but I'm sure it was them. Everyone knows who the culprits are. Who else would bother stealing chickens and damned sheep around here?'

'We'll investigate your complaint.'

'I damn well hope so!'

'Could we start with the outbuildings that were broken into?'

'Gerard will take you to talk to Davey, our estate manager,' he waves a dismissive hand. 'But if I were you I'd go straight to the Wood and fish them out one by one. Frankly, we're sick and tired of the lot of them. They're like damned vermin!'

'We'll start at the scene of the crime, if you don't mind, sir.'

'I don't mind where you start! As long as you take the matter in hand. Our solicitors are fighting a losing battle over the eviction order and the police sit around twiddling their thumbs... This is an outrage! One is no longer in charge of one's own land. It's all gone to the dogs.'

Dogs are barking Gillian and Erin off the estate. There is some howling too. Those hounds are thirsty for action. Released from their confinement they would no doubt tear the two women to shreds.

'Shut up!' Dave, the estate manager-cum-cook's son, orders the dogs and pulls on the lead. Squealing, the two beasts settle at his foot. He is a large man with a big beer gut and bloated face. He looks like a seasoned drinker with that face and bloodshot eyes. He waves Gillian on when she glances back to check the bloody Dobermans are contained. 'Yeah, yeah, carry on that way!' he nods to her, 'Cross the meadow – there be a path by the sideway, straight into the Wood!'

'What a pleasant lot they are!' Erin observes sarcastically as they tread on across the muddy courtyard and towards the wooden gate. They had to leave the car behind. There is no vehicular access to Sexton's Wood from the direction of the estate. They will have to return the same way. 'I just hope the bloody dogs are locked in when we come back for the car.'

'How did the thieves manage to get away with the loot, unnoticed?' Gillian wonders. 'Those dogs would've had them torn to pieces!'

'Unless they know them.'

'Or they had nothing to do with the theft. Probably there was no theft. My bet is his Lordship is putting together a case for eviction of those poor buggers from the woods.'

'You think?'

Gillian nods. She is sure they are wasting their time. Wasting police time was a crime last time she looked. Nevertheless, here they are shuffling through sheep droppings, on a mission of knee-capping the homeless on his lordship's orders. She hates it. At least the surroundings are tranquil and relaxing. Sheep graze contentedly and without sparing them a second glance. They look warm in their woolly gear. The path is messy, with muddy water standing in deep puddles that feed the ditch. The air is fresh and pungent with country scents. Further into Brambly Meadow, towards the wood, cows take over the job of trimming the grass from the sheep. On closer inspection, Gillian concludes that they are bullocks, not cows. Wouldn't the occupants of the nearby Sexton's Wood prefer beef to lamb? Gillian ponders their preferences. If they intended to steal livestock, aren't the bulls a bit closer to hand? Why go all the way towards the Weston Estate where those vicious Dobermans guard the stock while you have a perfectly delicious rump steak on your doorstep?

They enter the wood. It's old – the trees are large, with thick trunks, the undergrowth a plush blanket of autumnal leaves. The air smells musky and wet. All is quiet but for the creaking of branches. Gillian stabs the leaves with her foot – they fly at Erin. She kicks back and they have a short-lived battle of leaves, laughing and flapping their arms.

'I used to love playing with leaves when I was a kid,' Erin says.

'I still do.'

'Some things you never grow out of.'

'Always a child, me…' Gillian sobers up. 'You know, I can't remember when I last brought Tara to the woods. I can't remember kicking leaves at her, or playing hide and seek. She was a baby one minute and an adult the next – I missed her childhood somewhere along the way.'

'Nah, you just forget! If you asked her, she'd remember.'

'The way she is with me these days, she'd struggle to remember my name.'

'You're too harsh on her. And on yourself. Ease up! How's the wedding preparations?'

'That's another thing – I don't know. I'm not in the loop. I have to be there for her. My last chance before she sails into the horizon.'

'So be there – take some time off, go shopping with her, book a venue, surprise her.'

'Yeah, I'm thinking of doing just that.'

'Stop thinking – do it!'

'I think she'll resent whatever I do.'

'You're doing it again, you see!' Erin throws her arms up.

'Doing what?'

'Thinking!'

'Yeah, too much thinking is bad for you unless you're crime-solving. And crime-solving is what I do.'

'Don't hide behind your job, Gillian. You can give it a break for a couple of weeks – the world won't fall apart without you in the saddle. We can manage, you know, without you.'

'Well, thanks. I suppose,' Gillian shrugs her shoulders.

'You know what I mean,' Erin looks hard at her.

They have crossed the low-lying stream over a felled tree linking its steep banks. From here it is up a couple of hundred yards before they reach the homeless' shanty town. The slope is muddy and slippery. Gillian's wellies are caked in clay and the trek is like dancing on ice. 'They have great natural defences here, you have to give it to them.'

Erin agrees. 'I almost wish I had the guts to move in with them: no mortgage, no earthly concerns, just fresh air and camp fires.'

Indeed, a camp fire is in full swing, with a few people gathered around it. Their dwellings are well camouflaged. They are burrows or caves in the side of the hill, wedged under the exposed roots of the trees above. If it wasn't for the sheets of corrugated iron and scraps of cardboard, you could miss this place altogether.

It looks like they're having their lunch. Something is being roasted – the aroma of cooking meat pervades the air. From a distance, Gillian can tell it is some sort of an animal impaled on a spit. Game or lamb?

'It smells good? What is it?' she shouts towards the hunched figures around the fire. They gape at her and Erin impassively. They don't seem taken aback or frightened to see the two strangers approach. They're just impassive and indifferent. They are mostly young, but not adolescent – in their twenties or thirties; skinny, with ashen complexions, emaciated; lanky long hair, wispy beards, shoddy, cheap clothing the colours of which blend into one infinite shade of grey.

'What business of yours is that? Who are you?' One woman gets up and starts walking towards them. Wearing a beanie pulled over her eyes and a pair of frayed joggers, she is like the rest of them in appearance, but seems alert and assured in her stride. Her accent and mannerism is not what Gillian would expect from a *hobo*, as his lordship would have her referred to. She is polished and has class. Why is she here? What brought her here? What unfortunate sequence of misfortunes landed her in a homeless colony? As she approaches, Gillian notes her deep-brown hair and striking blue eyes. She is a good looking woman.

Gillian and Erin flash their ID cards at her.

'Wow, a detective inspector! That's a promotion for our humble lot,' the woman jeers, and Gillian is assured more than ever that the woman is not local, her accent clipped and clear.

'We received a complaint about theft of stock and supplies from the Weston Estate.'

'And you immediately thought it had something to do with us, naturally.'

'We're exploring all lines of inquiry.'

'Or is it that his highness pointed you in our direction?'

Gillian doesn't want to answer that question. She is uncomfortable being here and bothering these people as they, clearly, seem to be no bother to anyone. Erin says, 'May we have a word with you and your... friends? Perhaps you've seen something that may help us with our investigation.'

'I'm sure your mind is already made up, but come and join us for a bit of game.' The woman leads them to the camp fire. Others, gathered around it, make room for them. They don't look hostile.

'Things gone missin' on the Estate. The coppers here,' the woman introduces Gillian and Erin with a non-committal gesture, 'reckon *we can help with their inquiries.*' Chuckles and inarticulate grunts ripple out. A man passes a tin mug to Gillian. Dark-coloured liquid inside it smells like cheap wine. He doesn't smile at her, but he looks benign.

'No, thanks, I'm on duty,' she says, pushing the mug away. Frankly, she would be more inclined to have this wine than the brandy Joshua Weston-Jones offered her. 'So, would anyone have any information about the theft of livestock and produce on the Weston Estate? Sheep have gone missing...'

'Sheep?' another man looks incredulous in a mocking way, 'A whole fuckin' sheep gone AWOL? Did you know that, Izzie?' he looks at the self-appointed spokeswoman. She raises her shoulders and her eyebrows in a mocking gesture. They all laugh.

The man looks at Gillian, 'We ain't seen nuffin.'

'No, you haven't,' Gillian agrees. It's not like they're going to tell her even if they had. She is gazing at the spit roast. It is some kind of a medium size animal, which, for all

100

she knows, could be a dog. Or a sheep. The well-spoken woman catches her eye and says, 'Would you like a slice of roasted badger?'

'Badger?' Erin is incredulous.

'Yes, badger. They only get culled, we may as well put them to good use.'

Another pair of people, a man and a woman, stagger out of one of the huts. She is in a state of part undress. He is zipping up his trousers. The woman laughs. It's a drunken laughter. The man lights a cigarette and throws the match in the fire. 'What's that about?' he points to the two policewomen.

'Police. Someone's been stealing from the Estate.'

'Stealing, my arse!' the man snorts, and walks away, muttering curses under his breath.

'No one's seen anything,' the woman gets up, 'so if you aren't for a slice of badger, you won't mind if we tuck in?' The woman is clearly jeering. Another ripple of chuckling travels through the ranks of the homeless innocents.

Gillian takes out her card, 'If you do remember seeing anything suspicious…'

'We'll call you,' the woman finishes for her and takes the card. 'We do have a mobile phone. Bought, not stolen, as it happens.'

'Great. Thank you for your time,' Erin is keen to leave. She is right – they aren't going to extract any information out of these people. They are personae non-grata.

'Your name,' Gillian fixes the woman with a stern eye, 'We need your name for the record.'

'Tracy Beaker, of no fixed abode.' The woman is smirking.

'Of course you are. I take it Izzie is your middle name,' Gillian replies calmly.

'Izzie to friends. Isabella to everyone else.'

'And your surname?'

'Butler.' The woman isn't smirking any more.

Back in the office, Gillian runs the name through the computer. She is lucky. There is an Isabella Butler in the system, arrested a couple of times for disorderly behaviour and once for soliciting, a charge that was later dropped. Born in Bath, 20th May 1983, she would now be in her thirties, and that fits. Gillian turns off the computer and stares into space. Suddenly she feels very tired. Her mind is blank. She has no plans. No *inventorising* goes through her head. Carte blanche. For the first time in her life she is sure she doesn't want to do this: chasing after a bunch of homeless people who may be guilty of many a petty crime, but overall are harmless and pose no threat to society. They are brazenly being framed to pave the way for his lordship's bulldozers. Gillian resents being the puppet in his hands and letting him pull the strings. And then there is the suspicious death at Golden Autumn Retreat: that wretched Cherie Hornby and her dead mother. Gillian doesn't want to bully that poor woman - - she has just lost her mother. Yes, perhaps she had helped her die, but for the noblest of reasons, if mercy was one of them. She is probably in hell of her own making and needs no further punishment. And then back to his lordship's lost property. A vicious circle… What does it matter? What does it matter who, if anyone, stole the fat man's sheep?

Her annual leave is well overdue. She may as well take it.

# XI

Three days ago he made contact with his guide. They didn't talk online, just agreed the time and place. Haji arrived three hours earlier and surveyed the piazza with all its archways and narrow alleys, the church and all the shops and cafes. He then sat and watched the people weaving through the piazza. He can tell a tourist from an undercover officer. It's nothing to do with the uniform; it's in the posture, in the stride and in the eyes. No soldiers or police were to be seen anywhere in the piazza. If a sniper had been installed somewhere in one of the many top-floor flats in the night, Haji would soon find out. There was nothing he could do about that. He couldn't anticipate every possibility out there. There is always some risk involved. He is used to taking risks. They are well calculated risks, like who would fire a gun into a street full of people? The busy piazza was Haji's shield.

His guide, an inconspicuously ordinary man in his mid-forties with black wavy hair and smooth olive skin, arrived on foot, emerging from a corner shop selling souvenirs. Haji hadn't noticed him get there in the first place so he concluded the man was good at his job. He knew how to blend in better than Haji knew how to pick him out from the crowd. Haji decided he could trust the man as far as the passage to France was concerned, and that's all he needed him for. They shook hands in the Western way, and spoke English.

'Had a good trip, Sandman?'

'As good as it gets, my friend.'

Despite his relaxed smile, the guide who called himself Kamal was nervous: his hand was sweaty. That was good. Haji would be able to read him like a book.

They sat in one of the cafes and had Turkish coffee: black, in small glasses, with a lot of sugar. Kamal told him about the passage to France: they would drive west in Kamal's pickup van which they would leave in Saluzzo, then they would make the crossing to meet up with their French contact in Embrun.

That was three days ago.

After a steep ascent, they have reached the ridge. The air here is thinner than in the valley below, but Haji is used to altitude. He doesn't need to acclimatise. The mountains back in Afghanistan are as high and as steep. And they are as beautiful. Haji takes in the beauty of the sheer rock wall rising in front of him and the softer rolling landscape, with yellowing meadows dropping behind. The sky is lapis lazuli blue, perfect and virginal, like back home. Not a cloud to trap the air. Haji inhales through his nose and his mouth – the smell of freedom. It's colder up here – cleaner, very much like his home in Pandsher Valley at the foot of Shomali Plain. For a split second, Haji wishes to stay here. To live and die here. He does not want to go on. It isn't like him to stop and leave things undone, though, so he nods and hobbles on behind Kamal when he tells him they must press on and reach the cabin before the sun goes down.

He and his mujahedin brothers always try to reach their kishlaks before the sun drowns in the night. The Soviets don't operate in the night – they wouldn't risk it. That allows the guerrilla fighters to get a good night's sleep and be with their families. Haji longs to be with Svetlana. Every day he does; he can't think of anything else. Others love war. They relish the scent of blood and crave the kill. Not Haji. He isn't a warrior out of choice. He loves his wife and wants to be with her, grow melons and travel the world. He only kills to save himself and because he remembers his comrades and how they died at Tajbek Presidential Palace. It is his duty to avenge their death.

He joined Masud, the Lion of Pandsher, after escaping from Kabul. As a member of the Presidential Guard he stood no chance. He was a witness to the slaughter. The Russians could not afford to let him live even though he was married to one of them, even though he spoke their language as well as they did, even though he was a Muscovite. Svetlana came with him to hide in his kishlak, lie low and wait for the war to end. And they did just that at first, but soon the surprised faces of his comrades, their screams and their dead eyes got the better of him. He had to seek revenge. He had to kill a Russian man for each one of his butchered comrades, or his mind would find no peace.

He has been killing ever since. He is the king of ambush. With his chemistry degree, he can make an explosive out of cow dung. Today, the mujahedin have another victory to celebrate. They have ambushed a convoy of twenty oil tankers and lorries in the Salang Tunnel. Haji's strategically distributed mines dealt with the Russian tanks that escorted the convoy. The lorries were trapped in the tunnel, surrounded at both ends, with no escape routes in this hostile terrain. The rest was a stroll in the park. All that is left now is to wade through the bodies, find survivors and finish them off. Moans betray those not clever enough to play dead. They get a swift stab and stop wailing. Weapons are being pulled out of the white-knuckled hands of dead Soviets. Haji carries six machine guns slung over his shoulder. Yet he prefers to use his knife on the wounded enemy soldiers – it's quieter this way, calmer. They look surprised when he reaches for their throats and slashes them, as surprised as his comrades were at the Palace. And then, their eyes become as blissfully dead. He has come to think of them as glass eyes – you can see through them, but not into them. There is nothing there. Death is nothing.

'Siuda, pamagitje…*Here, help me...*' The call from another dying man draws Haji deeper into the tunnel. He finds him buried under the two bodies of his dead comrades. His chest is squashed, his face flushed red with the effort. A trickle of blood that must have poured out of his nose has dried around his lips like a clown's mouth. He sees Haji and whispers, blood gurgling out of his throat, 'Spasiba… *Thank you…*' His eyes aren't glass, not yet. They even smile. They don't know what's to come.

Without thinking Haji grabs the boy's head, but something stops him from slicing the boy's throat. Despite the blood and the bulging veins, he can see this Russian is just a child. He doesn't shave yet – there is no stubble on his chin. Haji is no child-killer. He pushes the weight of the two dead soldiers off the boy's chest to help him breathe. The boy cries in pain. His ribs must be broken. Haji is walking away without looking back. The boy's comrades will come tomorrow morning. They will find him and take him back home, to Russia.

When the operation is over and every mujahedin emerges from the tunnel and is accounted for, someone sets one of the capsized oil tankers on fire. The flames burst into the tunnel and overwhelm everything and everyone that's in it.

Including the boy.

Haji wishes he had finished him off in the first place.

The dusk is lit by the fires and a chain reaction of explosions follows. The spectacle must be visible from afar. Black smoke is pumped sky high. The mujahedin have to leave immediately and blend into the mountains – Soviet helicopters will be here in a matter of minutes and the mujahedin have nothing to take them down with. Not yet.

Haji negotiates a path clinging to a sheer rock wall by a narrow gorge. Sixty feet below the Pandsher River foams and bubbles, accompanying him down to the valley where Svetlana is waiting for him in their mud brick home on the south side of his fortified kishlak. He has left his loot, the machine guns and ammunition belts in the cave where the rest of the company have left their spoils of war. They all go home, dressed in turbans and long robes, looking like your everyday peasants. They will have a good meal and a chat with their wives, maybe mend a few broken tools and pots, and listen to their children play in the courtyard. The gloss of normality.

As he reaches the orchard of mulberries and apricots that is just outside the baked-brick wall, Haji hears the helicopters. He puts his hand to his eyes to shelter them from the rays of the setting sun and he sees two of the choppers hovering over the Salang Pass. They must have already discovered the carnage. That was fast by Soviet standards, Haji is glad he and his men have cleared the area so quickly. When the Russians see the extent of the destruction, they will come down to the villages looking for someone to blame. They might even come here.

Approaching his house, Haji can see Svetlana's slender figure hunched over the fire. She is cooking something, making supper for him, waiting so that they can have it together. Her veil has slid away from her head and the light from the frisky flames bounces off her fair hair, making it shine like gold. He picks up pace, almost runs towards her to grab her to lift her off the ground and hold her in his arms. She is a dove's feather in his embrace.

Her expression is solemn though. 'Have you heard the helicopters? They've been up and down for a couple of hours now.' She speaks in Russian to him, but she has been learning local dialect and can hold a basic conversation. Haji is so proud of her! He kisses her. 'Did you hear what I just said?' she asks, frowning.

'They'll go away,' he replies.

'They make me feel uneasy. Only three weeks ago, remember? That village was razed to the ground. It wasn't far from here. I worry…'

'Don't! Don't worry. They have their hands full. We keep them too busy to bother with villages. We steer them away.'

'Not busy enough to stop them from punishing innocent people.'

'No one is innocent. This is war. People die. Even if you let them live, they still die,' Haji suddenly remembers the young Russian soldier he tried to spare, in vain.

'I don't want to die... I don't want our baby to die...' she gazes at him intently, her intense blue eyes fixed on his.

Haji can't believe it. For a moment, he is convinced he must have misheard. 'Our baby? Are you pregnant?'

She nods. He snatches her hands, kisses them. He doesn't dare take her in his arms in case he breaks something inside her womb. His delicate, fragile Svetlana is carrying his child within that womb. 'We're having a baby...'

She keeps looking at him, something steely sneaking into her eyes. 'I don't want to die. I want our baby to live,' she repeats stubbornly.

'So do I! So do I!' He is blabbering, exuberant and drunk on the news. 'We must celebrate! Everyone must know!'

'Haji, my love, can't you see what's going on around us? I'm scared...'

'You can't be scared! I'm here to protect you- the two of you – with my life! You can't doubt me!'

'I don't, and I know you'll do everything for me, but it makes no difference. I'm still afraid... I can't bring a new life into this place... This war will never end – can't you see that!'

'The war will end! Like every war – it will run out of fuel; it'll fade away... You have my word!' He will fight to convince her. He is a fighter after all. She needs reassurance – lots of it. And there will be mood swings and strange cravings. Haji will weather the storm of this pregnancy. He will stand by her like she has always stood by him.

'When will it end?' she throws her arms in the air. 'I can't wait, and live like this!' She sweeps her hand around the room lit only faintly by the dying fire.

Haji doesn't understand the question. Admittedly, this isn't the luxury of their flat in *microrayon*, but it is all they need, and she loves it: their living-breathing home as she calls it, the *kyariz* well with crystal-cold water, their orchard… She said -

She said she loved it. She said she would love this life – this world of his - as long as he was here with her.

'I'm here with you. I'm here for you,' he reminds her, but it isn't enough. He knows it isn't.

The thump of a helicopter passing overhead adds to the unease they find themselves in. They should be celebrating, and yet they are arguing. The flatbread she has been cooking is burning.

'Haji, I want to protect our child – your child. I can't do it here. I don't know how. There are no doctors, no hospitals. What if…'

'Everyone will help, trust me! My whole family, my mother and my sister -'

'My family are in Moscow. And I'll get decent medical care there. I must go to have our baby there. You must let me. We owe it to our child.'

He is shaking his head, numb with disbelief and defiance.

'He – she – will be safe, warm, comfortable… will go to school, and…' she approaches him, takes his face in her hands and kisses his lips, 'we will be back with you as soon as this war is over. I promise. And you must promise me you won't let yourself get killed.'

So he promises her – a promise for a promise. He promises he will wait for her.

# XII

Heather decided to come with him.

He had to tell her it was young Tommy's tenth birthday because the boy's present came out of their joint account and the meal at Pizza Express would do too. She would find out sooner or later and she would resent it even more if he hadn't told her. She is resenting it nevertheless. But perhaps not as much. Staring at the droplets of rain that smash against the glass and are swept away by the relentless windscreen wipers, Heather remains resolutely silent as if, in her head, she is counting all those annihilated droplets. Oscar dares not interrupt her. From time to time, he glances at her from above the steering wheel. He fears she will spoil the evening, that her reason for coming is to do just that. What else could it be? She has never approved of his closeness with Katie, nor of his fondness for Tommy. She understands his motives better than anyone, but she doesn't approve – full stop.

'When I booked the table, I told them it was Tommy's birthday. They'll have a cake for him, with candles and all that malarkey,' Oscar warns his wife. She must be ready to join in the celebrations with the 'Happy Birthday' song, and the smiles and clapping. She chose to come with him; she has to conform. For the moment, she takes her eyes off the windscreen and responds with a tearful, pained gaze. Her eyes are welled up to the brim, perhaps due to all those crushed raindrops she's been watching so intently.

He pats her right knee, 'Really, Heather, there's no need...'

She whips her head away and fixes her eyes back on the rain-battered windscreen. Oscar's gaze follows hers, his eyes briefly focused on the windscreen pane and the splashing droplets driven by the wind to their tragic end. The red hue of the crossroad traffic lights filters through those droplets and for a brief second they form the blood-soaked face of Sergeant Butler with the lazy, thickening tracks of blood marking his dead face.

'For God's sake!' Heather screams and jolts him back into the present day, 'You jumped the red light! That car barely missed you!' Her face is contorted with agitation. A 4x4 is stationary at an odd angle behind them, sounding its horn angrily. A few other cars have come to a standstill on the junction. Oscar raises an apologetic hand to acknowledge the curses and waving fists, and continues slowly on his way.

'Sorry,' he says. 'It's the damned rain. Can't see anything.'

'You could have had us both killed!'

That statement stings.

'Sorry,' he repeats and reaches for Heather's hands, bundled into small fists in her lap. He squeezes them firmly. He already has a man's death on his conscience. Sergeant Richard Butler. He had him killed – sent him to his death in that Argentine bunker on the slope of Mount Langdon. A father-to-be, a father who would never lay his eyes on his daughter. Because Oscar had him killed.

'Just concentrate on your driving,' Heather instructs him.

Yes, just concentrate on surviving. He has been telling himself that for the past thirty-odd years. He had a duty of honour to discharge towards Butler's wife and child – an ongoing duty. He couldn't do that dead. Heather has always understood; she just doesn't approve. She can't bear Oscar's involvement with Katie: he was present at Izzie's birth; he was by Katie's side, holding her hand and telling her how proud Richard would be. He was the first man to kiss Izzie's chubby little hands. He cried with joy. And then he cried with sorrow when Izzie walked away, leaving Tommy behind like unwanted ballast, a dead weight that would drag her down if she stayed. So Oscar took on Tommy as his own, alongside Katie. They shared that weight and the tears that came with it. Tears shared with Katie, tears that he could never share with Heather. They have no children of their own, and she won't forgive him his adopted family. She resents every minute of it, every hour he spends growing closer with *that woman and that woman's child, and now grandchild.* She is jealous of everything that ties them together: the good and the bad, the very few joys and the very many tears. She has nothing to be jealous of, he keeps telling her that, but she won't listen. And maybe she is right, because it has just occurred to him that he doesn't want her there with Katie and Tommy. He wants them both only to himself. They are his whole world and Heather is now just a chore – his cumbersome duty. He doesn't know when and how the tables have been turned on Heather, but he knows that she would be ill-advised to test where his loyalties lie. His patience is at breaking point.

'Wow! Is it really mine?' Tommy's fingers are caressing the rod and sliding down to the reel where they get confused in the complex mechanism of ball bearings and flip-switches.

'Of course it's yours! From me and Heather, happy birthday!' Oscar feeds on Tommy's excitement. The present is spot on, just what the doctor ordered. He smiles at Katie, seeking her approval, but she can't see him because she's looking at Heather.

'Nothing to do with me,' Heather contradicts him with a shrug of her shoulders. 'I didn't even know what was in the box. In fact, I didn't know there was a box until this morning. I'm always the last one to know.'

Katie is puzzled. She doesn't know what to say to that. Has Heather said that on purpose? To humiliate Katie? Oscar feels like he should be apologising for his wife, and he knows that no apology would ever be enough. He bites his tongue. The air is heavy with discomfort. Only Tommy is at ease.

'When can I try it? Can you teach me, Oscar?'

'Well, we have that camping trip on the cards, don't we?' Oscar says. 'I know just the lake…'

'Yes!' Tommy punches the air, and the discomfort of the adults is pushed out into the stratosphere. 'When are we going?'

'I'm thinking next Saturday, if you have no other plans.'

'As if!' Tommy snorts, sparks of thrill jumping out of his nostrils.

'And if Nan is happy with that.'

'Nan?' Tommy has Katie in his grip, and he won't let her go until she says *yes*. Her eyes smile at the boy, and this time that smile spreads across her face and warms its way deep into Oscar's heart. God, he loves her! It must be in his eyes, and Heather can probably see it, but he doesn't care.

'Come on, Katie,' he grins, 'you can't break both our hearts!'

'Next Saturday?'

'Yep.'

She cocks her head to one side, teasing poor Tommy for a little while longer.

'Nan, I can't learn to fish in the bathtub, you know!'

'Hmm... You may be right there,' she has a beautiful smile when it touches on her eyes. 'OK then, next Saturday it is!'

Tommy springs to his feet. His arms close on his grandmother's shoulders and his face disappears in her thick, long hair. Oscar wishes they were his arms and his face. And he hopes that Richard doesn't mind, while watching from up there, how much he has come to usurp his love for his wife and grandson.

# XIII

'Just saying goodbye to my favourite patient,' Wanda is leaning over Yvonne's bed. She has to force a smile onto her lips – Yvonne is in a bad way. To make things worse, she is refusing to take food. Intravenous feeding can only go so far and Yvonne knows that. She claims she can't swallow; she claims her insides hurt more when she has eaten; she claims there is no point. Perhaps only the last claim is true.

Her eyes are out of focus, but she makes an attempt to look at Wanda, 'Who are you?'

Wanda isn't wearing her nurse's uniform. Her hair is loose and curly. She has put on a touch of makeup: eyeliner and lipstick. It is no wonder Yvonne doesn't recognise her. 'Wanda, your long-suffering nurse!' she forces another smile.

'Oh, Wanda! How you have changed… You're off to a party?'

'Going home, Yvonne! Going home today!'

'Good girl… Give a cuddle to your daughter from the dying old woman at the hospice, will you?'

'I'll give her a cuddle from my friend, Yvonne. I don't know any dying old woman, though.'

'Touché!' A weak smile softens Yvonne's face. She lifts her hand to search for Wanda's. Wanda sits on the side of her bed and squeezes Yvonne's hand. 'Good girl… Glad you came… I'll miss you… for as long as it takes me to die, that is.'

'Enough of dying, please.'

'That's easier said than done.'

'You must eat, help your body fight this…'

'Have a safe trip home,' Yvonne chooses to ignore Wanda's advice, which isn't surprising. She is as stubborn as they come. Wanda will miss her too.

Andrzej drives her to the airport – he's taken a day off. He said he had given a month's notice at work; he said the company had asked him to stay on for a bit longer to accompany new drivers on intercity routes, and to help with their training. He couldn't say no. They need him. Wanda won't argue with him. She will give him time and space. After all, he has agreed to pack it all in. It's just a matter of time. One month's separation won't kill anyone. She understands her husband; she knows what his work means to him. He will have to wean himself off being indispensable, but he will do it. He promised.

He has been sitting in the car, stiff and silent, while she babbled on about the surprise this would be for Paulina. The best gift they could give her! She won't believe her eyes! Grandma had been sworn to secrecy about Wanda's return home. It will be a cracker!

Andrzej drives and leaves the talking to Wanda. The traffic is awful, and it is getting late. He probably resents the detour to the hospice, but doesn't mention it. In passing, in between the torrents of exclamations, Wanda notes his reticence but blames it on the blues of their parting. It is only temporary. 'You know,' she suggests, 'I may as well put this month to good use and start looking for a flat. Mum said we could even find a small bungalow with the money we have if we go further afield, away from the city. I don't mind. Fresh air will be good for Paulina. I always wanted to have my own veggie patch! What do you think?'

He nods. 'Sounds good.'

They are rushing along, running and overtaking other travellers who seem to have time to spare to take it at their leisure and stroll lazily or stand in the middle of the floor, chatting. Andrzej has taken her wheelie suitcase from her and is carrying it, lifting it over other people's heads and scattered pieces of luggage. It was a good idea to check in electronically from home – at least she won't have to queue in the twisted, tightly packed line of passengers before check-in. Instead of hand luggage, Wanda is travelling with a huge teddy, a Paddington Bear, that will fill the whole space in the overhead compartment. Pauline will love him! He's bringing his own little suitcase with him.

They have reached the Passengers Only cut-off point. Andrzej takes her in his arms, the Paddington Bear squashed between them, and kisses her. It is an evasive kiss, on the forehead. He is also avoiding her eyes. Maybe they are welling up with tears – silly old boy!

'Right! Will Skype you tonight, but it'll be late... You can imagine how it'll be on arrival! It'll be a stampede! . Mum will've invited half the village.'

'I know. Don't worry. We can talk tomorrow.'

'I'll see what I can do, OK?'

He nods. 'You'd better be going.'

'And you'd better be joining me soon!' she laughs. 'I

want to see you home by Christmas!'

He shifts his gaze towards her at last. 'It won't be this Christmas, though…'

She has already executed half-a-turn away from him when his words catch her unawares. She almost loses her balance. 'What do you mean?'

'Like I said -'

'You didn't *say* anything! What do you mean?'

'They offered me more money. It's a promotion for me – supervising trainees. Really good money, Wanda! I couldn't say no, like I said… Another six months on that pay, and we will be able to afford -'

'You said a month!'

'I know – I said… They made me an offer I couldn't refuse. Only six months and I'll be with you by Easter.'

*Last call for passengers travelling to Krakow,* the announcer's voice cuts the space between them in half. There will be no more hugs, no more goodbye kisses. Wanda can't bring herself to touch him. 'You lied, you bastard!' she spits through her teeth and starts walking.

'I'll come for Christmas, if that's what you want!' Andrzej shouts after her. 'Talk later! Skype me, yeah?'

He has to rush back. He is on the late shift, already working with trainee drivers, already earning his big bucks. Wanda will change her mind when she discovers how much he can save in the next six months. She may even let him extend it to a year. The offer is on the table. The company want him to stay – they value him.

The bloody traffic is a nightmare. Andrzej weaves in and out of the fast lane, which isn't any faster than the rest of them. He is heading directly for the depot; no time to go home and get his sandwiches from the fridge. Damn it! It was that unexpected stop-over at the hospice. Wanda just had to wave goodbye to her patients. Perhaps she should reconsider leaving them in the first place? No, that's just mean thinking! She is better off at home with Paulina. She is right to be there. Paulina comes first. Andrzej comes second. He hopes he does! A cheeky smirk quivers on his lips. She'll get over it! Six months, maybe a year.

Miraculously, he clocks in with two minutes to spare. Genius! His student is already there – naturally. He is keen, and a quick learner. Young. From up North. He will do well, Andrzej will make sure of that. They will run the routine checks first, then Andrzej will let him take the wheel tonight.

'Hi, Malik! It's your lucky night – you're in charge! How does that sound?' Andrzej slaps Malik on the back affectionately.

Malik's face breaks into a rare grin. 'I thought you'd never ask!'

# XIV

'You're looking good.' This isn't an empty compliment. Perversely, prison seems to agree with Sean. Gillian expected to find a battered old man resigned to his self-inflicted fate, but he is far from that. The clean-shaven look suits him. His bright Irish eyes smile at her.

'I've been working out – weights mainly,' he says, 'Not much else to do here.'

'I see.'

'I have to be seen to be fit to survive in this jungle. Earning respect. I've got a few good years to go.'

'Sixteen, isn't it?'

'So the judge said.' The smile has vanished. 'Let's not talk about me. So… what brings you here?'

'I thought you may want to know how Corky is getting on.'

'And how is he getting on?'

'Slowly. Suffered a few minor injuries in skirmishes with Fritz over the territory, but the pecking order is now firmly in place and the boys stay out of each other's way.'

'Good.'

'He misses you.'

His eyes well up; he pinches his nose and laughs. 'Pity they don't allow dogs here. I'll have to complain about that.

Could do with someone to talk to.'

'I'll pop over from time to time.'

He rounds on her with a hard glare. 'Why would you? You hardly know me.'

'I hardly know myself. Too busy for retrospection... Anyway, I don't have to know you to like you, and I like you for some reason.'

'Thanks, but still -'

'It's easy to talk to you. For one, you aren't going anywhere – you may as well sit and listen,' she tries to crack a joke. He rewards her with a snort.

'I'm just saying you don't have to -'

'I know, but I've got too much time on my hands: I'm on leave.'

'Suspended?'

'No!' Gillian rolls her eyes. 'I'm on leave – a holiday, heard of that? Three weeks.'

'That doesn't sound like you.'

'I morphed into the new me. I'm seriously considering packing it all in – the police work. Sick and tired of it... I guess I'm an old-timer – I don't get the PR stuff or the bloody crime statistics analyses. The paperwork does my head in.'

'Can't teach an old dog new tricks?'

'Something like that. I'm going to enjoy life.'

'Good luck with that.'

'Tara is getting married...'

He nods as if contemplating the news, but his face is impassive. He only knew Tara for five minutes. Why should he care? Perhaps coming here to see him was a mistake. Gillian can't think of anything else to say. She feels rather

122

foolish. He is a stranger. Like so many people who have entered and exited her life without leaving a lasting effect, Sean has been a flash in the pan: intense when it happened, but without the staying power. It isn't his fault – it's hers. She is the one who skims on the surface, never allowing herself to peer deeper, to dive in and commit. She'd rather contend with that big black hole in her private life; she knows how to deal with it – you just pretend it isn't there and keep yourself occupied elsewhere. Don't complicate things, that's her preferred alternative to getting a life.

As if reading her thoughts, he says, 'I really don't think you should've come, Gillian.'

'No, I shouldn't.' She gets up, covers his hand with hers and smiles ruefully, 'Take care, Sean. I must dash.'

There is a moment of hesitation in his eyes. It seems he has changed his mind. He holds her hand for that little bit longer than he should. He is about to say something – something important, something personal – but decides against it. He says, 'Goodbye, DI Marsh.'

Gillian is taking her life seriously – the personal aspect of it. It isn't a large chunk of her life, and so far, it hasn't been the most important one, but this is about to change. She will catch up with Tara before the girl flies the nest, and that already means catching her mid-flight. Gillian has been regarding Tara's marriage to Charlie as the final nail in the coffin of their mother-daughter relationship, but now she sees it as an opportunity to show contrition and, hopefully, earn Tara's forgiveness. Three weeks. She has three weeks to make up for lost time. She will use her holiday wisely. In any event, she wouldn't know what to do with all that spare time on her hands. She's never holidayed before, not in the proper sense of the word. Doing nothing goes against the grain of her Calvinist mentality. She has inherited workaholic tendencies from her father. This is her first attempt at rehab.

Grace, Sasha's mother, is so much better at it! In her sweeping Jamaican fashion, she has beaten the hotel manager into submission. 'You give us respectable discounts on the rooms and we'll give you many happy, drinking guests. If people have somewhere to put down their weary heads, they're more likely to buy that one extra nightcap, no?'

'Well -' starts the manager. After the hard bargain driven so far by Grace with great virtuosity, his already ashen face is getting even greyer. 'Well, we have standard rates -'

That isn't an answer Grace expects to hear so she doesn't let him finish. 'Look here, if our guests have to drive home, they won't enjoy themselves 'cos they won't be able to have a drink. I don't want the guests at my daughter's wedding - and her best friend's wedding too - I don't want our guests to feel like they have to rush home! It's a big thing for us. We want everyone to enjoy themselves, don't we, Gillian?' She nudges Gillian, who blinks like a dazzled hedgehog in headlights. 'So two weddings, two lots of guests, two lots of paying customers – if that's not wholesale prices then I don't know what is!'

'We've already agreed on the twenty-five per cent off the venue hire,' the manager endeavours to point out the obvious, but that, to Grace, is yesterday's snow. She flays her arms like she is fighting off a swarm of wasps, 'No, no, no! That's sealed and dusted! We're talking the rooms now.

We can't have our guests sleeping in the car park, can we now? I couldn't look them in the eye!'

'Rooms will be reserved for your party as soon as I know the numbers.'

Grace glares at the manager, her huge eyes rounded in disbelief. 'You're not serious! You know what we're asking you, or am I not speaking English? Can we start talking business now, or shall we take it elsewhere? There are other hotels round here...'

The manager hunches under the threat. Even Gillian feels slightly intimidated, though she has nothing to fear: she's on Grace's side.

'Tell him, Gillian!' Grace despairs. 'Maybe he'll understand it better coming from you!'

'We have guests coming from afar, some of them from abroad... Jamaica, South Africa... They may need to stay longer than just one night.'

'You'll still make a hefty profit!' Grace stomps her plump foot on the plush, five-star carpet.

'Ten percent,' the manager clenches his teeth.

'Double it and we're all yours!'

OK, two middle-aged women may not be what the man is after. It may, in fact, have the opposite effect to what Grace intends, Gillian fears, but she is wrong. Just to close this hard bargain and make it to his therapist by the close of business, the hotel manager says, 'Done!'

Grace spits into her hand and offers it to the man to seal the deal.

'We have the venue and the rooms sorted,' Grace announces to the girls over a high tea in the hotel restaurant, which is on the house of course, compliments of the management. 'Don't worry, the cost is on us. What else are parents for? You just turn up and look gorgeous.'

'Thanks, Mum,' Sasha beams at Grace. 'Is Dad in on it?'

'On a need-to-know basis, if you must know.'

'Whoops!'

'He'll do as he's told, no?'

'He wouldn't dare not to!' Sasha laughs.

Tara is looking at Gillian. It has been a while since she looked at her that way. 'Thanks, Mum,' she echoes Sasha. Gillian smiles. God, she smiles! Everything inside her is warm and happy. 'Who is having the last macaroon?' She hopes it will be Tara. She loves macaroons – she used to before she stopped eating two years ago. A dreary, but distant past…

'That's mine,' Tara reaches for it. The smile inside Gillian grows wider and warmer.

'Did you know Tara's dad invited us to spend our honeymoon on his farm in South Africa?' Sasha announces.

'The four of you?'

'Well, yes! Sorry, you're not invited, Mum.'

'Never mind me. You just remember to say thank you when you get there.'

'My father won't be there. He will be staying in his house in Dorset after the wedding, until February, I think. We'll have the whole farm at our disposal. Hortensia will be there – she's always there. I can't wait for you to meet her, Sasha! She's a gem! She's this mother figure…'

Gillian wishes she was that mother figure, or just a plain mother to her daughter. She will most certainly try her best to achieve it in the short time that she has left. 'So all that's

126

left is your wedding dresses,' she chimes.

'And the bridesmaids',' Sasha gulps. 'We know what we want. This amazing snow-white chiffon for us, with fake fur – you know, because it's winter so we thought we'd make it Christmassy…'

'If we can afford them,' Tara rolls her eyes. 'But we can always dream… Otherwise -'

'No, no *otherwise*. We must make the dream come true,' Gillian has learned a thing or two from the formidable Grace. 'What else are parents for!'

Webber knocks on her door, yells *Gotcha!* when Gillian opens it, and pushes by her, heading straight for the kitchen. What on earth is he doing here? 'Haven't you got the kettle on?'

'Put it on, then.'

He does, then sniffs around the kitchen for signs of food. Gillian folds her arms and leans against the kitchen door frame.

'I thought I'd pay you a visit, see when you're coming back.'

'In three weeks.'

'Only we've a sweepstake at the station around your return day. The odds are seven to one that you'll be back within the first week. I bet a tenner.'

'You'll lose it.'

'Even if I were to tell you that Scarface was bringing someone from Bath to take over the Hornby case?'

'Even then.'

'Are you feeling all right?' He pauses, tilts his head and approaches her with the hot kettle in hand, slightly tilted and dripping hot water. Wisely, Fritz removes himself from the line of fire and vanishes under the table. From the safety of his hidey-hole, he gives out one warning yodel. Corky produces a short bark in response to that.

'Mind the hot water! You're scaring the animals!'

'No, honestly, Gillian! What's wrong with you?'

'Nothing! I'm on holiday.'

'That's what got me worried in the first place! Thought maybe you were ill…'

'Tara is getting married. I need time off work to get things ready.'

'Get things ready? Not you! It's a mid-life crisis, isn't it? Age catching up with you?'

'Fuck off, Webber.!'

He puts two mugs with milky tea on the bench-top and helps himself to two teaspoons of sugar.

'Me too,' Gillian says. She's still propping the door frame.

Webber puts the sugar in her tea. 'At least you still take sugar! I wasn't sure it was you. You didn't even phone in… So level with me - what's with the new you?' He sits down, rests his mug on a coaster and warms his hands around it.

She joins him at the table and takes a sip from her mug. The tea is too hot to drink, but she wants to hurry him up. 'You'd better be quick, Mark. Tara and Charlie will be here any minute. Then we're off to my parents with the wedding invite. Supper is waiting – I don't want to come across as a bad host, but I'm busy.'

'No, it isn't you… What the hell happened to you?'

'I don't know, Mark. I'm tired. Maybe I've burned out. I just stopped caring. At this very moment, all I care about is my daughter's big day. I want to be around when it happens, not running around the country, chasing shadows.'

'I understand that. Family comes first.'

'You should know that, of all people!' Mark is the prototype of a family man. Despite all adversity and despite Kate's depression, he has been holding his lot together, never easing up and never giving in to doubt.

'Yes, but after the wedding... you're back in action, right?'

'I don't know yet. I need to think it through.'

# XV

It is an apocalyptic sight – a large, flat area covered with torn huts, bits of tarpaulin flapping on broken structures, trying to take off; cardboard and corrugated iron strewn across the desolate muddy ground. There is graffiti written in Arabic on a billboard advertising Coca-Cola, which is serving as a wall of somebody's shack. Haji can't read Arabic, but he likes the lettering, which is like terraced arches and pointy minarets punctuated with one-eyed snakes. The writing is a reflection of the desert, and Haji is Sandman, a desert-man – he is bound to like it.

The smell is that of burning, and indeed many of the makeshift structures have been set on fire and are wholly or partially charred. Haji wanders into the camp, kicks a pot which tumbles away, bouncing on a stone and coming to an abrupt standstill. A poor excuse for a door in a poor excuse for a dwelling sways open. A young black man steps out. He eyes Haji with suspicion. 'What you want?'

So there are still people living in the Jungle, Haji discovers. People are like rats – they can make a home out of anything. Ingenious. Tenacious. Survivors. Haji has lots of respect for rats. He doesn't have to like them to respect them. He doesn't have to like people either, and many of them he doesn't like, particularly those he can't trust. But unlike with the rats, Haji has no respect for those people. The world should be rid of them.

'Nothing,' he tells the black man. 'What happened here?'

'You too late. Everyone gone – detention centre.'

'In the UK?'

'Ha, ha!' the black man makes a deep and resonating noise when he laughs. 'You wish!'

'You are still here,' Haji observes. 'And others,' he adds upon noticing two more heads popping from the dark interior of the dwelling. It is astounding how they managed to gather a mismatch of materials to reconstruct their shack and make it look like an integral part of the mess, so that it blends in perfectly.

'I stay. They go and come back from detention centre. Some do, some don't.'

'Any Afghans you know?'

'No. You go other place. You too late for the Jungle. Bulldozers come tomorrow. Police come. You go!' The black man waves him away.

'What about you?'

'I go the UK. Not detention centre.'

'Good luck.'

Haji walks away, swerving towards the motorway. He comes across more and more Jungle dwellers. There are those who are buried in everyday domesticity, cooking a meal using an oil drum as a stove. A group of younger men, who look no more than teenage boys, are playing cricket. Haji stops and watches. He listens to their arguments. They are Pakistani, a faint whiff of home...

So it isn't the end of the world. It isn't the Apocalypse. It isn't as bad as what he has left behind. Not half as bad. Not yet.

The burning smell was the same, though: acidic and suffocating. And the black smoke unfurled across the sky and made night out of the day. And people cried – those who were still alive cried for those who had been killed. Haji cried.

It had started with such promise. Haji had been given a three days' leave of absence, and left the British compound in Helmand Province to travel to Pandsher Valley for his little sister's wedding. It was going to be a big wedding in the best of Tajik tradition. Haji had not seen his sister in three years, since he had left the kishlak and joined the British in the fight against the Taliban. Haji had unfinished business with the Taliban – they were behind Masud's assassination and he wasn't going to let them walk over his country's grave unchallenged. He had become a much-valued interpreter working for the Coalition forces. It was one more war he had to fight before it was all over, once and for all. Before he could reclaim his old life.

But on that day, he wasn't a fighter – he was the big brother of the bride. He barely recognised her when he lay his eyes on her upon arriving in the kishlak. She was a princess, bathed in red and golden robes! She took Haji's breath away.

The family were all there, every generation of uncles and aunts, cousins and countless other relatives. No expense was spared for the feast. Some of the delicacies must have been smuggled from Pakistan. A band of local musicians brought their instruments and played old, well-known songs. People danced. It was as if time had retreated in its tracks. It was like it used to be before the wars began.

The only difference was the omnipotent weapons. Almost every male guest carried one, mainly machine guns, but also smaller pistols. Guns had become a way of life, so when some of them were discharged into the sky for a salute to the bride and groom, no one batted an eyelid. It was a celebration – exuberant, bubbly rat-tat-tat of machine guns drumming for joy. They flared in the night sky like fireworks.

The planes arrived within seconds. It was as if they were hidden nearby, waiting for an excuse to strike. There was no prior warning. Bombs rained on the kishlak for a few seconds, which seemed like an eternity. Though people ran, there was no escape. Splinters of homes, appliances and body parts flew in the air. And on it went, just as Haji thought that it could go no longer, that there was nothing left to destroy. After that it was just the ground and the rubble spewed onto it that was battered some more and bombed for good measure, in case there was a grain of resistance buried in it.

When it was over and only silence was left to drill into his brain, he crawled out from a collapsed well where he had been weathering the carnage. Like after the defeat at Tajbek Palace, he dared not stand up and walk; he shuffled instead, on his knees and elbows, searching for survivors. Anoosha, his little sister, the golden bride, was lying, half buried in the rubble, half bathed in her own blood. Her skin was still warm when he closed her eyes and stroked her cheek.

The soldiers came at dawn: two armed vehicles and no ambulance. They knew there was no point in bringing medics. Medics were a commodity reserved for the Allied

Forces, not the natives. Not to mention that they didn't expect to find any survivors. They were quite surprised to discover Haji hunched over his dead sister's body – stiff and cold by then.

He asked why; it was just a wedding... no Taliban here, only his little sister in her wedding robes... he wasn't making sense.

The American officer was at pains to explain. He didn't even look at Haji, but over his shoulder, into the dusty horizon. A big man he towered over Haji, his legs wide apart, arms folded on his chest, while Haji pulled himself up to his feet to identify himself and to stand to attention as a good soldier should. Once again, Haji was an inconvenient witness. Once again, he would be better off dead. And he was asking questions. Damned Haji!

'It's a war! Collateral damage, tragic as it is,' the officer closed the dialogue. He had wasted enough time talking to this inconsequential individual. It was a war.

Haji understood. He knew war better than anyone, better than the American officer, better than any Westerner. It was time to take that war to them. And it was down to Haji to give them a taste of collateral damage.

Despite the unexpected demolition of the Jungle, where Haji was to find Ferryman, he has no difficulty establishing contact with him in Calais. They have been expecting him to get in touch electronically, through the emergency channels. From then on it is business as usual. Ferryman appears to be a fully Westernised individual, though he says he is from Algeria. His reasons for helping Haji bring war to the West remain obscure throughout the duration of their Channel crossing. He talks mainly about his love of sailing and food. He also loves music. He shows Haji how to do the Moonwalk like Michael Jackson while they're listening to the album called *Thriller* and eating couscous with lamb.

The cutter is a single-mast boat, sleek and fast, and very luxurious. It bears no comparison with the glorified dinghy that brought Haji to Italy. Haji is the only passenger. No more refugees, no Boys with big, curious eyes that are willing to scan the night sky with Haji. No mothers with half-dead babies cuddling up to their barren breasts. Things are changing for the better the closer Haji gets to the UK. Now, it is just him, Ferryman, and Michael Jackson, travelling in style.

To stay under the radar and evade the ever more vigilant coastguards, they are planning to land in Cornwall.

'There are old smuggling routes through Cornwall, going back like hundreds of years,' Ferryman shares his historical knowledge with Haji. 'That's the best chance we have of sneaking in unnoticed.'

# XVI

Tara and Charlie are sitting on the sofa, holding hands. Gillian sits there too, but no-one's holding her hand. The sofa is the centrepiece of her parents' reception room, as they call it. Soft and comfortable, it is meant for guests, its only purpose being to make people want to stay. Gillian's mother has baked a cake, lemon drizzle because it is Tara's favourite. Time stands still in this house; there never is much rush.

'How big a piece do you want?' Mother asks Tara, suggesting with her knife a decent slice.

Tara nods. 'I am a pig, aren't I? But I love your lemon drizzle, Gran!'

'Who doesn't?' Father chimes in. 'I married your gran for her lemon drizzle!'

'I must get that recipe off you,' Gillian remembers.

'Whenever would you have the time to bake cakes!' Father laughs. 'Just come over here – that's your best bet at getting a slice.'

'I might yet surprise you. I'm thinking of quitting the Force and baking cakes.' Gillian says it matter-of-factly. She expects a shocked reaction, but to her surprise, everyone takes her announcement in their stride.

Tara says, 'I'll believe it when I see it.'

'Your mum has always been a bit of a hot-head. You never know... Once she gets something into that head of hers...'

'It'd be nice, though.'

Gillian is pleased to hear that: *it'd be nice though*... It means she is still considered viable mother material. And one day, a grandmother. 'I could look after my grandchildren – for a fee, of course.'

Charlie chokes on his tea. Tara laughs. Father says, 'That'll be our job, your mother's and mine.'

'When it comes to it.'

'I'll be onto it, then,' Charlie recovers from his bout of coughs. Gillian is sure that will make her parents blush, but they chuckle approvingly. Mother offers Charlie more cake *for stamina*.

When she stops laughing, Tara waves her arms, 'Calm down everyone! One thing at a time. We need to get married first!'

On the doorstep, Gillian's parents hug Tara and Charlie. The boy is already a family member, adoption papers and all. Gillian wishes she could be as natural and easy going with him as they are. She truly wants him to feel welcome in her life, despite their original stand-off. Wanting it is a start. She, too, gets a kiss from her mother and a bear hug from her father. It isn't often that she does – it's her own fault, really. She usually just flies in and out of their house, giving them no opportunity to as much as get up and walk her to the front door. Life can be so sweet when you slow down and let yourself watch it unfold. Living on the go is only half the fun, like having your cake without eating it.

She could get used to it. The life of leisure has its advantages. This stroll in Sexton's Wood is one of them. It's a chilly morning; frost has bitten into the undergrowth good and solid. The autumnal colours of the wood are misted by the frost. Mud is frozen into foot and tyre prints. With her hands in the pockets of her jacket, Gillian is treading deeper and deeper into the forest. She kicks leaves and they are briefly airborne, and then they float to the ground in a sweeping motion. Corky tries to catch them; manages to get a mouthful of them and spits them out fussily. He jumps onto his front paws – he looks comical, and maybe he means to. He is inviting her to play. Her mind is free of *inventorising*, free of thought. It's a liberating feeling. She could get used to it. The idea of returning to work fills her with dread. She clenches her stomach and suppresses the trepidation inside it. She can always give her notice, and walk away. She will.

She climbs the steep slope where the trees lean close to the ground as if they are hanging onto it for dear life. As she reaches the south facing ledge that overlooks the farmlands below, she comes across a bench. It wasn't there when Gillian was a child; when she used to come here with her father. Corky gives out a snap of a bark – a woman is sitting on the bench, scanning the view. She turns rapidly – an involuntary reaction to the dog's bark. It's the woman from the homeless colony, Isabella Butler – Izzie.

She eyes Gillian with suspicion, almost hostility. 'What now?' she snaps.

'Nothing,' Gillian shrugs her shoulders. 'Mind if I sit with you? There aren't any other seats around.'

'If you must.' Izzie reciprocates the shrug.

Gillian sits next to her, while Corky starts running circles around them.

'Your dog, I take it.'

'Friend's... Mine, really,' Gillian reflects. By the time Sean is out, Corky will be dead. He is her dog now.

'Nice. Always wanted to have a dog.'

'What stopped you?'

Isabella rounds on her with a stern gaze. 'Why do you want to know that?'

'Curiosity... Striking a friendly conversation,' Gillian scowls. She knows that striking a friendly conversation isn't quite her strength. She is rubbish at it and the woman can be excused for being suspicious of her intentions. 'Look, I'm not here on police business. I'm just taking a stroll in the wood, taking a dog for a walk...' She points to Corky.

'OK. Then you don't need to ask questions.'

'I guess I don't.'

They sit in silence for a few minutes, feasting on the view. It is breath-taking: rolling fields, pastures, small patches of hedge here and there, and far in the distance the roofs of the Weston Estate. Fed up with relentless tail-chasing, or perhaps dizzy, Corky settles at Gillian's feet, panting.

'I used to come here with my father when I was a little girl,' she tells the woman. It feels awkward - telling her that. Gillian is more in her element asking questions. But her questions are usually intrusive; she has just proven how unwelcome they are. 'It's been thirty-odd years since I came here the last time. I must have been eight. My dad and I built a shelter, out of branches and leaves. It was about the same time of year. We built a fire and sat around it, telling each other scary stories.'

'My father died before I was born. The Falklands... How is that for a scary story?' Isabella gets up from the bench. 'See you around.'

'You never told me anything about a day out with *that boy*. I'd have preferred it if you had told me first, before you made any promises. You put me on the spot,' Heather sounds hurt. She has been sounding hurt for years, and Oscar has learned to side-step her resentments.

He stops eating and is watching her as she stabs with her fork at the fishcake on her plate. He could put the straight facts to her: that if he had forewarned her, she would have said no; she would've cried and thrown tantrums to stop him. Putting her on the spot was part of the plan. Oscar, the cunning military strategist, has put his best foot forward, and now she has no choice but to live with it. And what is there to live with: a day fishing trip with a ten-year-old boy! Get over it! Naturally, Oscar isn't going to tell her any of that. 'I wasn't thinking, sorry, love...but what's done is done,' he says – philosophically and non-confrontationally – and gets on with his lunch.

He has a sneaky suspicion Heather won't let him get away with it. And she doesn't. 'You never think about me. About how it makes me feel! Your constant visits to see *that woman!* How you ingratiate yourself with her! Do you really think I didn't notice how you looked at her?'

Here we go! Oscar has lost his appetite. He has to think on his feet; he can't let her drag him onto this slippery trajectory. He puts his fork down, accepts Heather's challenging glare head-on, and says, looking her straight in the eye, without flinching, 'I'm responsible for her, for both of them. This is how it is, and how it will stay! Cut her some slack, Heather, for God's sake! She's lost her husband, lost her daughter, and I am to blame!'

'You think you are, but -'

'I'm not going to debate this with you.' More and more often, she drives him ballistic. What the hell does she know about anything! Has she ever lost anyone she loved? Has the rug ever been pulled out from under her feet?

'Of course not!' Her face and neck flush dark-red, as they always do when her blood pressure goes up. 'I don't want to talk about it, anyway! I can tell how you look at her. It's nothing to do with guilt. And that boy... What is he to you? You're not his family! You're not his grandfather! Stop acting like one!'

'He doesn't have any other family. He doesn't have a grandfather, nor a father. In case you haven't noticed, I'm the only male figure in that boy's life.' He is glad he is able to deflect her attention away from Katie.

'The same male figure you were in *Isabella*'s life? What good did that do for her? She still ran off; she was still a junkie!'

She knows how to strike where it really hurts. Bitch!

'I can only but try,' Oscar says calmly.

'Try? You've stopped trying for me years ago! You're obsessed with *that woman*. I prohibit you -'

He won't have it. He won't hear it. He puts his arms around her. 'I don't have to keep trying with you! I love you, Heather. You are my wife, and I adore you. When will you finally accept that?'

'Oh, I don't know...' She hangs her head down, a sign of

141

acquiescence. He can see the skin of her skull through her thinning hair. He thwarts a shudder, and kisses the top of her head.

'I do! I do know, you silly girl!' But he doesn't – he doesn't know when he started telling her all these lies. All he knows is that he wants to see Katie on Saturday, and take Tommy fishing. Heather can go to hell.

Wanda knows how to make him do things he doesn't want to do. She has always had him eating from the palm of her hand. And she has succeeded once again: two wretched weeks of absolute silence on her part, and Andrzej is in pieces. He is lost. He has no purpose. He cries at night, pushing his face into the pillow – the pillow that she has left behind, by his side. A reminder of her absence.

She has not allowed Paulina to speak to her dad, either. He keeps calling, Skyping, sending text messages every day, twice, thrice a day, only to face a wall of silence.

She has won. This afternoon, after work, after he spoke to Paul and apologised for pushing him from pillar to post in the last few weeks, he gave her what she wanted. He sent her a text: *Gave my month's notice. Be back home for Xmas. For good. X*

She replied instantly, as if she'd been sitting there with her mobile in hand, waiting for this moment, her response pre-typed, only one single button to be pressed: *Put on your computer. We'll Skype you. Now. X*

He throws himself at his laptop. Skype takes for ever to load – sometimes, when you most need it, the reception is shit. He urges the bloody thing to come on, pushes his fist between his teeth, 'Come on, you bastard!'

The ethereal sound of the ringtone ripples out, and here they are: his two angels.

'Daddy? Why are you crying?' Paulina is peering into the screen, having brought her little face right into the camera. It distorts her features, making her eyes bulge, her nose enormous and her lips like a fish-mouth. He sniffles, and laughs, then wipes his nose.

'Crying? Who's crying?' Bloody hell, he has to do something about all that crying!

'Mummy says I can make a wish for Christmas! That you will bring me whatever I wish for... Is that true?'

'Would Mummy ever lie to you?'

'No.'

'So it must be true! What is it, then? Shoot!'

'I can't think of anything,' her little face looks troubled, 'but you mustn't forget to come home, like you did before. You forgot... I didn't like that...You will remember this year, won't you?'

'OK.' Yes, he is crying. He is turning into an old woman. 'I'll bring you a little surprise.'

'Or a big surprise. I think I'd prefer a big one.'

Pippa is a little girl all over again. Age, worries and the tragedies of past years have peeled away from her one by one, and all that's left is sheer, child-like delight. She is twirling across the room, barefoot, having abandoned her slippers under the chair. Will's letter is pressed to her chest, held tight with both her hands. She is surprisingly light on her feet, considering her age and frailty, and those nasty varicose veins. The hem of her cotton dress is airborne. It nearly catches on the red-hot bars of the electric fire. Harald has to catch her in mid-flight and pull her away from it and into his arms. 'Come here, missy! You'll go up in smoke if you aren't careful! You skirt has almost caught fire!' He kisses her and feels her heart beat fast. Cuddled between them is the letter – Will's reply. It is like holding a newborn baby.

'Oh, I still can't believe it, Harry! He's coming! He's coming to us!' She is drunk on the news. Her eyes shine.

'You'd better believe it. Saturday night he'll be sat here in this room, having a chat with us. I bet you'll grill him about everything and anything – every girlfriend, every job he held, every place -' His voice snaps in half. All the things they have missed. Sixteen years of silence to be filled with words. Still, it won't be the same...

Pippa frees herself from his embrace. She can't stay still. She paces now, rubbing her hands, conniving a plan, 'You must stop me if I talk too much! Do you promise?' She doesn't even look at him or wait for his assurances; she presses on, 'I'll wait with the supper... Ah, something he used to love! Remember lamb chops? He used to love his chops! Mint sauce, baby potatoes. Oh, will they have new potatoes at this time of year? Are they in season?'

'The supermarket will have everything, don't worry.'

'I want to put the dinner on the table the moment he arrives, steaming hot... what time will that be?'

'The train will pull into the station at quarter to nine, precisely,' he reminds her for an umpteenth time. She will forget in the next few minutes, and will, no doubt, ask him again.

'What if there is a delay? What if the plane is late?'

'I'll call you from Heathrow if that happens.'

'Yes, you must…' Her eyes are dead serious as she fixes him with a round-eyed gaze, 'Call me even if it is on time. So that I know when to start on the dinner, so I don't worry…'

'I will.'

'Maybe I could have a word with Will, when you call?'

Before he agrees, she changes her mind. 'No, maybe not. I want to look at him when I speak to him. When I hear his voice, I want to see his face. It's so much better that way, don't you think?'

'Whatever you say, Pippa, whatever you say…'

# XVII

They decide to set off early to beat the morning traffic. Bath is a bottleneck throughout the day, so they will leave before six even though it is dark and miserable outside, and Malik in particular may find it impossible to get out of bed. But he is the first one up and going, splashing in the bathroom, cursing the cold, but soldiering on nonetheless. It would help if he wore something more than just his boxers, Ahmed thinks. His limbs are long and gristly, and his torso painfully skinny. His ribs are stamped into his skin. If you look at him, Malik is no more than a pubescent boy. Come to think about it, he is just that, having only just turned twenty.

They leave without breakfast – too excited to think about eating, not to mention that the fridge is empty and has been since Ahmed joined Malik on his late-night net surfing. Then the Snapchats, fast and furious; then their talks, meticulous planning and plotting. Ahmed didn't need convincing. After that day at the school gate, he has become duly converted to the cause. It wasn't a religious conversion, it wasn't as if he had suddenly experienced some sort of road to Damascus moment. In simple terms, it was Ahmed's pride – it wouldn't let him take humiliation without a fight. Ahmed wasn't one for turning the other cheek. He would spit back in their faces – an eye for an eye. He embraced the cause, body and soul.

Frost has settled onto the windscreen; it's almost impossible to scrape it off. They leave the car engine running for a few minutes, the fan spinning and blowing hot air, while they go back into the flat for a cup of tea. It isn't just the car that needs warming up.

On the landing, they run into Harry, who is taking out the rubbish. 'You're up bright and early,' he beams. He looks very much bright and bushy-tailed himself. He is always up at the crack of dawn – old people usually are; there is something in their constitution that won't let them waste any time of day. It could have something to do with the imminence of dying – the *carpe diem* thing. Something sharp stabs Ahmed in the gut, but he doesn't allow himself to acknowledge it. He knows it's fear, and fear is weakness. He refuses to think beyond the here and now. On reflection, this is also a form of *carpe diem*. He smiles back at Harry. They're on the same page even if Harry doesn't realise that.

'Looking good, Harry!' Malik says.

'I am good,' the old man chimes. 'Will is coming. We got a letter yesterday: he's flying in from Australia – this Saturday!'

'That's good news!'

Something is still drilling inside Ahmed's stomach – that knife being turned and twisted... 'This Saturday...' he echoes Harry, hopelessly.

'You must meet him. I know you'll like each other.'

'Yeah... I'd like that...' Ahmed is feeling positively sick. Saturday, of all days...

'Are you two off to somewhere?' Harry asks, eyeing Malik's backpack.

'Yeah, we're going on a little day trip – Cornwall.'
'Cornwall? It must be beautiful this time of year.'

It is beautiful. They have arrived too early for their agreed rendezvous. They are meeting Sandman at dusk, at around five thirty. To stretch out, they went for a walk, climbing up a cliff alongside the coastal path. There weren't many walkers around, only an older couple, who shouted a cheery hello. The views from the top of the cliff were amazing: an endless stretch of calm water blending into the wintry pale blue sky and, right at the foot of the cliff, sharp, metallic grey rocks and a bird of prey hovering, almost motionless, ready to swoop. They stood and watched the bird as it went down, hardly touching the surface of the sea, and taking off with a catch in its claws. Not suitably dressed for the chilly weather, they couldn't stay long and had to keep moving.

They returned to the car a few minutes ago. It is parked in a narrow, residential street of Charlestown, overlooking the fortified inlet where an old wooden schooner is moored, making you think you're in the middle of a Cornish period drama.

Malik turns on the engine for the heating to kick in. The radio comes on, too. The news is on. They listen in silence as the newsreader confirms that the new US president is Donald Trump.

'You see what I mean?' Malik squints at him. Ahmed knows exactly what he means. It goes without saying. They have no choice but to get on with it. No more preaching to the converted.

'It's time. Let's go,' he tells Malik.

They head for the rendezvous point in a secluded bay

148

with a small pebbly beach. Again, like the cliffs above, it is deserted. It's that time of year and the early onset of darkness puts off ramblers. As they approach, they can see a boat heading away from the shore. That must be the boat that has brought Sandman here. A figure emerges from behind a stack of large boulders: rather short, wiry and limping. Sandman.

Soon they are standing face to face: the two young and the one old man.

'Salaam alaykum,' the old man says without smiling. He has an open, Asiatic face which inspires trust. His eyes are narrow and small, buried under the heavy thick hoods of his eyelids. His complexion is weather-beaten and earthy. He doesn't have a beard, not the real traditional thing, but a few days' stubble, which is peppery grey. He doesn't shake their hands, but hugs them one by one, and kisses them on each cheek. The kisses feel bizarrely paternal. Sandman has the presence of something grander than you, something eternal. No wonder they call him Sandman, a man made of countless pieces. At least, that's what Ahmed thinks. It's his interpretation of the man's name. It suits him, so he won't be asking him what his real name is. What does it matter, anyway? Would he even tell? The idea is for them to remain strangers.

In the car, Ahmed drives and Malik takes Sandman through the finer points of the plan. 'We've all the components at the ready. It took me over a year to assemble the stuff, bit by small bit not to arouse suspicions.'

'Very wise of you,' says Sandman. His accent is thicker than tar, but his English is grammatically correct and clear.

149

'We've enough to make two devices: one for you and the other one for us.'

'I'm going for the military target?' There is a hint of anxiety in Sandman's voice. Ahmed wonders why. Surely, he's not afraid! Seasoned mujahedin like him!

'The Wensbury Plains MOD base, yes,' Malik's voice, on the other hand, is bristling with excitement. 'The train traverses Wensbury Plains. We'll intercept it immediately after Sexton's Canning station – it's the last stop before Bath. Once the train driver is incapacitated, I'll take over -'

'Malik is a trainee train driver,' Ahmed adds and laughs, enjoying the word play, which seems to be lost on the other two.

'I am,' Malik says, proud as punch. 'I'll stop the train in the middle of the Plains – you get off there and head due east. It'll be about two miles to the base. I say about 'cos you can't get a true satellite picture, or any accurate map, but I went there a couple of times, travelled on foot right to the fence of the base. No one saw me; it isn't properly manned, not the outer perimeter at least.'

'That's good,' says Sandman. 'I'll find it.'

'You'll have time, plenty of it. About twenty minutes after you get off, we'll roll into Bath, and there'll be fireworks galore! It's the start of the Christmas shopping season – perfect target, perfect timing,' Ahmed can see in the rear view mirror that Malik is grinning. He has devised this plan – it's his baby. 'I'm guessing all rescue and emergency services will be diverted to Bath. That'll give you time and opportunity to sneak into the base and cause maximum damage.'

'God willing,' Sandman nods his head slowly.

# XVIII

The terminal has its own tube station. It is enormous, throbbing with people: passing, running, pushing, overtaking, stopping and taking off again, speaking in foreign tongues Harald can't begin to comprehend. He has landed on an alien planet. Heathrow is a whole planet in its own right, and Harald Winterbourne is stranded in the middle of it, gagging for air.

It is way too warm. The air is strangely dry and powdery. Despite his considerable height, Harald is an ant dwarfed by this transitory world. He has stopped and is trying to read an electronic board full of endless entries that keep moving upwards and disappearing before he has a chance to get his head around them. He can't see the flight from Singapore, the one Will is on. The fact that he is five hours too early may have something to do with it.

Something drives into his back, blunt and painful. 'Oh, I am so sorry!' cries a woman with a trolley topped with a toddler sitting astride a gigantic piece of luggage. She sounds Australian.

'Don't worry,' Harald assures her.

'I don't know what I'm doing!' she despairs. 'My husband was picking me up – he's late. I can't get hold of him on the phone. I'm so sorry! I don't know why I'm telling you all this!'

'You've just arrived from Australia?'

'Yes, visiting my husband's parents. It'll be their first time with Gemma,' she smiles at the toddler, who is eyeing Harald with big, bewildered eyes.

'I'm picking up my son, also from Australia,' Harald explains his presence in the middle of this huge hall. 'Only I'm a touch too early. I don't know which gate to go to.'

'It's all very confusing, isn't it? Do you know the flight number?'

'Yes, I've got it here.' He hands her the piece of paper where Pippa in her small, lyrical hand wrote all the details.

The woman glances at it. 'It's not due until six o-nine!' She gives Harald a puzzled look, probably suspecting him of being an escapee from a mental asylum.

He straightens his back, trying to look in charge of his whereabouts and his general direction. 'Yes, I know. Like I said, I am early. Would you like any help with your luggage?' He changes the subject. 'I've got time on my hands…'

'Ah, I shouldn't -'

'Lisa!' A man is running towards them, waving his hand, a distressed and guilty expression on his flushed face.

'Rob! Where have you been!'

He catches up with her, kisses her, then the little girl, Gemma, who still looks rather confused as to who is who – very much like Harald himself.

'Traffic! Bloody traffic! Roadworks all the way! The whole bloody motorway is dug up! Don't ask! Let's go. I'm parked in a Drop Off zone… Before they tow me away!' He relieves the woman of the trolley and pushes it forcefully towards some invisible exit. The little girl, Gemma, waves to Harald from the top of the trolley.

'Bye, bye!' She smiles at last.

Harald waves back.

At last, the electronic display board is showing Will's flight! Harald was beginning to doubt this was for real. He started thinking he had dreamt it all up, that Will wasn't coming at all and that he, Harald, was a confused old man suffering from illusions. He had to call Pippa at home and ask her to check the flight details. He ran his forefinger across the flight itinerary Will has sent, digit by digit, letter by letter as he recited the number. She kept asking if he was all right – as if! She kept saying she wished she was there with Harald. So did he – he wished that too.

He has been standing by this gate in the Arrivals Hall for God only knows how long. His legs are a bit wobbly: it may be tiredness or his nerves. He has a headache; he's been straining his eyes to examine every passenger emerging from the gate. Could he miss Will? He hasn't seen him since he was a boy of seventeen! People change. Though a father should be able to recognise his own son in a crowd of strangers, surely! Harald doubts himself. Those wobbly legs are letting him down. He really ought to sit down, but if he does, he will miss Will. More and more people are gathered by the gate. Harald holds on to his prime vantage point at the front of the crowd by sheer willpower. His vision becomes blunt. The constant movement of people renders him giddy. Then it all stops.

The movement stops. The frame freezes. Clarity returns to his eyes. They are fixed on a singular vision – Harald himself. As he was thirty-five years ago. The same height and build, the same posture, even the hat: a leather cowboy hat. He used to wear that same hat. Where is it now?

'Will!' he waves just as Will spots him of his own accord, his face breaking into a wide smile, his hand reaching for his hat and waving it back at Harald.

'Dad!'

Harald can't execute a single step forward. Bolted to the floor, he waits for his long-lost son to come to him, and embrace him, and hold him up as he shakes in his arms. 'You haven't changed, Dad! Same old big oaf!' Will has tears in his eyes. They look glassy. Harald can't contain his own. They make their way down to his chin.

'You've grown up! Look at you,' he mumbles. 'You're a man!'

Having pulled away to look at each other, they hug again – a hug that lasts for ever because Harald finds it impossible to tear himself away from Will. He's not letting him go. Never again.

Will pats his back in a manly gesture, and keeps patting it until, finally, Harald lets go.

'We'd better be going. We've a train to catch. Mum's waiting with supper... You know how she is... if we're late -' He breaks off. 'Oh my dear God! We thought we'd never see you again!'

'Sorry, Dad. I had to sort myself out.'

'I know... I know. Don't be sorry. You've nothing to be sorry for. It's me -'

'No!' Will stops him firmly. 'We're not going there.'

'Quite right, quite right.'

'So Mum's waiting at home? In Bath?'

'Yes. We've a train to catch from Paddington. The nineteen twelve to Bristol, Temple Meads. We must be going. Let me help you with your luggage. The supper, you see, it can't wait!' He's babbling pointlessly.

They get to Paddington in good time for Harald to give Pippa a call.

'Something happened...' she says faintly when she answers, on the first ring, 'He hasn't come...'

'No, no! He has! I thought I'd call you to let you know we're on track... He's here, with me! Will can't wait to talk to you, to see you!'

'Oh...' she gulps. He can envisage her face. That makes him smile.

'Do you want to have a word with him? He's right here, beside me.' Will smiles, but Harald can see he is nervous, probably as nervous as his mother on the other side of the line.

'Oh dear! I don't know...' She is breathing fast.

'Just say hello. Come on, girl!'

'All right, yes! No! No, I want to see his face when I talk to him. I really do... I want to hold his hands, feel... Not now, not while he's standing in the middle of a train station. I may not be able to hear him properly... I'll miss his first words to me. I can't miss that... I want to hear every word! I'm deaf, you know!' She attempts to inject some lightness into her fear, irrational fear as it is, but nonetheless, real.

'That's all right. Don't worry, my love. We'll be there in no time. It's only a couple of hours. Not even that.'

As soon as the train rolls into the station, they board it. They find their pre-booked seats. Will leaves his backpack in the luggage area. It is too big to go in the overhead compartment. Harald takes comfort from the size of it. 'You're staying for a while, I hope?' he dares to ask.

'I'm thinking of staying for good, Dad.'

The door is shut, the train screeches as the brakes are released, and they are on their way.

# XIX

The weather has been catastrophically bad. It rained all day yesterday, wild winds uprooting a few trees and making some pathways non-negotiable. The temperature has dropped, too. It only adds to the atmosphere. Oscar and Tommy are huddled up in the rowing boat like two thieves in the night. It is still raining, but the wind has subsided so at least they aren't tossed and flung around the lake. Large raindrops hit the surface of the water, causing splashes and then ripples. 'It's like an air raid,' Tommy enthuses. 'We've been learning 'bout that at school.' He grins. His two front teeth are large and white, like Richard's. He still has his small and sharp milk canines. He keeps poking them with his tongue. Apparently, they are wobbly. Oscar remembers his milk teeth; he used to put them under the pillow for the Tooth Fairy. Things he has forgotten... You forget your childhood if you have no children and grandchildren of your own. It drifts away from you, into the mist of your ageing memory. Tommy has brought it back to the surface, fished it out from the depths. Oscar wishes Tommy was his. He could relive the antics of his distant boyhood through him. With him.

'We could be like Spitfire pilots,' Tommy seems to be able to read Oscar's mind. 'Like we got shot down over the

English Channel, and here we are – scrambling for dry land -'

'In a leaking old dinghy -'

'And it's getting dark, and we're hungry as hell!' Tommy is probably speaking from the heart. They had a bag of chips each before they left the station, and nothing since.

'We'd better catch something to eat before we starve to death.'

They gaze at the surface of the lake, unsettled by the rain, at the spot where they have dropped the bait. Dusk has settled in and the heavy clouds steal whatever is left of daylight.

'Tell me about Granddad, about the Falklands,' Tommy asks. He wants to know all the details, so he can impress Robert. It's time he knew: he's old enough. 'Gran told me you were there when he was killed.' The boy's eyes shine, reflecting in the black mirror of water.

'We were storming Mount Langdon. In the night. Very poor visibility, just like now. The mountain was heavily defended. The Argentines lay down constant fire. Relentless. There was this bunker in a cave – there was no way of getting to it head-on, no way of leaving it behind. There was a hail of machine gun fire streaming out of it. We had to take it to move on, or it would have our arses, one by one. Your granddad, and another man, Corporal Walsh... they were given orders to take the bunker and disarm the gunner. Your granddad led the mission. We could only provide cover for a while, then the two of them were on their own. Your granddad went in first, with his bayonet fixed onto his rifle. He stabbed in the dark... He must've thought he got the bastard, but... the gunner was still alive, his finger on the trigger. He pressed it just as your grandfather sunk his bayonet into his chest. He made it possible for us to take the mountain. He died a hero's death, your granddad: Sergeant Richard Butler...' Oscar marvels how his worst nightmare can be retold so calmly and so logically. And in so few words. Quickly. Only the nightmare lasts for eternity.

'Nan said I could have his Military Cross when I'm eighteen!'

'That's only eight years from now.'

'I'll get my own, too, to add to it, you know?'

'How's that?'

'I'm gonna be a soldier. With the Parachute Regiment, like you and Granddad!'

'Does your grandmother know?'

'No. And don't tell her either. You know how she is,' Tommy winks at Oscar as if it is a joke, 'she'll only say no. But I'll still do it, you know?'

'I'm guessing you will. I'd do the same if I were you.'

'I knew you'd understand... Did you always want to be a para?'

'Whoa!' Oscar yells in reply. He has a catch. A small, imperceptible jerk of the hook is followed by another one. Oscar releases some of the tying rod and then pulls and locks it in. It's a big one: heavy and determined to break away free. It stands no chance.

Tommy carries the catch in the bait bucket. It's heavy – what with all the water, not to mention the massive trout – but Tommy doesn't mind; he soldiers on. The bucket bumps against his thigh; water sprays out. 'Gran loves rainbow trout!' Tommy says as they finally reach the station and find

159

two seats to rest while waiting for their train to arrive: the eight-o-five to Temple Meads, via Bath. 'You must tell her we caught it. She won't believe me. She'll think we bought it in a shop.'

'I'll tell her, don't you worry! My fisherman's reputation is at stake here,' Oscar is laughing. Maybe Katie will ask him to stay for a late supper: grilled trout. He would love that. They could sit at the table, the three of them, like a family. Oscar wants nothing more.

'How long till the train comes?'

'Fifteen minutes.'

Tommy's teeth are chattering and his lips are slightly purple. Oscar realises the boy is cold. And hungry. 'Wait here. I'll get you some hot chocolate and something to eat.' A small café at the station sells hot chocolate and coffee from a vending machine. They also have some pre-packed cakes. Oscar buys two hot chocolates and two flapjacks, and carries them to the waiting room where Tommy is guarding their catch.

'Here, drink while it's hot. I don't want you to catch your death,' Oscar tells the boy. 'Your nan would never forgive me if that happened on my watch!'

Sexton's train station is an old Victorian building with all the trimmings and inconveniences of the yesteryear: it is small and draughty, with stone-tiled floors polished to shiny perfection due to over a century of busy foot traffic, and with uncomfortable hardwood benches. It is pretty, though: it has a clock tower, an intricate lace of railings and balustrades, and a flyover pedestrian bridge leading to the platforms.

Gillian has offered to drive the boys to the station, and then to pick them up again later, at ten past midnight when they return – drunk and disorderly – from their stag night. She has four of them in her car: Charlie, sitting next to her, looking so prim and proper that you would be excused for thinking he is the blushing bride, not the raucous stag. The other three, Sasha's Rhys and their two best men, Joe and Adrian, are in the back seat, cracking half-indecent jokes, burning with excitement. It is the thinly veiled prospect of a thinly veiled stripper that has got their pulses racing. Frequent references to the lady's big blue eyes accompanied by their twitchy-finger gesticulation confirm Gillian's suspicions. Charlie is doing his best to divert her attention away from Joe and Adrian, and their lewd innuendoes. Entertaining Gillian with conversation isn't easy though, he is soon reminded. She isn't one for casual chit-chat. Her eyes keep darting to the back seat and *the lady's big blue eyes*. She catches Rhys's eyes in the rear view mirror. He smiles sheepishly, embarrassed that Gillian, at her age, has to reckon with the excesses of the boys' unbridled depravity. She smiles back – grins, in fact; she'd laugh at their ribald humour if that was appropriate. Which it isn't. After all, she is the bride's mother, one of these boys' mother-in-law to be. Poor Charlie! What is he getting himself into!

'Thanks for chauffeuring us around,' he insists on distracting her.

'No problem. At least I can do something useful, and keep an eye on you, like I promised Tara.' She says it, her face straight as an arrow. Charlie gives her a missive of a troubled look. She laughs, 'Of course I didn't. Just trying to make up for lost time – you know, make friends with my daughter's future husband.'

'Thanks,' he nods with understanding. He must've forgiven her for the stand-off in their early relations.

'Don't mention it.'

Joe bursts out in a thunder of laughter. Gillian has the disturbing impression he's laughing at her and Charlie. She is wrong, of course. Joe slams poor Rhys on the back and says, 'It'll stay between us, scout's honour, you dirty bastard!'

Gillian wishes she could hear what has made Joe laugh. She has missed it, bummer!

The parking area in front of the station is small and crowded with London commuters' cars. They'll be coming on the train the boys are taking on their onward journey to Bath. They'll be coming on that train, getting into their cars and driving themselves to their homes in the picture-perfect villages in Sexton's immediate vicinity. But by the time they vacate the parking slots, Gillian will be gone too. She needs a parking space now. She finds a Disabled space and takes it with a guilty crunch in her stomach. 'Right, I can't stay here long,' she mutters, directing the stags to hit the road.

They are climbing out of the car, thanking her politely and waving to Corky who is squashed behind the back seat. Gillian is planning to take him for a walk on The Green while she is at this end of town. The Green, with its gravelled paths, is the only dry bit of land left in Sexton's where a dog can have a runabout without drowning in mud. The rain of the last few days has been unrelenting.

Charlie pats Corky on the head, 'Be good, man,' he tells the dog. Gillian wonders what the hell he's thinking. Corky is probably wondering the same thing.

162

'Thanks again, Gillian.'

'No worries. I'll be waiting somewhere here at quarter past twelve, yeah?'

'Thanks!' He shuts the door, catching the buckle of the passenger seatbelt in it. That makes a grating noise. Apologetically, Charlie opens the door and pushes the seatbelt inside. 'Sorry,' he mumbles and scuttles to join Rhys and the other two as they swagger into the station building like a gang of rowdy bandits, hollering and laughing. Gillian winds down the windows to clear the air and let out the alcohol fumes. The boys have had a few drinks for the road and the car stinks to high heaven.

Three other men follow Charlie and his pack into the station. Two of them are young and agile, the third one is older; he has a nasty limp.

Brothers in arms, Ahmed muses - they are brothers in arms: Sandman, Malik and Ahmed, and the bond between them is stronger than blood, stronger than love. Yet they don't know each other, not really. Ahmed and Malik share a flat. They only met for the first time when they came to Bath to study. Before that, they were strangers. Sandman is even more of a mystery. They don't even know his real name. They don't know where he was born, where his homeland is. They know nothing about him and he knows nothing about them, and yet there is a bond between them. They share a mission, each for his own reasons, but the mission is the same, as is the object of their hatred. Paying back in kind: hatred for hatred. At least, that's what Ahmed tells himself so there is order and reason in his mind and a purpose to his actions. He is a rational man; things must make sense. What he is about

163

to do must make sense. Payment in kind to restore balance. Natural justice. Revenge. Justified force. Necessity... There is a word out there for how he feels. There is a word for everything in this clever world of ours. Ahmed must find it. All sorts of words fly off Malik's tongue, and he believes in them. Ahmed does too, as he now has faith in something that is greater than him, but he hasn't found a word yet that fits him personally. Maybe there isn't such a word. Maybe no word can express it... The bond. The mission. Natural justice. Revenge. Necessity. Sandman...

There is no individual person behind Sandman, no frail, weak humanity. All there is to him is a purpose. In the few days that he stayed with them at their flat in Bath, Ahmed has learned nothing about the man. He doubts Sandman himself remembers any of his past or knows who he is. He is a phantom. But, bizarrely, Ahmed trusts him with his life – with what is left of it, that is. Sandman won't retreat. He won't change his mind. He won't abandon their mission until it is done.

They drove to Sexton's Canning in a car which they left in the centre of town, parked on a double yellow line, booby-trapped. It was Sandman's idea. They won't need that car anymore. It is full of their DNA. He, for one, does not wish to be traced. He is Sandman – he leaves no traces behind. Ahmed and Malik agree. Malik is keen for maximum damage to be done. Ahmed doesn't want his mother to know it was him. She wouldn't understand. She would cry and blame herself, and all those bastards would let her take the blame.

What blame? Ahmed asks himself. There is no blame, only glory. He must believe that. Justify that in his mind.

'We're like Butch Cassidy and the Sundance Kid,' he says.

Malik laughs. 'Yeah! It was a damn good film!'

Sandman looks at them without comprehension. His hooded eyes don't so much as blink. Of course, he doesn't know what they're talking about. He hasn't seen *Butch Cassidy and the Sundance Kid*. 'It's about two men, outlaws. They go down in style, their guns blazing,' Ahmed explains to Sandman.

'Outlaws?' Sandman asks.

'Like… criminals – thieves - from the Wild West.'

'Thieves get their hands cut off, where I come from. It's not good to steal, no good.'

They approach the station. A bunch of young men, loud-mouthed and drunk, are entering the building. There are four of them: disorderly and bawdy. 'Catch up with them,' Sandman instructs Ahmed and Malik. 'It will look like we're with them. Less suspicious.'

Sandman is a cunning fox.

They attach themselves to the group. As it happens, apart from Sandman, they're all the same age. They look like they're mates. They queue up for the tickets. Ahmed finds it amusing that he and Malik are buying tickets for the train they're going to blow up. Ironic. He smirks at the thought. A young boy, ten, maybe eleven, is staring at him. Ahmed winks and the boy smiles. He is there with his grandfather, a bait bucket and a set of fishing rods popped against a bench next to him. Sandman is also looking at the pair. His face is like a carved stone, his eyes expressionless. Ahmed stops smirking. He wishes the boy and his granddad were waiting for a different train. Or perhaps they're just picking someone up. Ahmed tells himself that is the case.

The arrival of the eight-o-five to Bristol Temple Meads, via Bath, on platform two is announced through the loud speaker. That's their train. The group of loud young men head for the platform, as does the boy and his grandfather. The boy grabs the bucket and leans against its weight as he carries it through the door. The grandfather follows, laden with fishing rods.

'Do you think the fish is gonna be alive when we get home?' the boy asks his grandfather.

'Oh yeah, definitely.'

'Maybe we can let it swim for a while in the bathtub... Do you think Nan would let me keep it?'

'What? As a pet?' The old man laughs.

'Why not?'

'We can always ask her when get there, but I've a feeling -'

'Leave it to me. I'll ask her nicely.'

The train rolls into the station, and they all board it. Ahmed, Malik and Sandman find seats in the same carriage as the boy and his grandfather. The drunken young men are restless. A typical stag outing. They take their seats, and then, just as the train jerks into motion, they decide to get up and relocate to the front. The front of the train is a bad idea, Ahmed assesses their chances. But then again, no one on this train is really safe. With the amount of explosives Ahmed carries in his backpack, they're all doomed.

# XX

The foul-mouthed young men move on, leaving the carriage peaceful and quiet. Since they entered the station, Oscar has found their behaviour overbearing and quite intolerable – a shock to the system after the soothing silence of the lake. He has tensed up inside, bracing himself for an unpleasant journey home. He is relieved they've gone to make a nuisance of themselves somewhere else. The youth these days – they have nothing to focus on, that's their problem.

Oscar is surprised however that they have left behind the other two. He was under the impression that they were all together, but now he is not so sure. The other two young men resolutely remain in this carriage, sitting arm in arm, with another - older – man keeping them company. Oscar thought the old man was travelling on his own, but he was obviously wrong. These three are together. He wonders what makes him think that. They have nothing in common; they aren't even talking to each other. They just sit there, the old man stone-faced, the two young ones agitated. One of the them keeps checking his watch, over and over again. The other one is playing with his fingers – bending them one by one, then tapping them on his knees, looking nervously around. At some point he catches Oscar's eye, and both he and Oscar look away. But Oscar keeps watching from the corner of his eye. His old soldier's instinct tells him something is not right. These three men sitting together are not right. Especially the older one. His clothes. He is wearing normal clothes, nothing out of the ordinary, except – Oscar notes – his clothes are brand new. There is a label sticking out from his rolled-up sleeve. His jeans are too big, held up by a belt. His jacket is a couple of sizes too large as well. It is as if someone has bought these garments for him without knowing his height and build. The style of the clothes – something is not right with that, either. Oscar can't put his finger on it, but it isn't right for that man. He looks uncomfortable in his oversized trousers and padded gilet with a furred hood. Something else is wrong. It is this one thing that makes these three men belong together even though they purport not to know each other. They have exactly the same backpacks: camouflage green canvas, the same make, the same style and size. They keep their bags on the floor, between their legs. Identical bags. A coincidence? Oscar doesn't believe in coincidences.

'What's wrong, Oscar?' Tommy pulls his sleeve. He speaks loudly, thus attracting the attention of other passengers, including the three men, who are now gazing in Oscar's direction, intrigued and somewhat alarmed.

'Nothing… something in my eye, I think,' Oscar rubs his left eye. 'Oh, there, it's gone!' He blinks theatrically.

'I thought you were asleep. Remember, you told me, in the Paras they taught you to sleep with your eyes open. Remember?'

Oscar mumbles something indistinctly. Damn it! Something fishy is going on! His instincts are never wrong. 'Shall we call your grandma to tell her we're on the way?

Where's your phone?'

'But we just called her, remember? At the station!' Tommy frowns.

'Yes, yes… She might want to know we're on the move now.' Oscar wishes now that he had his mobile phone on him. Damn it! He has left it at home as he refused to be harassed by Heather. He wanted to be left alone: him and Tommy, and the wilderness. Damn it!

As if on cue the two young men get up, pick up one of the backpacks, and leave the compartment. The old man doesn't move. Was Oscar wrong? Were they, after all, thrown together randomly. He scans the carriage: most of the seats are taken. Perhaps that was it: the three men landed in the only available seats, and they happened to be next to each other. He breathes in relief. He doesn't have to worry about Tommy, about putting him in some jeopardy. It's only Oscar's overactive imagination. He must stop sniffing danger at every corner. This isn't the Falklands. Nothing is going to happen, for God's sake!

'So have you decided if our catch ends up on the table or in the bathtub?' he returns his full attention to Tommy.

'Um…'

Tommy is telling him about his plans for the fish, his face animated, excited and round-eyed, but Oscar stops listening.

The old man has got up, too. He picks up his backpack, rather gingerly, and puts his on his back, almost in slow motion, as if it contained something fragile, like glass. He heads for the door. There isn't a station anytime soon. The next station is Bath. Until then, the train traverses Wensbury Plains with no stops. A good twenty minutes without stopping. Where is that old man going? This is not right.

Oscar bends over Tommy and grabs his arm. 'Now, Tommy, listen carefully,' he exhales into the boy's round-eyed face, 'Don't ask any questions. I want you to go down between the seats and roll up into a ball. Can you do that? Cover your head. Stay on the floor. Stay that way until I come back, OK?'

'Where are you going?'

'I need to follow that man,' Oscar points discreetly to the old Asian man, who is now standing on the link between the carriages, facing the door.

'Where is he going?'

'I don't know yet. Remember? No questions. If something doesn't look right – you'll know when that is – I want you to take out your mobile and dial 999.'

'Is something wrong?' Tommy looks frightened. Vulnerable. A little boy Oscar is leaving on his own. Like he did the boy's grandfather... He mustn't dwell on it. He must follow his instinct.

'That's what I'm going to find out. Stay put, soldier!'

'Sir!' Tommy pushes forward his scrawny, ten-year-old chest.

Harald is watching his son. After the long aeroplane journey, Will is asleep, lulled into a nap by the monotony of the train journey. He has propped his head on the window pane, which reflects his profile in multiple layers. His chin is lifted, his mouth slightly ajar and his breathing slow and peaceful. His face hasn't changed. He is the same little boy Harald has got etched into this paternal memory – his little boy. The features are still soft and smooth, and he still wears the African suntan. Perhaps the Australian sun paints your skin the same way the African one does. All of a sudden, Harald wants to go back. It's a physical sensation in his gut, like a hunger pain – he is so desperate to go back and face the African sun. Somehow, Will has brought a hint of it with him, on his skin and in his scent. Harald inhales it. How he has missed his boy! How he has missed his homeland in Africa! And now they are both here, before him, asleep.

There is something innocent in a sleeping man's face. In Will's case it is the innocence of his boyhood, from before... before that day when their world had ended.

He is back, and Harald's world is back on track, too. A stray tear rolls down his cheek. He doesn't care if anyone sees it. Harald is crying with joy. It is joy and relief, and pain that clutches at his chest. A good pain – a pain that reminds him that he is still alive.

He has an urgent impulse to touch Will. Perhaps he needs to make sure he isn't dreaming this whole moment up. He leans forward, his face close to his son's, so close that Will's steady breathing brushes against Harald's cheeks, and he stretches his hand and strokes the boy's hair. Will stirs, opens his eyes and squints, dazzled by the artificial light on the train. 'Dad?' he asks with disbelief, as if he has forgotten that they are together again, father and son, going home to Mum.

'Yes, Will,' Harald smiles and withdraws his hand. 'Did I wake you? Sorry.'

'Have we arrived?' Will sits up, but his eyes are confused and heavy-lidded, and keen to drift again into slumber.

'No, not yet. Close your eyes, go back to sleep. I'll wake you up when we're almost there.'

'Sorry, I'm not much company. I'm feeling knackered,

suddenly...'

'We have lots of time to catch up on things,' Harald pats him on the knee. 'Plenty of time... Plus you don't want to repeat yourself, do you now? You'd still have to repeat everything to Mum. She won't take it from me. You may as well save your breath.'

'OK, if you say so -' and he closes his eyes again, even before he finishes the sentence.

They have plenty of time. A lifetime. Will is here to stay – he said so. God, what a reversal of fortunes! Harald is thanking his lucky stars. He leans into his seat, throws his head back and gazes at the other passengers. He is smiling at them. He wants to tell them to keep going, even if it may be tough from time to time, because there is joy and happiness at the end of all that suffering. There always is – that's what natural justice is about. One woman smiles back at him. She is in her forties or fifties, sitting next to a man the same age. The man is doing something on his laptop, looking frazzled, scowling. His fingers dance lightly on the keyboard. The woman isn't doing anything other than staring into space until she catches Harald's eye and the smiles follow. Harald nods as the woman, playfully, ruffles her man's hair. In his turn, the man glances at her surprised, his fingers playing musical statues over the keyboard of his laptop. 'What was that for?' he asks.

'Don't know,' the woman tells him, but that makes him smile. So now there are three of them smiling. It's a chain reaction Harald has started.

He moves with his eyes to two young ladies, both of whom are occupied on their telephones. They can't see him, but Harald keeps smiling. One of them comes across something amusing on her phone – she shows it to the other one. They giggle and they look up and see Harald. He keeps smiling. They scuttle with their eyes, but their giggles intensify. Harald chuckles. He is delighted.

The door to the carriage opens behind him. Harald can feel the whiff of cold air and the clanking sound of the running train; then the door closes, the sound is muffled. Two men hurry through the carriage, heading towards the front of the train. They walk briskly without looking for seats. They are just passing. Harald recognises them. At least, he is sure he recognised the one at the back –

'Ahmed!' he calls out. The young man's head turns and he gazes at Harald, his eyes strangely out of focus. 'Ahmed! It's me, Harald! What are you doing here? What a coincidence! Come and meet my-'

Ahmed doesn't seem to know who Harald is. He turns away from him, brisk and unsmiling, and presses forward. For a split second, Harald doubts his own eyes. That wasn't Ahmed. It was someone looking just like him. And the other one – that wasn't Malik, either.

Ahmed's stomach turns. He feels lightheaded, faint. He has to stop and breathe. Black specks swirl before his eyes. 'Wait!' he shouts, and pauses, squatting on the platform between two carriages, his head between his knees. He swallows repeatedly, not wanting to throw up.

'What the fuck are you doing?' Malik glares at him, pacing over him like a caged animal. 'Let's go!' For the millionth time he glances at his wristwatch. 'We've got two minutes to stop the fucking train for Sandman to get off. Let's go!'

'That was Harry -' Ahmed experiences another wave of nausea.

'What?'

'Harry's on the train… With his son…'

'So what?'

'For fuck's sake, we can't -'

'Get up!' Malik pulls him by the scruff of his neck. 'We've no time for this shit. Now!'

'Haven't you heard me?'

'I heard you all right!' He's holding him up, his fist grasping the lapels of his jacket, his face contorted with fury. 'No turning back, hear me? Harry'll have to join the party.' He drags Ahmed to the next door – the last door on this train, the door that leads to the final carriage. 'Come on! Don't go soft on me now!'

Bright light floods Ahmed's eyes as he braves the narrow corridor of the crowded carriage. The four young men – the stag party from Sexton's Canning – are having a whale of a good time. They are cracking jokes and chatting up a bunch of women, all wearing pink bunny ears. A hen party and a stag do – such a small world! The women are sniggering, their cheeks burning with excitement. The men are thundering with laughter. Two of the men are sitting down, the other two standing up, blocking the passageway. Malik and Ahmed have to squeeze between them, exchanging polite and apologetic smiles. One of them, a long-faced fair-head with a freckly forehead and pale eyelashes, says, pointing to the front of the train, 'Where you going, mate? There's no seats there, just the train driver. Tis how far you can go.' He is looking straight into Ahmed's eyes as he pushes by him, face to face. Ahmed says, 'Sorry. Thanks.'

He follows Malik, who doesn't stop.

Malik tears the door open and they burst in on the driver. Taken aback, he stares at them for one uncomprehending second, his round face slowly setting into a bizarre, inexplicable expression of something bordering on pleasant surprise. 'Malik?'

For the first time Malik pauses. He too is taken aback. He knows the driver. He may even change his mind. Ahmed takes one tentative step backwards.

'Step away from the steering, Andrzej,' Malik orders the driver, addressing him by his name. 'We're armed. We carry explosives – do you understand?' He slows down and it seems like an eternity when he repeats the instructions. 'Step away. Lie down on the floor, face down. I'm taking over.'

'You lost your mind, yes?' the driver says, his accent thick. 'Playing tricks on me, Malik, are you?'

'Move! Now!' Malik barks, but the driver only moves in order to block Malik's access to the dashboard.

'You don't want to fight me, Malik. I've a black belt -'

Malik pulls out a knife and shoves it in the man's face. 'Stop the fucking train!'

The driver dodges Malik's first thrust, which slashes through the air. Malik tries again but this time the driver grabs his wrist and pulls it towards him, which sends Malik off balance. They tumble onto the steering wheel. The train seems to be gaining speed. Malik is paralysed in the driver's arms, and is forced to drop the knife. 'Get him!' he hisses at Ahmed over the man's shoulder.

Ahmed, too, is paralysed – with inaction. But this only lasts for a split second. He is sure now the driver has Malik under control. All Ahmed has to do is to dispose of the explosives. Before it's too late. He opens the door. The wind hits him sideways, almost lifts him from the train, which is now travelling with doubled speed. The two fighting men must have pressed the accelerator, a gas pedal, or whatever it is that makes the train go faster. Having regained his balance, Ahmed swings the backpack with the explosives, intent on throwing it as far away from the moving train as is humanly possible.

The train enters a sharp bend. And suddenly, without any prior warning, it stops in its tracks, the grating sound of its brakes like a screech of a prehistoric raptor.

Ahmed, still holding onto to the backpack, is tossed out of the train and into the dark night like a burning cigarette butt into a pool of flammable black oil.

In the distance, the train rushes over the ancient Roman-built viaduct above the village of Little Horton. Its progress seems to be faster than usual. Perhaps it's just Gillian's perception. The trains are so much faster these days. She throws the ball for Corky, and he goes for it full gallop. In fact, he starts running in the direction his instinct takes him before the ball leaves Gillian's hand. Then he disappears behind a bush.

The Green is dark and empty at this time of the night. The last few days of rain have not done much to entice ramblers to the park. And it's getting colder. The weather forecast says that wintry temperatures are on the way from the Arctic – just for some meteorological diversity, to keep people guessing what the next day may bring. Gillian doesn't mind a bit of frost to shackle the mud. She hates it when the animals stagger indoors with dirty paws and carry the filth onto the carpets.

As soon as the train is gone, all that is left is the vibrating silence that slowly dies away. She can now hear Corky squelching through the mud in search of the ball. He is making snorting, grunting noises, having probably stuck his nose where it doesn't belong.

Gillian loves the tranquillity of an empty park. Trees are slowly beginning to shed their green foliage, sporting nothing more than twisted black silhouettes against the starry sky. She breathes in, contemplating what life could be like if she wasn't a copper. Would she make a decent –

What? She wonders. What could she do for a drastic career twist? Become a lollipop lady? There is probably a long waiting list for that.

Corky returns with the ball, and proudly deposits it at Gillian's feet. He sits back, his tongue dangling, and watches her predatorily as she picks up the ball. She is about to throw it again when a violent firework in the distance lights up the sky.

She instantly knows: it's the train.

# XXI

She bundles the dog onto the back seat. Corky is putting up some resistance; he whimpers and pushes his tail between his hind legs – he is frightened by the explosion. Gillian starts the engine and takes off. She is there, at the scene, within minutes. It is the notorious bend where the rail line circumvents Little Horton and where visibility is poor. In the seventies, another train was derailed in the same spot, culminating in four casualties. A speed limit had been in place ever since, and no further incidents have occurred until today.

She could tell the train was going way too fast.

Now, she can also tell that speed wasn't the only cause. She steps out of the car, slams the door shut behind her, leaving Corky cowering on the seat. She approaches the train with caution. The first carriage has come off the rails, rolled down the bank and is lying on its side. It has dragged the second carriage halfway down with it. That one is hanging precariously with its nose up in the air, threatening to tip over any minute. The last two carriages are disjointed, looking like a broken leg with a bone sticking out.

There is a smoking crater before Gillian. This, she thinks, must be what caused the derailment. This is what hurled the train off its tracks. She stares with horror at the human remains scattered within the circumference of the crater. They are charred and bloodied – unrecognisable body parts belonging to somebody: maybe one, maybe two people.

With a hand shaking uncontrollably, she takes out her mobile, 'DI Marsh. We've an emergency situation two minutes west beyond the Little Horton viaduct. A train is derailed. Casualties, multiple injuries, deaths… We need ambulances. Now!'

'Dispatching! We've received a 999 call a couple of minutes ago. From a child! We thought it was a hoax.'

'It isn't! Send the bloody ambulances now!' Gillian is angry. 'Ah, hang on! Call in the counter-terrorism and bomb squads as well – this looks like a terror attack.'

She rings off. She can't risk approaching the first two carriages. There may still be explosives on board, plus the carriages look dangerously unstable. The passengers must be evacuated as a matter of urgency however. A few bewildered individuals are beginning to emerge from the back carriages, staggering away from the train, screaming and crying. It's dark. Confused people are running in all directions. It will be impossible to contain them in one place. Lights are flickering inside the train. There is the danger of electrocution on top of everything else.

Where is Charlie? Where are the boys? She doesn't know which end of the train they have boarded. She runs towards the third carriage, climbs up the steps and yanks the door open. The door opposite is already open – some people must have got out that way. She can hear cries for help. A man is holding the limp body of a woman in his arms. The flickering lights animate her wide-opened eyes. There is a small trickle of blood from her temple. The man is wailing and shaking her. Her head flips from side to side as the flashing lights hit and animate her dead face in a grotesquely bizarre spectacle. Gillian approaches, steps onto a broken laptop whose screen cracks under her foot. 'Sir, you must leave the train. Now!'

'What about my wife?' he looks at her pleadingly as if it was within her power to bring the woman back to life. 'Do something!'

Gillian tries to feel for the woman's pulse. There isn't any. 'She's dead.'

'Who are you?' the man demands.

'The police.'

'I'm taking her with me,' he decides and tries to lift the woman's body. He is too weak and staggers, trips over the broken laptop, and both he and his wife drop to the floor. The man weeps, 'Annie! Annie...'

Two young women are staring at the whole scene in horror. They are perfectly immobilised in their seats. Everything has fallen from the racks and the seats. Gillian steps over pieces of luggage and gets the two girls up on their feet, pushing them towards the door and out of the train. 'Emergency services are on their way. Wait for them! Can you hear me?' They don't answer, but they do as they are told and leave the train. Gillian has to pick up the grieving man by his shoulders to tear him away from his dead wife. 'Later,' she tells him, 'Not now. Later!' She doesn't know exactly what she means to say, but strangely he nods and lets her lead him to the exit.

She passes by two men who are seated opposite each other: one elderly, his body sprawled on the seat awkwardly; the other one younger – both unresponsive. Gillian assesses her chances of carrying them out. She's too small, too weak. They will have to wait for the paramedics. She presses on. Across the gangway connection. Another door is hanging open. More people are trickling out of the train. Disoriented. Confused. She directs them away. This train could be a ticking bomb.

Wedged between two seats she finds a small boy: nine or ten years old. He is sitting with his knees drawn up to his chin, his mouth gaping. In his hand is a mobile phone. He seems to be unaccompanied by an adult. Gillian squats in front of him. 'Hi. I'm Gillian. What's your name?'

'I'm not really supposed to talk to strangers,' he says calmly, but there is hesitation in his eyes.

'I'm not a stranger. I'm the police,' Gillian retorts and shows the boy her ID.

'Good,' the boy exhales heavily. 'I called the police. It was ages ago! I thought you were never coming!'

'You called 999?'

'Oscar told me to.'

Gillian looks around. 'Who is Oscar? Where is he?'

'He's my friend… my nan's friend. I mean he was my granddad's commanding officer. In the Paras. He knows what to do -'

'I see. So where is he now?'

'He's following a suspect,' the boy informs her with all possible gravity in his tone.

'OK…' Gillian doesn't know what to make of this. Little boys have huge imaginations. 'Are Oscar and the suspect still on the train?'

'No, course not. The suspect pulled the emergency brake and got off. That's how it all happened – the train stopping... It was like an air raid, you know! I told them when I called 999.'

'I see.'

'Oscar is following him. He told me he would go after him just before it all happened. Oscar knew something was fishy about that man. And he was right. Oscar is always right, you know? He is a real Major! He said I must call 999 - if it didn't feel right - and I must tell them... He knows these things, Oscar does.' The boy is blabbering. He is clearly in a state of shock, but Gillian realises he is telling the truth. This isn't the figment of a little boy's imagination. The sole fact that the adult, Oscar, is gone and that he has left the boy behind on the train, can only mean one thing: the boy is telling the truth and Oscar is following a suspect. He must have concluded that leaving the boy on the train would be safer than taking him with him.

'Which way did they go? Can you point me in the right direction?'

The boy points to the hanging exit door. 'They went through that door. Then I don't know which way. Oscar told me to hide between the seats.'

'OK, let me get you off this train,' Gillian reaches out to the boy, who accepts her hand. She walks him to the door and helps him down to the ground. She leads him to a group of passengers cowering at a safe distance. 'Take care of him. The Emergency Services are on their way.'

'Come here,' a woman puts a jacket over the boy's body and hugs him. He is shivering badly. 'What's your name?'

'Tommy Butler.'

'Tommy,' Gillian leans over him, 'I'm going to go and find your friend Oscar, all right? Can I trust you with a

182

message for when my colleagues arrive?'

'The cops?'

'Yes. DS Webber. Ask for DS Webber.'

'Course you can trust me! I've got it all in hand, you know!'

'Can you tell him exactly what you told me. I'm DI Marsh. Will you remember?'

'Yes, ma'am!' Tommy nods in earnest.

Gillian jumps out of the door Tommy has pointed out to her, and runs straight on. Time is of the essence, she has no doubt about that. If the suspect carries explosives, he may be heading for the MOD base on Wensbury Plains at best, or for the nearest populated area in the worst case scenario. Either way there is no time to waste. Assuming Oscar is indeed a trained military man Gillian may be able to rely on his backing. He may be well trained for tracking down the suspect. Armed Response are on their way, too. They'll soon join in the search for the suspect. If all goes well, they may yet be able to prevent this bloodbath from getting any worse.

Luckily, the sky is clear tonight and the bright stars shed a modicum of light on her path. The ground is squelchy, still wet and treacherous from the days of incessant rain. It isn't easy to run. Her shoes are caked with mud. She feels heavy-footed. The chill of the cloudless night is beginning to bite, but Gillian is now running. Her stride is measured and steady. She has to catch up with the two men. In her assessment, they have about fifteen or twenty minutes head-start on her. She can only hope that Oscar, a supposed army major, won't do anything stupid on his own and that he will wait for backup.

A single shot bursts through the air.

It comes from her right-hand side. She stops and listens for more, but no more shots follow. She turns right and runs. She can feel her heart wrestling with her ribcage. Her breath burns her lungs, but she doesn't slow down. She has been going for ten minutes, maybe longer. She could be closing in on whatever – whoever – awaits her in the dark. She is afraid to use her mobile as a torch. There is no telling who is out there with a gun in their hand. The night produces no sounds. No sounds of fighting. No sounds of calling for help. Only her own wheezy breathing. For all she knows, someone – she hopes it is the suspect – is dead.

A body is slumped on the ground. It is no more than a black, tangled silhouette curled up into a messy bundle. It could be the man, Oscar. Or the other man – the suspect. Gillian tries to hold her breath as she approaches, but the man can hear her. 'Here,' he whispers, 'Here…'

'Who are you? Your name?' She stands behind him, knowing that he is incapable of twisting his body to face her. He is definitely injured. But he may be holding a gun.

'Oscar Holt… I'm…' he struggles to speak.

'DI Marsh. Help is on its way.' Gillian is reassured that the other man is nowhere near. Gone. She puts on her mobile's torch to take a closer look. The man on the ground – Oscar Holt – is in a bad way. He has been shot in the torso, on the left-hand side: the blood has soaked his clothes in that area. He has suffered considerable blood loss already. Gillian takes off her jacket and pushes it hard into the man's left side. This may slow down the bleeding until the medics arrive. 'Your little friend, Tommy, told me you were following a suspect.'

'Thank God he's all right! He is a good boy, Tommy...'
Oscar nods and winces as he tries to brief her. 'The suspect
is Asian, around sixty, maybe older. He's heading for the
military base... with a backpack full of explosives, I
suspect...' He is breathing fast, shallow puffs of air like a
woman giving birth. 'He pulled an emergency brake over
the... the Little Horton viaduct... Two accomplices on the
train. I heard an explosion... it happened at the same time...
I think it was an explosion...'

'Yes,' Gillian nods. 'Stay still.'

'You must go after him. Leave me here. He's slow...
Limping. I may've inflicted some damage... We struggled.
He shot me, but... I managed to wrestle the gun out of his
hand... threw it in the grass... He isn't armed... Apart from
the explosives, in a canvas backpack. Go!'

'I need to call for help. I can't leave you here! You'll
bleed to death!' Gillian whips out her mobile. There is no
signal. There wouldn't be in such close proximity to a
military base. Still, she can dial 999 and ask for an
ambulance. She gives the operator as precise co-ordinates as
she can.

'Go! For God's sake, go!' Oscar urges her. 'I'll be
fine...'

Gillian doesn't have to be asked twice. She lights her
torch and searches the ground. 'Which way did you throw
that gun?'

Oscar tries to point over his head. She directs the beam of
her torch in that direction. The light skips and dances on the
wet grass. At last, it bounces off a shiny metallic surface.
The gun. She picks it up, slides it behind the belt of her
trousers. The gun feels cold and heavy. 'Found the gun,' she

tells Oscar and waits for more encouragement from him.

He obliges. 'Go woman! Before it's too late! It's an order...'

She runs.

A lone figure is limping hurriedly. Away from her. He is a short, wiry man who despite his disability is surprisingly light on his feet. There is a backpack on his shoulders, under a fur-trimmed hood. Gillian draws the gun and holds it with both her hands, pointing at the man. 'Stop! Put your hands up!'

He does stop and turns around to face her. There are only a few yards between them. He has narrow, deep-set eyes and when he looks at her it seems like he is smiling. Oddly, his lips break into the semblance of a smile when he says in a hoarse voice, 'Svetlana?'

It is more of a question than a statement. He examines her, his head cocked slightly, his lips repeating slowly, incredulously, 'Svetlana... *Tyh vozvraschiwah...*'

'I said, put your hands up!' Gillian repeats. Her voice and her hands are shaking. She is sure he can't hear her. He is smiling at her, for God's sake! 'Put your hands up slowly where I can see them.'

He makes a few steps forward towards her. He is an old man and a bit unsteady, and she should really be helping him to stay up on his feet. That's her first instinct. She can't possibly shoot an old man. What if she's got the wrong man? Not to mention that trusting smile of his. 'Svetlana...'

He is walking towards her. It's a trick. Gillian pulls the trigger and aims at the sky. The shot ricochets against the stars and it stops the suspect in his tracks. It shakes him awake. His eyes open wide for one second and now they are really looking at Gillian. She says, 'One more step and I will shoot.'

'I have explosives on my back,' he tells her something she already knows. His accent is broad, foreign. He speaks surprisingly softly, considering that what he says is a deadly threat. 'You shoot, we both die. Except I don't mind dying.'

'Put your hands up!'

He doesn't listen. He lowers his backpack to the ground and squats over it. He lifts the flap. 'I give you five minutes to run, then I detonate it,' he tells her in the same calm, soft tone. As if he is promising her a treat. But his eyes are cold steel. He means business.

Gillian knows she won't shoot him. She can't kill a man, and even if she could, the whole bag of explosives would blow both him and her to smithereens. She could miss – her hands are shaking uncontrollably. She has no choice. At least, if he blows himself up here and now, in the middle of the deserted plains, no one else will die. If she runs now... She knows she only has five minutes to put some distance between herself and the bomb. She runs.

# XXII

She stumbles and lands face down in muddy, smelly water. Her side collides with a large stone. Pain shoots through her ribcage. For a split second, she thinks she'll faint. As she gets up, her head goes into a spin and she feels nauseous. Blood must've drained from her brain. She kneels for a while, wasting precious seconds. It is more her willpower than her muscles that hoist her back up to her feet. She tries to run, but it's like moving through liquid tar. She forces her body to run. From a distance this looks like a disjointed breakdance. Slowly, she regains her balance. She must keep going. How much time has she had already? She has lost track of it. She must not fall again. She takes out her mobile and, with wet fingers, tries to screen touch it to get the torch on. The phone doesn't respond. Gillian curses, 'Fuck! Fuck! Fuck!'

She dries her fingers on her trousers, and tries again. This time the torch comes on. She breaks into a panicky sprint, the beam of the torch slashing darkness like a laser sabre.

The five minutes must be up. Why has nothing happened? Has he been bluffing? Should she turn back and arrest him. She is the one with the gun!

'Who's there?' the thin, weak voice of Oscar Holt travels from a few yards ahead. 'Help me…'

'It's me. I'm back.' She slumps next to him. The jacket she has left with him is completely saturated with blood. She pulls it off him. It weighs a ton. She grabs his hand by the wrist and pulls his arm over her neck. 'Come on, help me here! Hang on to me! I'm going to get you up, on your feet -'

He resists. 'Why did you come back? Why did you abandon the pursuit? He's going to -'

'What he was going to do was to blow himself up and take me with him! Come on! Up!' Oscar is heavy and cannot support himself, leaning on her with all his body mass, but she's got him. 'Let's go! Let's get you -'

An explosion shatters the silence of the night. It seems like it is only a few steps away. Even though she has been expecting it, it takes her aback and she falls with the weight of Oscar Holt on top of her. 'That's him,' she whispers. She doesn't know why she's whispering. The man is probably dead and she has nothing to fear now. But fear is exactly what is making her heart pound like a ram. She is about to implode.

She wriggles from under Oscar and pulls him by both his arms onto her back. She doesn't know where her strength has come from. 'Hold on to me, Oscar!' All she can hear in reply is a very faint and hoarse intake of breath. She takes a few steps forward. Oscar's feet are dragging behind her, catching in the undergrowth in an attempt to slow her down, but she is pressing forward regardless.

The bark is unmistakable. 'Corky! Here, Corky!'

He is with her within seconds, jumping, sniffing, whimpering. 'Good boy... Did you bring help?'

The dog barks and runs off. What the hell...

Soon he is back, still barking. Human voices calling.

'Here!' Gillian shouts, but the sound that comes out of her is suppressed by the weight she is carrying.

Black figures cut across the field. She recognises Webber. He recognises her, 'Gillian! Fucking hell! I thought you were in that blast!' He levels up with her. 'Who's that?'

'Oscar Holt. Injured. Been shot. We need to get him help quickly. He's bleeding to death…'

The paramedics materialise with a stretcher.

Webber takes the weight of Oscar Holt onto his shoulders to help him onto the stretcher. 'You're all right, sir? Speak to me. Can you hear me?'

Oscar Holt slides from Mark's embrace and falls to the ground. Mark kneels over him, puts his ear to his mouth. 'He's not breathing.'

'Step aside,' one of the paramedics tells Webber.

'Stop the bleeding!' Gillian yells. 'He's unconscious but he's alive. Just stop the bleeding!'

The paramedic gets up. 'He's dead. We're too late.'

Gillian feels sick. She staggers in a circle and throws up. 'Shit! Shit! Shit!'

'It's not your fault,' Mark tries to comfort her, his hand on her back.

She shakes it off. 'Of course it is! I left him and went after the suspect. I should've stayed with him… brought him back sooner! Fuck!' She hits her forehead with the flat of her palm.

'You went after the suspect? Did he get away?'

'He's just detonated the bomb,' she tells Webber.

'It was him? Just one man?'

'Yeah. Gave me five minutes to run before he did it. God

knows why!'

'Better not ask…'

'He's probably dead.'

'The bomb squad are there by now. He's either dead or they've got him.'

'I don't mind either way.' Gillian exhales. At last, her lungs aren't burning anymore. She has recovered her breath. 'Why aren't you with them?'

'I was bloody well looking for you, wasn't I! You told Tommy, didn't you?' Mark has raised his voice. He never does that unless he is beside himself.

'Tommy… How will I tell him about his friend, Oscar? Fuck!'

'We didn't know which bloody way to go! You should've waited for backup! Scarfe will be having a word with you…' Mark is telling her as they're walking briskly, following the men with the stretcher and Oscar Holt's body on it. 'Luckily, I saw Corky in your car. I let him out, and he was after you like a shot. We just followed him -'

'Good boy, Corky…' Gillian glances at the dog, who is right beside her leg, trotting contently, his job done.

'How many casualties are there on the train?'

'We don't know yet. It'll be a while before we do. And just to make things worse, a booby-trapped car went off as the Vehicle Recovery were putting it on tow. One of the workers is dead. It's your worst fucking nightmare! We can't deal with this shit on our own - counter-terrorism lot have taken charge of the scene.'

'I need to get on that train.'

'No way! They won't let you. Anyway, haven't you had enough?'

Gillian pauses, looks Mark straight in the eye, and there he can see her steely determination. She says, 'Charlie and the boys were on that train.'

The hospital seems in chaos. The entire medical staff has been mobilised: nurses and doctors are running from patient to patient, tripping over each other; all the operating theatres are in simultaneous use; every ward has been commissioned to accommodate casualties that are still pouring in. The Accident & Emergency area is swamped, people are camping on chairs, some directly on the floor, wrapped in grey blankets and metallic-silver thermals. The noise is harrowing: moans, sobs and wailing. Some of the casualties have been sent to other hospitals, mainly Bath and a small number to Bristol.

Gillian is standing by the main entrance, waiting for Tara to arrive and watching more and more ambulances unload their cargoes at the door and take off, sirens blazing, to collect more wounded. Some lie on stretchers and wait until someone finally wheels them indoors. Others try to wobble inside on their own. Blood is smudged on the floors like mud – crimson footprints and flamboyant brushstrokes of sliding footwear. As if someone has gone mad.

As soon as Gillian managed to establish that Charlie had been air-lifted to hospital, she called Tara. It was the hardest telephone call she ever had to make. Because Tara was with Sasha, and Rhys was dead.

She wasn't there with the girls to see Sasha's reaction, but she heard it. She heard the, 'You're kidding me, right?' followed by a nervous laugh. Then the chilling silence. Then Sasha's panic-stricken, defiant voice on the phone, 'What did you say? You weren't talking about Rhys… It isn't Rhys – tell me it is NOT Rhys!'

'I'm sorry, Sasha. I'm so sorry…'

And finally the almost voiceless cry, like a rattling hiss.

The phone must have slid away from Sasha's hand. Gillian could hear a distant, muted conversation between the girls. *It isn't true… She's lying…*

*She wouldn't… lie.*

*He's not dead! We're getting married!*

*Come here!*

Muffled sobs – Tara was probably hugging her friend, Sasha's face and her cries buried in Tara's embrace.

It was a good couple of minutes before Tara picked up the phone again. 'Mum, I'm going to call Sasha's mum. I'll ring off now. As soon as she's here I'll be on my way to the hospital. Don't go anywhere… Please, be there…' Gillian detected a childlike fear in Tara's voice, the fear of being left alone to deal with something that was too big, too scary to even contemplate.

'I'll be waiting for you at the main entrance.'

She has been waiting now for half an hour, maybe longer. In all the bedlam, with people coming and going in the middle of the night, it is difficult to spot that one singular person. Gillian is worried she has missed Tara. She is worried that Tara is on her own, dashing along endless hospital corridors, looking for the man she loves. The man Tara loves and Gillian doesn't – though she bloody well should at least try to like him! A pang of guilty conscience stabs at Gillian's gut. She feels guilty, irrationally responsible for what happened to Charlie. Can something bad happen to people because we don't like them? Did Gillian somehow, sub-consciously, wish Charlie ill? She could've driven the boys all the way to Bath. That would have saved them. All of them: Rhys, Joe, and Adrian. And Charlie Outhwaite. As it is, Charlie is fighting for his life. The other three are dead. Just like that! Because she didn't have the time to drive them to Bath. Because they took that cursed train. How will she ever explain that to Tara? To Sasha.

She can see a tall, willowy figure hurrying from the car park, towards the well-lit hospital entrance. It's Tara. Gillian waves to her and shouts her name, but her voice and gestures are drowned in the general commotion of the hospital foyer. She runs towards her daughter and shudders to discover that the girl is only wearing a flimsy T-shirt and leggings. She draws her into her arms. 'You'll catch your death!' she admonishes her and instantly realises how ridiculous that must sound.

'Do you know where he is? What's going on?' Tara is shivering in her mother's arms as they walk towards the entrance.

'He's in the operating theatre, undergoing surgery. He has lost lots of blood... They trying to save his leg, that's all I know.'

A small gasp escapes Tara when she hears about the leg. Now, in the full light of the foyer, Gillian can see her daughter's face. It is ghostly white. Her eyes are frightened, her lips trembling just like her whole body.

Gillian leads Tara to the first floor where, she knows, the surgery is taking place. They stand in the corridor, by the door through which they are not permitted to go. Tara is leaning against the wall and squeezing her mother's hand.

Squeezing it so hard that it hurts. 'Mum, tell me he'll be all right... I'll believe you... if you say -'

'He'll be fine,' Gillian would say anything, do anything to ease her child's distress.

'He has to be. He wouldn't do this to me.'

Time passes. They are both slumped on the floor – there aren't any chairs to sit in, all having been moved to A&E. It's been several hours. No news is good news, Gillian assures Tara. The shock has rendered her very tired and confused. She has stopped watching the door and is now staring vacantly at the white wall in front of her. She is still holding Gillian's hand, but her grip is loose and limp. No words can take her out of this state, so Gillian doesn't try to speak. An hour ago, when it finally occurred to her, she called Charlie's parents. They are on their way, but they've got a long way to come from Kent. They may not make it in time.

In time for what?

At last the door swings open. The doctor is brief, almost unsympathetic, but then he has to rush off to the next patient – he has no time for pleasantries. The good news is that Charlie is still alive. They've tried to re-attach the tendons and ligaments of his shattered leg; time will tell if that worked. The bad news is that he has lost a lot of blood and there is some brain swelling. He is in a critical condition. The doctors have done everything they could. It's up to Charlie now. There is nothing Tara and Gillian can do here, either. They can't see him yet. They should go home, but they can't do that. They are waiting for Charlie's parents to arrive. At least, Charlie's parents can live in hope for the time being. Unlike Rhys's parents. And Joe's. And Adrian's.

# XXIII

This is relativity theory in action: a night, a day and another night gone by in the blink of an eye. The time is in a state of dizzying flux. Gillian has slept for a couple of short hours, so short that she isn't quite sure if she's got the right date. It is possible that time has not shifted forward at all and she is trapped in some time bubble.

She is up in her bed; Fritz is gawping at her, meowing. He is hungry and not too pleased with her. He doesn't like the strangers sleeping in the spare bedroom: Theresa and Jerry, Charlie's parents. They have shut the door in his face. He is not used to people coming into his home and restricting his free rein of the house. They had nowhere else to go, an argument that is lost on Fritz.

They all came home late yesterday night, only once they were sure that Charlie was out of danger – as far out of danger as he could be. He is stable now, but still critical. The scan has revealed some damage to his bones and soft tissue in various places, but nothing the doctors can't deal with. He is in an induced coma until the swelling in his brain is reduced. So the danger is stabilised, but still present and pending. They found that out last night. A night and a day of anxious anticipation felt like a single lash of a whip, it went so quickly.

Gillian drags herself out of bed. She opens her wardrobe – there, concealed amongst her clothes, hangs Tara's wedding dress. She hid it there so that Charlie wouldn't see it before their big day – that'd be bad luck. Bad luck! How ironic! Gillian cringes. She pulls out the dress and suspends it from the wardrobe door. Such a beautiful thing! She caresses the immaculate softness of the satin and runs her forefinger over the elaborate pattern of the lace on the bodice. It is silver-white, out of this world. Will Tara wear it? Will she marry Charlie? Will he live?

Gillian shoves the dress back into the wardrobe and shuts the door. She goes to the bathroom – she doesn't have to wait her turn today. It's all hers. She longs to hear the usual commotion inside it, the banter between Tara and Charlie over the towel or the way each of them squeezes the toothpaste out of the tube, but today there is none of that. She takes a shower, brushes her teeth and looks in the mirror to find her face gaunt and her eyes framed in black circles. On the landing, she pauses by Tara's door and listens to the comforting silence. At least Tara is asleep.

She puts the TV on and feeds the animals. Corky knows to be patient, but Fritz expels a few indignant yodels before swooping on his bowl. Her toast gets cold on the plate while she takes her coffee to the sitting room, and surfs for the latest news. It doesn't take long. The media are buzzing with what will become to be known as *the Sexton's Bombing*.

With the images of the derailed train and disjointed carriages in the background, the reporter confirms the death toll. 'Thirteen people are dead, including the train driver, and a further eight are fighting for their lives at the Western National Hospital. Fifty-two passengers suffered various, non-life threatening injuries; some are still hospitalised. The majority of the casualties occurred in the first two carriages which sustained the heaviest impact from the bomb explosion. A hotline number at the bottom of the screen has been provided for people trying to track down missing relatives who could have been on that train. The police are hard at work trying to identify all the victims and to piece together the sequence of events. They have called for witnesses. I have with me Chief Superintendent Alec Scarfe.'

The camera swings away from the reporter, and in motion, catches Beatrice Pennyworth, the long-forgotten PR guru of Sexton's Constabulary. From under which rock did she crawl? A blast from the past! She is always on hand when trouble brews – the more trouble the more indispensable Ms Pennyworth is. Things must be really bad if they had to call upon her services. Gillian dislikes the woman intensely. She is all about damage control and censure. With her in the picture, the facts will be buried and *official versions* will take their place.

'Chief Superintendent, can you now confirm that this was a terrorist attack?'

'No terrorist group, as yet, has claimed any responsibility for this, but yes – we have reason to believe that it was. We are still gathering evidence however and will only be able to comment in full in due course. Naturally, our sympathy is with the victims and their families.' Beatrice Pennyworth is nodding behind Scarfe.

'Is it true that the perpetrator is still at large?'

Ms Pennyworth taps Scarfe on the shoulder. 'That'll be all at this point,' he says as if on cue. 'We'll call a press conference when we have more information available.'

'But is it true?' the reporter is relentless and the cameraman is still pointing the lens at Scarfe's face.

He pauses. 'We advise that the public remain vigilant. Our forces are on high alert. We are looking to members of the public for any information relating to this incident.'

So the bastard is still at large, Gillian interprets Scarface's words. She gets dressed and heads for the station.

Sexton's CID is as bad as the hospital was. It is in utter chaos. Neither DS Webber nor DC Macfadyen are in. Gillian is told they've been working flat out in the last twenty-four hours and have subsequently been sent home. As a matter of fact, the local bobby is neither wanted nor desired on this case. MI5 and the Counter-Terrorism Squad have taken over the police headquarters and the investigation. MI5, Counter-Terrorism and of course, Ms Pennyworth. PC Miller is manning the desk and heartily advises Gillian to bugger off home, too. He's heard about her antics following the suspect without backup, 'It won't be long before Scarface starts looking for someone to take the blame for the slip he gave us. You're best advised to stay out of sight.'

'So it's true he got away?'

'Yeah, he did. Gone with the wind. No sign of him.'

'How the hell did he manage to get away? He can't possibly know the area, he isn't local. He sounded foreign. He can't have been working on his own...'

'What do I know?' The constable shrugs his shoulders.

Gillian leaves Miller on the desk and heads for Forensics to talk to Jon Riley. To her relief, he is at his desk, deep in his work, which isn't something you can bank on at this early hour. Most likely, he never went home for the night. This is an educated guess: Jon looks like he has been dragged through hedge backwards, and smells even worse. Streaks of his long, wispy hair have escaped from the bun held by two chopsticks on top of his head. There are sweat patches gradually spreading from his armpits. His desk, as usual, is a dump.

'Hi Jon! What can you tell me about the train attack?' she shoots from the hip.

'Nothing,' he shoots back. ''Tis confidential stuff. Intelligence – top secret. I'm working for MI5 for the minute. My lips are sealed, I am afraid. But how are you otherwise? I heard you played hide and seek with the suspect? Neat!'

'Come on, Jon! It's me you're talking to!' Gillian plants herself in an empty plastic chair next to Riley. She isn't going anywhere until he talks to her. She knows that he knows that. She just needs to play his game – the hard to get game. 'I'll tell you what I know.'

'What do you know?'

'You first.'

'Between you and me, yeah? Nothing leaks to the media.'

'As if I would!'

'OK, what do you want to know?'

'How it happened, to start with. How many perpetrators? Details, Jon – something you're good at.'

'It looks like it was just the one bloke.'

'Just one?'

'For now, yes. The explosion occurred outside the train. He must've planted the explosives by the rail tracks, over that infamous Little Horton's bend, you know where the -'

'Yes, I know the history of it. Get to the point, Jon, please.'

'We're still looking into it, but like I said, he planted the bomb by the tracks, and waited – detonated it just as the first carriage hit the point. It could've been a sensor. We're going through the debris-'

Gillian interrupts him, 'He can't have been waiting outside. He was on the train! The boy, Tommy, saw him on the train. The man he shot dead, Oscar Holt, he followed him from the train. Someone else planted the bomb. He wasn't working alone, I knew it!'

Riley clearly doesn't like to be contradicted, 'Not quite. He could've planted the bomb beforehand, then got on the train -'

'And what? Take the chance that he doesn't get blown to kingdom-come with the rest of the passengers? Bearing in mind, he was carrying explosives with him, in a backpack -'

'DI Marsh! My office!' Scarfe is standing over them, blowing steam from both his ears.

'You've broken every rule in the book, Marsh!' He is banging his desk with his fist, as is his habit whenever he talks to Gillian. Talking to Gillian is inadvertently quite violent. 'You did not call for backup -'

'I did, sir! I remember distinctly calling -'

But he can't hear her. 'You left a message with a little boy and took off, unarmed, after a dangerous suspect! I am surprised you're standing here in front of me, still alive! Surprised, and frankly, I don't know what to do with you anymore! You're lucky you're not dead, but I have the misfortune of having to deal with you and the consequences of your actions! Sometimes I wish you were de -' He catches himself saying that and gawps at her, bewildered and befuddled. 'You could've been killed in that blast, you realise that?!'

'Yes, sir!'

'You did not follow the protocol -'

'I wasn't on duty, sir!' Gillian decides to intervene and avert the course of her down-the-drain career. 'I wasn't on duty! I'm on holiday, you may recall... I acted in my private capacity, as a civilian, so to speak.'

'A civilian?'

'Yes, exactly that! The perpetrator was on the run and I was in hot pursuit, sir! With another man who had put himself in danger by following him directly, I had no choice... I tried to effect a citizen's arrest.'

'Citizen's arrest?' Scarface echoes again.

'Yes, sir! Remember, I wasn't on duty. I'm on holiday -'

'Then get the hell out of here! Before I start a disciplinary against you! You're not supposed to be here, so don't be! Otherwise I have no choice but to have you suspended pending the investigation into your conduct.'

'But, sir -'

'No! You're not here. You're on holiday!' He is beginning to calm down, having seen a way out of this sticky situation. 'Besides, we are not handling this case. It's out of our hands. It's the MI5 and Counter-Terrorism lot. Our role is purely supportive. Out of our depth... And you,' he points his finger in her face, 'are out of here all together.'

'Sir!'

On her way out, Gillian bumps into Beatrice Pennyworth. 'DI Marsh, enjoy what's left of your holiday,' she smirks, making Gillian's skin crawl.

She is glad she isn't on the case. She shouldn't be. She should be with Tara and Charlie, supporting them, like any decent mother would. It took Scarface's wrath to make her realise that. Gillian decides to leave this mess behind. She isn't supposed to touch it anyway. She is out of her depth! And that's a fact.

Back at home, she realises that everyone is still fast asleep. The events of the last twenty-four hours have exhausted them on every level. A glance at the clock tells her it is only a few minutes after nine. She, too, is absolutely knackered. All the emotions and dramas have taken a bit longer to catch up with her. But now she is dead to the world. It is an enormous effort to drag herself to bed. She nearly trips over the cat, who once again is demanding food. She ignores him and slumps into bed, fully-clothed.

Something cold and metallic is wedged under her back. She shifts to one side to find the gun.

It is a .44 Magnum with a rubber handle. Gillian picks it up and examines it slowly. There are still four bullets in the chamber, only two having been fired – the one that killed Oscar Holt and the warning shot she fired into the sky instead of the terrorist's forehead. Gillian flicks the chamber back in and slides the gun under her bed. She will have to think about it. She is too tired now for any rational thought, not to mention that it wouldn't be in her best interest to reveal to Scarfe that despite being in possession of this weapon she had failed to apprehend the perpetrator. She should, of course, have surrendered it straightaway. That's the protocol. Except that she wasn't thinking. She didn't even remember she had it. It must have fallen out from behind her belt when she dropped dead in bed last night. And now... Now, it's too complicated to return it. Anyway, she is to stay away from the investigation... Tired... She may bury it and forget it. It's too much trouble to declare it now. Maybe later, when she is in full control of her faculties.

She closes her eyes and is gone.

The banging on the door is not subtle. Corky barks, sensing a serious intrusion. Gillian is shaken awake and stumbles down the stairs in a daze. It occurs to her, irrationally, that the terrorist has followed her to her house and has come to silence her. After all, she may be one of very few people who saw his face.

She presses her back against the wall and asks nervously, wishing she has brought that bloody gun with her, 'Who is it?'

'Eduard Gosling, MI5. We've met.'

'Have we?'

'At the Protect training.'

Yes, she remembers the stuck up, 007-type with his upper-class accent and an expensive suit. She opens the door. Two plain-dressed men, followed by Gosling, barge in. Corky and Fritz stand their ground, shoulder to shoulder in the hallway. Corky growls. The men halt, and the beasts and men stare at each other, a classic Mexican stand-off.

'They aren't very sociable,' Gillian informs them. 'Sorry, I didn't have the time to send them to finishing school.'

Gosling presents a Roger Moore smile. Under any other circumstances, he could charm the pants off Gillian, but at this very moment she finds him plain irritating. The house invasion is not something she needs at this time. As if on cue, there are footsteps on the landing.

'Mum? What time is it?' Tara's voice sounds hollow.

'It's too early. Go back to sleep! I'll wake you when we're meant to go! They said lunchtime, remember?'

'Is someone there with you?'

'No! I mean – yes. Just people from work. Don't worry! Go back to bed!' She turns to Gosling, 'This isn't really a good time, sir! My daughter's fiancé was on that train – he's in a critical condition in the hospital.' She sees no compassion or understanding in his eyes, so she adds emphatically, 'And I am on holiday.'

'Just a few questions, DI Marsh. You'll appreciate you're the only one who can give us his description.'

Gillian sighs. She knows she has to cooperate. This may also be an opportunity to share her suspicions. 'OK, I'll come with you. I can describe one of them for you. Don't know about the others.'

'We believe he was working alone. A lone wolf.'

'I think you're wrong,' she retorts and gives him a short rundown while in the car.

By the time she returns home, the artist's impression of the suspect is on the midday news. It is vague and not quite 100%, but that's the best she could achieve. It was dark and she stood a few yards away from him for only a minute or so. She isn't sure she would recognise him now. They have run his description by Tommy and other passengers, and they more or less agree with Gillian that the man was short and wiry, in his sixties, and with distinct Asiatic features – particularly the heavily hooded eyes. Unfortunately, there aren't that many witnesses, and most of them, like Tommy, are unreliable. What Tommy remembered however was the man's clothes, especially his green gilet with a fur-trimmed hood. That piece of information makes it to the news, too.

'The identity of this man is as yet unknown, but the police believe the man was working alone. If you see him, do not approach. He is dangerous and may be armed.'

So they didn't believe her when she said he had accomplices. Oh well...

Gillian turns off the TV. It's time to go back to the hospital. She puts on the kettle for the coffee and climbs the stairs to wake up Tara and the Outhwaites. Tara's door is open and her bed is empty. She looks in the spare room. Theresa and Jerry are gone as well. They've gone to the hospital without waiting for her. Damn it!

# XXIV

He froze. He hesitated.

Hesitation could have cost him his life. Haji is not one for suicide bombing. It's not his way. He is not religious enough to believe in martyrdom and heavenly virgins. He is a scientist, a rational man. But he froze.

It was the woman – she appeared from nowhere. Her small stature and blonde hair, and her face – from a distance –

He froze because for that one split second he thought Svetlana had come back to him.

Then he heard the woman speak, and the moment was gone.

He wanted to grab it and hold on to it, but it wasn't there anymore. So he let her go. He had to let her go. And that too could have cost him his life. It still might.

He gave himself – and her – enough time to get away before he detonated the explosives, using the mobile phone remote device. He should have killed her first. He may yet pay the price of his hesitation.

Haji is contemplating the events of last night. Ahmed and Malik must be dead. Their bomb exploded just as he pulled the emergency brake. He knew the train had gone too far. He knew it would add a couple of miles to his trek to the military base. He knew something had gone wrong. Not quite to plan. They intended to die, but not as they had: pointlessly. The train was meant to reach Bath to strike at the heart of it, like a bullet. Not everything goes to plan; that is a hazard of war.

The man who followed him from the train – that wasn't meant to happen. He clearly had some military training, but still was no match for Haji. Haji lives war. That man stood no chance, hard as he tried. He is probably dead and poses no more threat to Haji. Unlike the woman. She saw his face. She looked him straight in the eye. And now they're looking for him, high and low. The hunt is on – he can sense it. It is a bit harder in this alien terrain to blend into the background. Haji is no city man. He has to steer away from populated areas. Because of the woman, his face must be plastered on every lamppost. That's OK. Haji is in no hurry to meet people. But sooner or later, he will have to. He has no provisions. He wasn't planning for a lengthy time out in the wild. It was meant to be a snake-strike type of operation: quick and light. Back home for dinner.

Only which home? Whose home?

Under the cover of darkness, he waded upstream the river so that any dogs they sent after him would lose his scent. The water was freezing cold and it soaked through Haji's boots and trousers, slowing him down in his retreat. Once he had put a reasonable distance between himself and his pursuers, he decided to rest. He had to trust his wits. Going back towards the town of Sexton's Canning was a good idea. Everyone would think he would be heading as far away as possible from the scene. Returning to it was the least risky thing to do. So that's exactly what he has been doing after a decent day of sleep, holed up in a concrete, bunker-like structure, abandoned in the middle of nowhere. It was a perfect shelter for him.

From the moment the traffic on the nearby road died out and the stars sprang up in the sky to light his path, Haji has been back on the road. He is looking for a quiet, uninhabited woodland – it will be ideal for him to lie low for a few days, maybe weeks. Things are looking up. If they haven't tracked him down in the first twenty-four hours, his chances are good.

He sees the thick, ragged outline of a wood not too far away. He thinks it is maybe a quarter of a kilometre across fields separated by low, neatly trimmed hedges. He abandons the road and dives into the fields, heading for the wood.

Sounds of a scuffle reach him from beyond a line of brambles on the outskirts of the wood. A woman is crying out, but her scream is muffled and dies out. Haji heads in the direction of the noise. A man is grunting and puffing. There is a commotion and the woman shouts again. She is shouting for help. Haji peers over the thicket. Two people are on the ground; a man is on top, his trousers down at his ankles. Beneath him must be the woman. She is putting up a decent fight: she bit the man's hand and he had to take it off her mouth. 'Get off me, you bastard!' she is panting and trying to push his bulk from her.

'Shut up, and be a good girl!' He pins both her hands over her head and wedges himself between her legs. 'Don't force me to slap you! We wouldn't want to rearrange your face, would we now?'

'Fuck you!' she spits in his face.

The man chuckles. 'You may find that it is you who's being fucked!' And he gets on with his business.

Haji is about to move on. That man's business isn't his after all. He does not want to make his presence known in these parts. It is of course interesting to discover how the Westerners carry themselves on their home turf. It isn't far from what they got up to in Afghanistan. But then, that was war; this is home. Everyone to his own...

The woman is weeping, 'Please, don't do that to me...'

The man doesn't acknowledge her plea in any way. He pushes into her and huffs with content, his arse rising and falling; the woman crying. She gazes up, away from the man's face, and this is when she sees Haji. Her plea transfers to him. Just through her eyes, but eyes are often much more expressive than words. Haji cannot stand there and do nothing. What that man is doing is not right.

Without thinking, Haji picks up a fairly large bough that has materialised under his feet as if on cue. He sways it and smashes the man over the head with it. The contented grunting stops and the man slumps face down onto the woman beneath him. Haji regrets it the moment he has done it. This is his second mistake in the last forty-eight hours. More mistakes than he's made in years. It's the foreign world. It has disorientated him.

He will have to kill the woman now. She has seen him. The man may live. He is probably unconscious and will come to, but he doesn't know who gave him the bump on his head. It's a pity. Haji doesn't want to kill the woman. It'd be a waste... In a way, he has helped her, and now - she pushes the man's bulk off and wriggles from under him. She grabs the bough from Haji's hand and, with a wild howl, starts hitting. Blow after blow at the man's face and head. It's a frenzied attack. The man comes to after the first blow, puts up a protective arm to his face, but she smashes it, and goes on until he is perfectly still. She has made mincemeat out of his face. There is blood everywhere. She is covered in blood that sprayed from the man. She even has it on her face. She is wheezing, exhausted with the effort, when she finally discards the bough and collapses next to the body. 'Done,' she says, and gazes at Haji. 'Thanks.'

He is taken aback. He has seen fury many a time before but not from a woman. He wouldn't want to cross her.

But he'll have to kill her. Because she has seen him.

He knows what has to be done, but against his better judgment, he waits.

She says, 'Will you help me bury him?'

'Is he your husband?'

The woman laughs. It isn't a jolly laughter. It's hard and bitter. 'No,' she tells him what he has guessed already. 'He's a fucking bastard. Deserved what he got. Can you help me hide his body?'

Haji nods. Change of plans. She is not going to betray him. She has just killed a man. She wants to keep quiet about it and so she will have to keep quiet about ever meeting Haji. He and she are bound to secrecy by this. It may yet prove very useful to Haji. The woman owes him. It is her turn to help him.

They start digging: she with the bough with which she has just killed the *fucking bastard*, Haji with his bare hands. Under the brambles the soil is soft, especially because it has been raining for a few days. It's easy to excavate a shallow grave, but the deeper they go the harder it gets. There are roots aplenty and the soil becomes compact and rocky. They stop digging.

They get hold of the body, Haji by the arms, the woman by the legs. It is then that Haji sees the man's boots. Solid boots. Haji's are wet and heavy, and frankly very uncomfortable. They have been scraping Haji's feet, opening up old wounds and making him wince with pain with every step.

'Hold on,' he drops the corpse on the ground. 'I need his shoes. And his trousers.'

The woman doesn't ask any questions. She seems to be on the same page as Haji – practical about things. He is beginning to like her. She helps him pull the man's trousers off, which isn't that difficult considering that he has already dropped them to do the deed. Then they take off his boots and his socks, one from each foot. Haji puts on his new attire. The boots feel particularly comfortable. They are good quality, soft leather. Good. Haji can hike a few miles yet in these. He smiles at the woman and she smiles back.

'Good choice,' she says.

They bury the *fucking bastard*, which by all accounts is a very becoming title for the man, in the shallow grave, without his trousers, his dick out. Haji finds that quite amusing. They cover the grave with leaves and moss. Haji has no illusions that sooner or later the body will be found. The question is how soon. How much time does he have to move on?

'Who is he?' he asks her. 'How soon will they start looking for the fucking bastard?'

'Soon,' she tells him. 'He's the landowner here. A big shot.'

'Not good,' Haji shakes his head. 'I don't want to be found.'

'Neither do I. I've more to worry about than you – I killed him, not you. But he deserved it.'

'Yes, you told me that.' Haji attempts to take the bough out of her hand; she resists and hangs on to it as if the piece of wood has moulded itself into her. 'We'll have to burn it,' Haji explains patiently. 'Your clothes, too. You are covered in his blood. Where is your home? Do you live alone?'

She surrenders the bough to him and says, 'Come with me.' She starts walking deeper into the wood, and Haji follows.

She doesn't have a home. And she doesn't live alone. The first thing Haji sees is the light from a camp fire. It's right in the heart of the wood, in a small clearing. There is one person hunched over the fire, drinking from a beer can and muttering something to himself. Or herself. It is just a lump of a person, wrapped up in layers of grey clothes and a beanie hat drawn over his or her hair. As they approach, Haji discovers that there are caves under a scarp, their entrances covered with all manner of materials: corrugated iron, cardboard, even a blanket. This isn't the England Haji has expected to find or indeed seen so far. But he thinks it agreeable. In fact, it makes him feel right at home. It reminds him of the network of caves and tunnels in the Pandsher Valley – his home for some years, long years when he fought the Soviets. Who would've thought he would find them here, in England? He always thought people here lived in stone castles and glass cities. Not quite. This is a small world after all.

The woman tosses the bloodied bough into the fire, and it flickers with newly found strength. 'Chuck the stuff in,' she points to Haji's old clothes that he has been carrying after changing into the *fucking bastard's* garments. He does it. His wet trousers dampen the fire for a bit, but it picks up in an instant.

'Shit!' the person hunched over the fire is staring at the woman, shocked at the blood on her face and the wild look in her eyes. 'What the fuck?' Haji realises the person is a man, but he is emaciated and narrow-faced, like a ferret. His hair is long. He could easily be mistaken for an old woman, until he speaks.

'Nothing, Ron. It's not worth talking about,' the woman informs him.

'Yeah?' he says, his interest extinguished. He takes another sip from his beer can.

The woman starts taking off her blood-stained clothes. She throws her hoodie into the fire. Underneath she isn't wearing much, just a flimsy top, light green. She is painfully skinny. Haji could count all her ribs if he cared to. She has small breasts, perky, by which he can tell she is fairly young, in her late twenties or early thirties. She has beautiful chestnut-coloured hair, which spills out of her beanie when she chucks that onto the pyre.

'Have you been to the cemetery?' she inquires of her friend, Ron.

He nods. 'There,' he points towards the entrance to the caves, 'three gallons. Went with Sally this morning.'

The woman goes and fetches a metal canister. She pours water out of it and washes the blood from her face. She sits in front of the fire and starts rubbing her arms vigorously.

She is shaking. She must be cold in that flimsy top of hers. Haji takes off his gilet and throws it over her shoulders. 'Keep it,' he says. 'I don't like the fur. It makes me think of a dead animal.'

'Thanks,' the woman nods. Her eyes are hollow. Perhaps she isn't shaking because of the cold. Perhaps it's her emotions. With the light from the fire she looks vulnerable and frightened. Her face isn't a happy one.

'Who the fuck is that?' Ron has spotted Haji.

'A friend. My friend,' the woman informs him, and turns to Haji, 'What's your name?'

'A friend and you don't know his name?' Ron chuckles. He doesn't have pretty teeth – rotten.

'They call me Sandman,' Haji says.

'Come and sit with us, Sandman,' the woman offers him a seat on a log, next to her. He sits down and, instantly feels weary – very weary.

'Sandman is staying with us for a while,' the woman says.

Ron nods. 'Wanna beer?' he addresses Haji.

'I don't drink beer. Water – water would be good.'

The woman pours water from the canister into a tin cup and passes it to Haji. 'They call me Izzie. Welcome to my home.'

# XXV

She had the supper ready for nine o'clock. She had calculated it would take them fifteen minutes: five minutes to catch a taxi and another ten to travel from the train station. There is not much traffic late at night. The lamb chops were ready and kept warm in the oven. Baby potatoes sat in the pot under a lid, on the hot plate. The broccoli and peas would only take a few minutes – she didn't want to overcook them. Mint sauce was in the fridge, made from fresh mint that Harry had brought from the supermarket that very same morning, before he boarded the train for Heathrow. There was lemon and lime cheesecake that Pippa had made herself, like she used to in the old days, back on the farm. White wine was cooling in the fridge alongside a few bottles of South African Castle lager and Australian Fosters; red wine was on the rack just in case Will preferred it. God knows what he drank. The last time they sat together to a family dinner he was only a youngster. It was a few days before he turned eighteen; he drank Fanta then. Now, sixteen years later, he is a man and Pippa doesn't know anything about him. This is about to change.

She had dyed her hair, a subtle copper tint. It was one of those do-it-yourself tinctures, but it came out all right; she was pleased with it. She really wanted to look the way Will remembered her, as if time had stood still and nothing had been lost between now and then. She put on an old dress, the one with red flowers, the one she used to wear for special occasions back in Zimbabwe. He would remember that dress. The red flowers complemented the copper tint in her hair.

When the key didn't turn in the door at nine o'clock sharp, Pippa wasn't alarmed. Not in the least. It was all down to the festive season, with legions of shoppers in Bath and the fever of Christmas… It is near impossible to catch a taxi at this time of year. Maybe they decided to walk home. Maybe Harry wanted to show Will how beautiful Bath was at night, especially with the Christmas lights winking from every window. Harry would be likely to do that. He loved these late-night walks. Both he and Pippa loved them. They would often venture into the night, hand in hand, wrapped in their scarves and mittens - a pair of harmless Peeping Toms, sneaking under the cover of darkness, peering into windows and stealing curious glances into other people's lives. Harry probably wanted to share some of that magic with Will, which would be perfectly understandable had it not been for the lamb chops getting dry in the oven and the baby potatoes getting cold in the pot. Silly old Harry forgot all about that! She would have to give him a piece of her mind!

She stood in the window lit by the twinkling white fairy lights that Harry had draped around the window frame, and watched the street below. Every new passer-by made her heart beat faster and she clapped her hands only to discover that it wasn't Harry and Will. She saw a couple stroll along, holding hands and kissing; she saw a group of youngsters fooling around, laughing out loud in their hoarse pubescent voices; she saw a woman with bags of shopping nearly fall as she missed her footing on that treacherous corner with a loose slab; she saw a man jump out of a car and drag out a Christmas tree from the back seat. She kept vigil, her heart leaping from time to time and sinking again to the depth of her stomach. When the grandfather clock struck ten, she felt sick.

She had been avoiding it, some irrational fear stopping her from picking up the receiver, but now she had no choice – she dialled Harry's mobile phone. He didn't pick it up and she went to the voicemail. 'Harry? Harry, where are you? Call me, please. Call me as soon as you get this message!' she clenched her fist around the receiver. 'The supper is getting cold. Come home. I really -' The phone beeped and she was cut short. She had to put the phone down, an idea she found intolerable. A few minutes later she tried again, and again she ended up leaving the same message, only more urgent, more hysterical. She was hurling herself between the window and the telephone in the hallway, breathless and panic-stricken.

Some minutes later, she could bear her helplessness no longer and so she went downstairs to the flat in the basement, having resolved to ask Ahmed and Malik for help. They would know what to do, who to contact to find out if the train had arrived on time. She rang their bell, but judging by the silence and the darkness inside the flat, she could guess that they weren't in. Yet, she refused to accept it. Perhaps they'd had an early night and were crashed out in bed? She banged on the door until her fist hurt. No answer. She was on her own.

She thought of heading for the train station. Of course,

that's what she would do! She threw on her coat and her shoes, and braved the night. She had no patience to hail a taxi and wait for it, so she walked. She cut a striking figure in the night: a disoriented old woman with a crazed look in her eye. People passing her were oblivious to her plight, going about their business, hurrying to their loved ones who waited for them at home. Pippa could wait no longer. The twinkling festive lights felt like an insult, as if someone – an evil and boastful clown - was having a laugh at her. She winced at them and buried her head deeper into the collar of her coat. She felt no cold even though the night was beginning to glimmer with frost.

The train station was quiet and almost empty. That was reassuring. She approached the man in the ticket office. 'The train from London, from Paddington – is it delayed?' she enquired.

'Speak into the grille, please, madam. I didn't catch that.'

She cleared her throat, stretched her neck and put her lips to the microphone. 'My husband and son are late. They were on the train from Paddington, London. It was due to arrive at five to nine. Has there been a delay?' She was just about controlling the tremor in her voice.

The man's eyes rounded, 'You didn't hear? There was an… an accident. The train was derailed. They said it was a terrorist attack.'

She stared at him, thinking he didn't understand her question. She had asked about the train from London, not about the world's latest calamities. What was he on about? 'No, you don't understand. I'd like to know about the train from London Paddington. It should've -'

'Ma'am, there is a number you can call, a dedicated

emergency number. I'll write it down for you,' he looked up the number and scribbled it on a piece of paper and passed it through the ticket tray. 'Here… They'll be able to tell you if your son and your… did you say both your son and your husband were on that train?' He gazed at her, a deeply sympathetic scowl crumpling his forehead. 'If you call this number they'll tell you if… if they're all right.'

She picked up the piece of paper and gazed at it, puzzled. She looked up at the ticket man. He nodded weak encouragement. She frowned, resigned to the fact that clearly the man was unable – or unwilling – to assist her with her inquiry. She scrunched the paper and, absently, shoved it into her coat pocket. 'I have to go home,' she informed the man. 'We've probably missed each other. They're most likely waiting for me at home, wondering where I am.'

On unsteady feet Pippa Winterbourne headed back home. She was in no hurry, her main priority was to keep her balance. On a couple of occasions, she had to grasp a railing or lean on a wall in order to regain her breath. Everything seemed a bit blurred and slow-moving. Sounds were dragging in time as if she was listening to one of those old-fashioned stretched tapes. It was that drunken sensation she had not experienced in a very long time. She was concerned someone might think she'd had too much to drink. At her age!

She was taking her time. Somehow, she knew that once she was in the flat she would no longer be able to escape the fact that it was empty. Harry and Will had not made it home. She peered into people's faces, hoping against reason that Harry or Will would smile back at her. One man asked her if she was all right, if she needed anything. She shook her head, apologised for staring and ran away. She stumbled and nearly fell. The stranger called after her, 'Are you sure you're OK?'

'Quite sure!' she nodded.

She arrived to a dark, empty building. She climbed the stairs up to her flat. The lights in the window were twinkling, just as she had left them.

'Harry?' she called from the threshold.

No answer. She went in.

As she stood, in her coat and shoes, she slumped into a chair. And she sat there, facing the door, waiting.

Time drags into infinity when you have nothing else to do but wait. She has been sitting in wait for several hours. The grandfather clock in the lounge struck five times some twenty minutes ago, each of those twenty minutes a stretch of eternity. She hears a knock on the door. She doesn't question it, doesn't ask herself why Harry can't be bothered to use his own key. She gets up, proceeds to the door and opens it. Two people in police uniform greet her and produce their ID cards; one man and the other one, a woman. Even now, Pippa is not surprised.

'Mrs Winterbourne?'

'Yes.'

'May we come in?'

'Yes... I was just about to call you. I've your number somewhere here, in my pocket,' she starts fumbling through her pockets.

'Let's go inside,' the policewoman takes her gently by the elbow and guides her into the lounge. 'Sit down, please.

We have bad news, I'm afraid -'

Pippa screams. She can't bear to hear to it. She can't. She puts her hands to her ears and screams.

'Tea or coffee?' The flight attendant is smiling at her, balancing two steaming jugs in her hands. She is wearing bright red lipstick; her attire is an immaculate suit, fitted perfectly to her petite figure.

'Coffee, please.' Wanda needs a boost – she's been up all night. Since the call.

The friendly stewardess pours her coffee. 'Milk?' she suggests.

'I don't know... I don't care! Just put it down!' Wanda snaps at the woman, who gawps at her, piqued. What has she done to deserve this rudeness? What makes people think that just because they paid their airfare they can abuse the crew? She glances at her colleague on the opposite side of the trolley, and shrugs her shoulders with an exaggerated sigh. 'Here you are, madam,' she says pointedly.

'I'm sorry... Thank you... My husband...' Wanda stammers, picks up the cup and brings it to her lips only to scald them. She doesn't feel the heat, though the man sitting in the seat next to her, winces in sympathy with her burnt lips. He and the stewardess exchange looks. The stewardess' is that of *I've seen it all before*... The man, on the other hand, is concerned. And he has reason to be. Wanda puts the cup down awkwardly, it tips and the hot, black coffee spills. It drips off her tray, into her neighbour's lap. He jumps in his seat to avoid the liquid staining his trousers.

'What are you doing! Look what you're doing!' he shrills.

Wanda stares at him, horrified. 'I'm sorry...' She is trying to stop the flow with her hand. That only earns her another alarmed glare.

The man calls for the flight attendant, 'Excuse me! Can you please -'

She glances over her shoulder, and shakes her head. 'Let me,' she comes to the rescue with a cloth.

'I'm sorry,' Wanda repeats.

'Do you have any spare seats?' the man demands. 'Only this is my best suit, and my seat is now all wet -'

'Yes,' the flight attendant is only too happy to assist. 'If you come with me, sir.' They depart, huffing and puffing, both deeply affronted by Wanda's antics.

'I'm sorry...'

She doesn't know what she's doing. It is all too surreal to take at face value: her being on this plane back to the UK after swearing she would never go back again; her going back nevertheless. To identify Andrzej's body.

The phone call came in the early hours of the morning. It was three o'clock, the night still thick and cold outside. The moment the phone rang Wanda knew it wasn't an ordinary call. She sat up in bed and listened to it. Her mother must have been doing the same from her bedroom. She, too, wasn't answering it. She, too, was numbed with knowing...

Paulina woke up and trotted to Wanda's bed. 'Mum? Why's the phone ringing?'

'I don't know.'

'Aren't you going to answer it?'

'Yes.'

She had to. It was for her. She threw on her dressing gown and went downstairs. Her mother was already there, poised by the telephone, her hand massaging her chest, her eyes fixed on Wanda. 'What can it be? No one ever calls at this hour... What time is it in England? Could it be Andrzej?'

'Hallo?' Wanda put the receiver to her ear.

'May I speak to Mrs Sokolowski?' A foreign accent bruising Wanda's surname.

'You are speaking to her. What is this about? At this time...' she mustered the courage to feign the displeasure at being awoken at an ungodly hour.

'My name is Tracey Goulding. I'm with the police -'

'Has something happened?' Wanda inhaled, feeling the air flood her lungs. She reached for her mother's hand. Her eyes told her what she already knew and what the policewoman was just about to confirm. Her worst fear.

'I'm afraid so. I'm afraid -'

*What is it with them being so afraid, always afraid so*, a rebellious thought shouted inside Wanda's skull. 'Just tell me!' she shouted into the receiver, her wits leaving her.

'There was an accident. The train your husband was driving last night was derailed.'

'No, no...' she was muttering into the phone. She had watched it on the late night bulletin on television – the suspected terror attack in England. A South Western train to Bristol Temple Meads. Andrzej could've been the driver. She hoped to God he wasn't. She acted as if he hadn't been. She and her mother talked about all that vicious terrorism everywhere you go, everywhere you step. Spreading all over Europe, like the Plague. She talked about it as if it had nothing to do with her personally. As if it was *their* problem, whoever *they* were. She put distance between herself and the terror, which, horrendous as it was, had no bearing on her life. She had gone to bed, put the lights off, listened for a while and when nothing happened, let herself drift into sleep.

Until the phone had rung.

'Your husband was one of the victims. He's dead.'

'No, no...'

'I'm very sorry.'

'No... This... How can you be sure?'

'He was the driver of that train, and... We need you to come and identify the body.'

Tracey Goulding is waiting for her at the Arrivals. She is a biggish, voluptuous woman – a Mother-bear type. She puts her arm around Wanda and rubs her back. 'Are you all right?'

'I... I spilled coffee on the plane,' Wanda feels compelled to explain the stain on her skirt.

Tracey Goulding nods thoughtfully. 'Please, come with me. Have you got any luggage to collect before we go?'

'Luggage?' Wanda stares at her without comprehension.

'Main luggage.'

'No. I've this bag,' Wanda lifts her handbag.

'Okay. I'll take you to the mortuary to -'

Wanda shudders.

'Sorry.'

They get into a police car. Tracey Goulding is driving. The traffic is atrocious. So is the weather – foggy, disorientating. Tracey has to focus on the road. She says nothing. Wanda says nothing. It is like a voyage into the Afterlife. It has been feeling surreal right from the start.

There should be a way to wake up from this nightmare.

But Wanda can't find a way.

Like a lamb to the slaughter, she follows Tracey up to the Mortuary building, then down a flight of stairs, into the basement. How fitting for the mortuary to be located under the ground...

The body is lying on a trolley in impersonal surroundings, not at all in a nice quiet room filled with white flowers and incense. For some reason, Wanda has imagined it to be more like a funeral parlour. It isn't.

Two more people are with the body. They introduce themselves, but she can't hear them.

'Are you ready?' Tracey Goulding asks.

How ready can anybody be? Ever? Wanda nods.

One of the people lifts the white sheet to reveal Andrzej's tranquil face. It is grey, the lips are faint purple; a cut on his left temple is clean of blood, almost like a line drawn with one of Paulina's crayons. The stillness in his features is not like him, but it is him.

'Is it your husband, Andrzej Sokolowski?'

'He was coming home,' she must tell them that. 'For Christmas... And he was coming to stay, do you understand? He was to stay with us for good.'

Tracey Goulding guides her out of the room. Wanda's legs buckle under her. Luckily there is a chair, a soft chair to sit in.

'Can I get you something? Coffee?' Tracey Goulding offers.

'No, not a coffee. I'll only spill it.'

226

# XXVI

Haji is up for his share of work. Yesterday he set up some traps and today he brought three decent size hares. He skinned them skilfully – it seems skinning a hare is just the same as skinning any other wild animal. A hare has plenty of lean meat. A good winter stew was what this lot of misfits needed. Haji broke into the allotments by the canal and requisitioned potatoes, carrots, parsnip – even some herbs. The wood and the allotments provide rich pickings. He investigated the Weston Estate from a safe distance over a couple of days, and decided to give it a wide berth. Primarily, because of the dogs; they would follow his scent into the camp and bring trouble. Haji doesn't need trouble. He is having a break from trouble.

He has been lying low for nearly a week now. This place and these people are God-sent: oblivious to the goings-on and detached from the world. Coming here was like stepping into another dimension. Haji has struck it lucky.

They are misfits, but a nice lot. Maybe because they are all misfits, they do not judge him. Nor do they ask him any questions. Maybe because they just can't be bothered. They aren't bothered with much at all. From time to time, someone goes to the town – called Sexton's – and brings provisions. Not everyone is equally good at that. Some, like

Ron, spend all their benefit money on booze. Ron drinks away most of it by the time he gets back to the camp, but occasionally even he produces a six-pack to share with the others. When he does, the festivities – and crudities – carry on through the night until they are all falling off their feet. The following day, they aren't half as jovial as the previous night, but they are still loud and foul-mouthed. And so it goes on. There is a rhythm to their lifestyle – an excess followed by a lull, and back to excesses with a vengeance. Sally and Twitch are on methadone, but that's not a big deal, they say. It keeps them alive. Without it, they'd be long gone – *down the drain*, as Twitch puts it. He says he is a veteran. No one has lasted as long as he has. He says he's forty, *or thereabouts*. That's ancient in junkie years, especially if *you're all with it*. Haji isn't convinced Twitch is all with it; for one, he can't understand a word he says. The rare comments that Twitch makes, Izzie translates for him. Twitch is *as pikey as they come*, Haji is reliably informed by Sally; *it takes time to get your head around what the fuck he be on about. Mostly bollocks!*

'Tis fuckin' amazin'!' Sally is licking her chops. Haji's stew is a hit. 'A fuckin' feast for the kings!'

'Wan' a beer, like?' Ron is offering one of his own. That means a lot. That is a mark of respect.

Haji shakes his head. 'You know I don't drink.'

'Suit yerself!' Ron grins, displaying the stumps of his incisors. He promptly retreats his beer can and snaps it open; raises it to Haji, 'I drink for you, Sandman!' He pours it down his throat.

Twitch says something animatedly, and spits in the fire.

'Yer right there, Twitch,' Sally seems to agree. 'Sandman

be a saint if he weren't Muslim!' They chuckle, pleased with themselves and their sharp observations. They know more than they let on.

Haji smiles. He forgot how to smile but this lot – they just reminded him how to go about the business of being jolly. 'I am not a religious man.'

'Who said you was?' Sally ribs Twitch, and they are in stitches, almost falling off the log. Anything will make them happy. Haji envies them. They have nothing on their conscience. Maybe he should get drunk one day, to water down his memories? Except that he can't afford to be off guard. He has to watch out for himself at all times. He is watching them, too, even when they are just larking about, harmless as mutton.

Ron has fallen asleep. It's uncanny how he can simply freeze in a most awkward sitting position, and drift off. Right now, his head is dangling between his shoulders, his jaw dropped, but he still has a firm grip on his beer can, which he is holding, slightly tilted, over his drawn-up knees. Izzie puts a blanket over him, and he wakes briefly, mumbles something, and resumes his position.

Haji takes out his drawing pad, and starts sketching Ron with his tilted beer can. No one bats an eyelid. So he is a saint, and a Picasso! It's all the same to this lot. He likes his newly found freedom. It is a freedom. Of sorts.

Izzie returns his gilet to him. 'Thanks, Sandman. Have it back.'

'You can keep it,' he tells.

'No, I don't need it. I've got my own. You need it more than I do – it gets cold at night.'

'I don't feel cold.'

'Nevertheless. It's yours.' She throws it over his shoulders.

Twitch starts twitching funny and winking at Sally. And she ribs him again and bursts into a throaty laughter. By now, Haji can tell that this amounts to an indecent proposal, and its keen acceptance. The two of them get up, elbowing and hugging each other in turns, and stagger away from the fire. Soon, they'll be making their usual grunts and squeals, and then they will come out for a joint. Which they will share with everyone except Haji, who is a habit-free saint, of course.

'I used to love drawing,' Izzie tells him. 'Drawing and acrylics... When I was a little girl. A lifetime ago.'

'You are not that old.'

'I feel that old.'

'You don't look old. I will draw you and show you. Do you like that?'

She shrugs, which means that yes, she would like that. Haji leaves Ron's portrait unfinished, and moves to the next page of his pad. Izzie is a graceful subject. Her outline is sinuous and uninterrupted. It flows like a river. Her eyes are large and blue, born under the same blue sky as Svetlana's, but her hair – deep chestnut brown and shiny – brings back the memory of Haji's sister on her wedding day. That, too, was a lifetime ago.

He is pleased with his sketch. He has captured her strength and her frailty, wrought into one.

She says, 'Thank you.'

He says, 'Believe me, this is my pleasure.'

'I don't mean the drawing.'

'Ah!' He nods, because he knows she means his timely

intervention. 'It was nothing.'

'It was everything. To me it was.'

'OK.' He is focusing on the bone structure of her long, thin fingers. Hands are notoriously difficult to draw. Her chin is resting on the back of her hand which is cupped over her knee. Her hand is part of her face. She is gazing into the fire.

'I never told this to anyone, but I can tell you. We already share one secret. What's another one?'

'OK. What would you like to tell me?' Nothing is likely to shock him. No secret. She may as well get it off her chest.

'I have a son. I haven't seen him since he was born.'

'I see.' Haji does understand: he has a son. He hasn't seen him at all. It hurts, but to him, there is no relief in talking about it. He can't bear thinking about it, never mind speaking of it.

'I don't want to see him.'

This Haji doesn't see as well as the first part. He, on the other hand, would die to see his son. Just once.

'I was hardly eighteen. I was raped. Brutally raped. I was young and trusting. It was at a party, with people I knew... I was drunk and probably drugged. He thought I wouldn't remember, but I did. I still do. I remember I couldn't lift a finger to fight back. It looked like I was OK with it. Not a single scratch mark on me. He knew how to go about it without leaving any marks... I couldn't complain to the police. No one would believe me. He said I was a slut. I believed him. I hated myself. Nine months later, I gave birth to a child. A son. I couldn't bring myself to look at him – all I saw was that man. I saw that man in my son's eyes. I ran away. Spent years on the streets, on drugs...'

231

Haji is outlining her mouth and adding final touches to the childlike curvature of her upper lip, a downward arch forming seconds before the child bursts into tears. This expression is so fleeting, but he got it – he captured it!

'You know, I never had a father. I thought he would've stood up for me if he lived... He would've protected me. My father was a soldier.'

'He would've if he could, yes. That's what soldiers do, but yes, they don't live long lives.' Haji never says anything unless he is sure of it. He is sure, being a soldier himself, that yes, her father would've protected her, if he had been there at the right time and at the right place. That however, he knows from experience, doesn't happen often.

'You protected me, Sandman. If you had been there, ten years ago, it would've never happened.'

'I don't know about that,' he shakes his head. 'I let people die, couldn't save them...' this is the closest he has ever come to confiding in someone. He trusts this girl. Once again, it's a mistake to trust people, but if there's anyone he can trust, it's Izzie. Because she trusts him.

The portrait is nearly finished: a beautiful, long-necked woman with a child's grimace quivering on her lips and long fingers curling up into a white-knuckled fist. She lifts her eyes towards Haji, 'It's stupid really, but I've come to think of you as my father. I imagine, if he lived, he would be like you. Looking after me, not letting anything bad happen.'

'If I can help it, I will look after you, God willing.' It's only a manner of speech because Haji doesn't believe in God. But he believes in what he says – every word of it.

# XXVII

Charlie is out of danger, and fully awake. Against all the odds, his youth and vitality have conquered death, but that's just his body. His spirit is crushed and quite beyond repair. He is semi-reclined in his bed, his leg holding him in place like a convict's ball and chain. 'I saw them. I could've stopped them,' he mutters.

'Saw who?' Tara leans over, peers into his eyes and squeezes his hand, which she has been holding since arriving by his bedside, to the exclusion of everyone else.

'Those two – bastard-terrorists. I recognised them straight away when the cops showed me their mugshots. I could've stopped them! They pushed by me – I said, "Where you going, mate?", but I let them pass! I let them do it! Rhys, Joe, Adrian… they'd be alive now -' Sobs shake his body. He pulls his hand out of Tara's and presses his fist between his teeth to muffle the crying. 'It's my fault they're dead. My fault…'

'No, no… Stop this now, Charlie! None of it is your fault!' Theresa is shaking with fury, or despair. Hasn't her son suffered enough? He doesn't deserve all this anguish and guilt! 'Tell him, Jerry! Tell him!'

Jerry looks bewildered. He is not a strong man and doesn't know how to exert his authority; he doesn't believe he has any. Anyway, he can't fathom what Charlie is talking about. 'Don't upset yourself, son. You must rest,' he stammers, hapless.

'Those two, Dad,' Charlie insists on prolonging his mental torment, 'I don't know their names, but I remember their faces. I was stood up – there was no seats in that carriage - I was blocking their passage – they pushed by me – heading for the driver's door. One of them looked at me – I told him, "No seats up there…" He heard me, but they weren't looking for seats, were they? The bastards! They were gonna hold up the train, and I could've stopped them!'

'No, you couldn't,' Gillian says. She is the only one who is calm and composed, the only one who gets what he is talking about. Perhaps, because of her job, she's used to keeping a cool head under fire and to analyse facts without emotional engagement. Perhaps it is because she's made that way – detached. Be as it may, she won't be swept away by this river of grief. 'If you'd tried to stop them, you too would be dead. It's a simple fact -'

'Mum – don't!' Tara fixes her with a warning glare. What has she said wrong?

'Sometimes I wish I was,' Charlie mumbles under his breath.

The nurse sends them away – it's time for Charlie's meds; then he needs to rest. The more he rests, the quicker his recovery. He turns his head away when they say goodbye, even when Tara tries to kiss him. It's those damned emotions: they play a man for a fool. Gillian has never been any good at making sense of emotions. Tara tries to teach her a thing or two. 'Next time, Mum, say nothing.

234

OK? You aren't helping - only making things worse.'

'Yes, of course… What was I thinking!' Gillian agrees, keen to please her daughter. She glances furtively at the Outhwaites. Are they angry with her, too? It's hard to tell. Jerry is holding Theresa around the elbow, carrying her weight as if she's about to sink to the floor.

'This isn't over yet, not by far,' Theresa sniffles. 'When will we have our son back?'

'One small step at a time. At least he's alive.'

Gillian is about to agree with that statement when she collides with a diminutive elderly woman. Both of them break into a profuse apology. 'I'm sorry! I wasn't looking!' There is a tint of a South African, or Zimbabwean, accent in the old lady's voice. Gillian recognises it instantly. It brings back the memories of her life in Kwa-Zulu Natal.

Pippa has brought grapes and chocolates, as you do for people confined in hospitals. She had to take a bus this time as she can't afford the taxi any more. Everything is so expensive, she has realised recently. But not the bus. She is a bus-pass holder, a fact which has been buried somewhere at the back of her mind for years. She has always regarded the little card bearing not the most flattering photo of her as rather useless, but now, suddenly, it has become absolutely indispensable. She saves money on transport so that she can spend it on grapes and chocolates, and sometimes on something small for herself. Yesterday, she bought a new scarf. Her excuse is that the winter is unusually chilly this year, but the scarf is also pretty and soft; it rejuvenates her when she wraps it around her neck, covering the scruffiness of it. She must look her best, of course.

She enters the ward and finds him awake and smiling at her. So he has noticed her new scarf! Pippa blushes.

'I brought you some grapes, and chocolates.' She kisses him on the cheek. 'We'd better hide them in the drawer, before the nurses catch us!' Dexterously, she conceals the box of chocolates in the depths of his bedside table.

'Thanks, Mum!'

'Don't you *mum* me, Harry! I'm doing this for you, but really! You ought to be more careful in future,' she scolds him gently, playfully. She doesn't mean to be harsh on him, but God! – didn't he give her a fright! Getting himself into trouble like that! She nearly lost him! What would she do without him if the unthinkable had happened, if she had lost him! She can't bear the thought of it! She sits on the side of his bed and gazes lovingly at his handsome, manly face. She strokes his hand where the big needle is attached with a plaster. 'Oh, Harry, Harry, what shall I do with you?' she admonishes him, a twinkle of mischief in her eyes.

He grasps her hand and kisses it.

'Do you think the nurses may object if we kiss, properly kiss?' she asks.

A little tear comes from nowhere and rolls down his cheek.

'What's that for?' Pippa pulls a hankie out of her bag and wipes away the unruly tear. 'Anyway, you're right – we shouldn't be kissing. Not in public... When you come home...'

She picks up a grape from the punnet and feeds it to him. He crushes it with his teeth, smiles, tells her the grapes are yum. He is so good-looking, her Harry! A magnet for women! 'You'd better not chase after the nurses,' she chuckles. She knows he won't. He only has eyes for her.

A nurse wanders in. Fortunately, she is rather heavy and unattractive. And she isn't in the first bloom of youth.

'Nurse!' Pippa takes this opportunity to inquire, 'When will you be releasing my husband? I feel he will recover much better at home.'

The nurse looks at her awkwardly; then her eyes travel to Harry, questioning and puzzled. He shakes his head. A little secret between them? Pippa cocks her head, a nip of suspicion tearing on the edge of her mind. 'I don't suppose you'd know,' she says aloofly. 'I'd better speak to the doctor, hadn't I?'

'Yes, Mrs Winterbourne,' the nurse concurs. Her voice is low and tired. No, Harry wouldn't find her in the least attractive. 'Visiting hours are over. You can come back tomorrow, at ten.'

'I was just leaving. I've a bus to catch.' Pippa shrugs her shoulders, none too pleased about the nurse's manners. She leans over and, with all due propriety, kisses Harry on the forehead. 'I'll see you tomorrow, darling.'

She leaves the room and, mercifully, hears nothing of the exchange that takes place following her departure:

'Your mother, I take it?'

'Yes. My father died on that train, you know?'

'Everyone knows. The hospital is full of casualties. I had to cut my holiday short.'

'Yes, I can imagine. My mother can't get her head around his death. She thinks I am him, and I don't know how to tell her…'

'Poor thing. Bless her! Let her believe what she wants to believe. The brain has ways of protecting itself against

237

shock.'

The bomber's parents look dignified and innocuous: he, a well-presented man of Middle-Eastern origins, with a neatly trimmed beard and tinted rimless glasses; she, slim, with dark soulful eyes, an upright posture and long black hair threaded with silver. Both are wearing smart, Western clothes. Both are well-spoken despite the remnants of foreign accents. They are Iranian, having come to Britain after the Islamic Revolution of 1979 – refugees from religious persecution, the voiceover informs the viewer. How ironic, Gillian marvels.

Pain is howling from the depths of the woman's eyes which are crumbling with red veins. The man's eyes are hidden behind his dark glasses, but his pain is in his voice. Gillian watches them and wonders: what is it about? Is it about the loss of their only son, or is it about the fact that he turned out to be heartless killer? Which is worse?

It is notable that, although they sit arm in arm on a stylish sofa, they do not hold hands and their bodies do not touch. They are isolated in their respective pain. It is as if they do not dare to draw solace from each other. Perhaps one blames the other one for what happened?

The man continues, 'And we'd like to say how very sorry we are for... to all the families of the victims. We feel their pain -'

'How dare he?' Theresa asks.

'We didn't see it coming. If our son committed this...' the man swallows hard and takes off his misted glasses, revealing his swollen eyes, 'then he is not our son.'

'He didn't do it!' the woman interrupts him, passionate

and defiant. 'I didn't bring him up like that! Ahmed wouldn't have done this! He wouldn't! He was a kind, decent -'

Tara points the remote at the screen, and the TV goes blank. 'That's enough,' she says.

'They're in denial,' Jerry comments. 'You don't have it in you to believe it, as a parent, you don't have it in you...'

'You'd know if Charlie was up to no good - I'd know – it's a mother's intuition,' Theresa contradicts her husband, 'but, you see, we'll never be in that place. Charlie would never do anything like that.'

Gillian stops herself from pointing out the glaring flaw in Theresa's argument. Tara has warned her to say nothing.

# XXVIII

Jerry has shoved his and Theresa's small suitcases into the boot of his estate car, and is sitting behind the wheel, waiting for his wife. Theresa has given Gillian a hearty hug, which made Gillian feel awkward. As usual. She is invariably discomfited by random acts of familiarity and affection from people she considers strangers, which includes almost everyone. She is relieved when Theresa redirects her attention to Tara. They hold each other for a while, their intimacy even more disconcerting to Gillian than the hug she has had to endure. Is she jealous of their closeness? She tells herself she shouldn't be – at least her daughter is inclined to engage in healthy human interaction.

'Thank you for having us,' Jerry smiles from the car.

'Any time, Jerry. I'll see you both on Friday.'

'If that's OK?'

'Any time, as I said.'

They are going home for the week, back to work, back to their everyday lives. Charlie is out of danger and on a fast route to recovery. The doctors are delighted with him. His parents can breathe again, live again.

Theresa has let go of Tara and, in one last attempt to evoke some form of an emotive response from Gillian, grabs her hand. 'I couldn't wish for a better in-law. Thank you,

Gill,' she enthuses. Gillian winces. She definitely doesn't like being called *Gill*. She smiles weakly and waves them goodbye, deep down dreading Friday already. In a mirror reflection of his mistress's feelings, Corky growls at her feet and simply cannot hold himself back from barking farewell to the house guests. 'Bad dog, Corky!' Gillian admonishes him without meaning it. Instantly, overcome by guilt, he flattens his ears and gives his mistress an apologetic gaze. He can read her like a book. He knows she's growling inwardly and he regrets betraying her feelings like that.

Tara pats the dog on the head, 'It's all right, boy'.

Gillian raises an eyebrow, 'That's what I'd call giving the dog mixed messages.'

'I know.' Tara throws her hands up in a gesture of surrender, 'Guilty as charged.' She tenderly touches her mother's shoulder. 'Thanks, Mum.'

'Whatever for?'

'For everything,' she shrugs and pulls away. 'Dad's coming on Thursday, remember?'

No, Gillian didn't remember that small fact. 'Oh,' she continues growling inside her head. 'With the wedding off, I thought there was a change of plans…'

'He still wants to be here for me, and for Charlie.'

'Yes, of course he does. Let's go inside before we freeze.' It is a chilly evening. Frost glistens in the light of a street lamp.

'I think I ought to go and see Sasha,' Tara says, unable to conceal her reluctance. 'I've been putting it off. I just don't know what to say to her… Isn't that selfish?'

'Yeah, it probably is,' Gillian regrets it the moment she says it. 'I mean -'

'I know what you mean. It's all right, Mum. I have to go and see her – as simple as that. I just feel guilty that Charlie is… you know, and Rhys – isn't.'

'It's not your fault.'

'I know that, but I just don't know what to say. What words can I say to her to make it sound meaningful? She's my best friend and I don't know what to say to her.'

'Say nothing. Just be her friend. Just be there.'

Tara kisses her cheek, 'Words of wisdom, Mum. I'm impressed! Where did you come by them?'

'Right…' Gillian knows when she is being mocked, especially when it is her own child who does the mocking. 'Off you go! Before I charge you for my wisdom.'

When Tara is gone, Gillian decides that rattling around an empty house, and tripping over the cat and the dog, isn't the best way to spend Friday evening. Work is what she needs. She has been having withdrawal symptoms in the last two weeks of work deprivation, which other people refer to as holiday. She is not due back until Tuesday, but a flying visit shouldn't hurt anyone. Scarfe won't be there – he never is beyond three p.m. on Fridays. This will give her a quiet moment to catch up on the latest developments and to speak to Jon about that troubling little doubt that has been niggling at the back of her mind since she spoke to Charlie.

She was wrong. Scarface is there: in the ivory tower of his closed-door office, conferring with Ms Pennyworth and a posh-sounding bloke from MI5, of which fact she is appraised by Webber the moment she enters the building. 'Scarfe's been at it flat out, day and night. His career is on the line for as long as that bastard bomber is still on the

242

'loose,' he informs her.

'It's been over a week,' she comments, an atypical note of sympathy for the Super in her voice. It's common knowledge: if the fugitive hasn't been apprehended within the first twenty-four hours, the chances of ever finding him diminish at an alarming rate.

'Eight days,' Webber confirms. 'We have all the airports and the bus and train stations covered. We have all Ahmed Usmani's and Malik Sadat's contacts under surveillance – nothing… The bastard has vanished into thin air. We don't even have his identity.'

'Talking about Usmani, is that the one who allegedly detonated the bomb?'

'Yeah, Ahmed Usmani. Did you watch that Panorama programme where they interviewed his parents?'

Gillian nods absent-mindedly. She is thinking of Ahmed Usmani. They got it wrong. She needs to clear this with Forensic and raise it with the Chief Super.

Scarfe's office door swings open, releasing Ms Pennyworth into the world like a plague. She totters on her high heels, passing by Gillian and Webber without acknowledging either of them. She is definitely frazzled, which is a pleasing thought. She is followed by the posh-speaking, and by all accounts, poshly dressed MI5 agent. He too isn't aware of the existence of such mere mortals as the two police detectives. But Chief Superintendent Scarfe takes instant notice of them. 'DI Marsh!' he hollers from his office and crooks his finger in her direction. 'If you have a minute.'

Great opportunity! Gillian marches in. Normally, Scarfe doesn't waste time on courtesies, and neither does Gillian, 'Sir, about the train bombing – Ahmed Usmani couldn't have detonated that bomb... I don't think he could. He wasn't there – I mean -'

'Detective Inspector, we have experts on this case. They've turned the scene inside out and there's evidence at hand. In fact, my advice is that Usmani is the very person who did it. But that isn't any of your concern. I see you're back -'

Gillian is dismayed. 'Just passing by, sir. I'm not due back until Tuesday.'

He doesn't seem to hear her. 'So I'd like you to take personal charge of a missing person inquiry: Joshua Weston-Jones has been missing for a week now. My hands are full and, frankly, it's bedlam here, so I need you to look into this ASAP.'

'Sir.' Gillian turns on her heel and takes herself out of Scarfe's office. There is no point arguing with him – that will only make him more obstinate. But she has her priorities straight: she'll talk to Riley first.

'Mark, pop over to the Weston Estate, do some sniffing around. His highness has gone off on his travels without telling anyone.'

'I can't, Gillian. I'm up to my eyes with the Hornby case. Time doesn't stand still when you're away, I told you, didn't I!'

Gillian pauses. 'So who is the new SIO?'

'DCI Grayson. On loan from Bath.'

'Now that I'm back, I intend to take over that investigation.'

'I'd like to see you try,' Webber snorts, amused. 'You haven't met DCI Grayson. Scarface is a pussy cat by comparison.'

'Is he a tiger, our Mr Grayson?' Gillian's laughter comes out as a rattle. 'Oh well, he'll have to bugger off back to his cosy little cage in Bath and mind his Jane Austen collection. This is my turf.'

Webber performs bizarre facial contortions, rolling his eyes and nodding his head like a spooked horse. Is this the onset of a well-overdue mental breakdown? She will have to ask him about the situation at home, with Kate. Later. Now, she asks for the Hornby case files to find their way to her desk by Tuesday.

'You'll have to have DCI Grayson's permission, ma'am.' Webber goes all formal on her.

'Grayson's permission? Grayson can go whistle. I want those files, Mark. And stop calling me a bloody madam. What's wrong with you?'

'Sir!'

*Sir?* Now Gillian is certain: Webber needs a break – before he breaks down. Poor bastard! She is about to tell him to go home and have a lie down when a male voice interjects:

'DI Marsh, I presume?'

She turns to find herself face to chest with a very large man with a pale Nordic complexion, red beard, and the bearings of a Viking. He is standing with his legs wide apart, presumably to accommodate what is between them, and holds the thick clubs of his arms folded on his wide chest.

'DCI Grayson. Nice to meet you, at last. I've heard a lot about you, DI Marsh. You're a good detective, but, nevertheless - no, thanks…'

'No thanks for what?'

'I won't need your help with the Hornby case. I have it

245

well in hand. And I've got DS Webber working on it with me.' It is at this point that he flexes his fist and his bones cracks. If there was anything in his hand, it'd be crushed.

Gillian isn't intimidated. She says, 'I've got a few theories regarding the use of the packing tape...'

'I've got a few of my own. Like I said: no, thanks.'

'Suit yourself.' Gillian wants to punch him in the gut, but that would probably break a few bones in her hand. So she executes the verbal punch with all the contempt that man deserves: 'Sir!'

He nods and swaggers off. Arsehole.

She is not giving in – not by far – and she'll resume this battle on Tuesday, when she's officially back in the saddle. For now, she turns to Erin. 'Okay, DC Macfadyen, it's you then. Off you go to the Weston estate.'

Erin scowls. She didn't like the Westons the first time she and Gillian had the misfortune to meet them.

Gillian doesn't care: rather Erin than her. And it is a matter of principle: she won't do as she is told and she won't be demoted to do tasks a constable could do just as well. She tells Erin, 'Just go and feign some interest, ask some questions. Talk to Weston-Jones senior. Get Uniform to interview all his minions. The usual tokenistic crap. I'm off. I must catch Riley.'

Jon Riley is busy. He's having a takeaway curry, judging by the pungent aroma. Poppadom crumbs litter his keyboard. The tomato sauce stains on his shirt and his general washed-out look indicate that he hasn't been home or, if he has, he slept in his clothes and came back to work wearing yesterday's attire.

'Gillian, my lovely,' he beams from above a fork-full, 'you always catch me in flagrante delicto! I'm in the middle of my dinner, as you can see.' He points to the array of plastic containers. 'I'd ask you to join me, but... it's all gone.'

'It's fine, Jon, I'm not hungry. I've just had breakfast. I want to talk to you about the train bombing.'

Riley screws up his chubby face in disappointment, 'I've been talking about nothing else... It's coming out of my ears. I don't even get to go home nowadays.'

'I can tell, but that's out of choice, I guess.'

'Well, let's put it this way: no one's waiting for me at home... You know the type: a sweet, size ten twenty-something with a shepherd's pie in the oven and -'

'Yes, Jon, I'm sorry to hear that,' Gillian cuts in, knowing he won't stop whinnying on his own accord. 'Humour me. It's important.'

'Everything is always important with you Gillian. But as far as I recall, you're not on that case.'

She ignores his unhelpful remark. 'Are you sure one of them detonated the bomb outside the train -'

'Positive. The bloody thing went off just as the head of the train rolled over the bend, and it was there – on the ground, not on the train.'

'And the bomber?'

'He was there too, just off the railway tracks, bang on in the middle of it, if you excuse the pun,' Riley grins. His warped sense of humour never deserts him, no matter what the circumstances. Perhaps that's his way of dealing with the horrors.

'Ahmed Usmani?'

247

'That's the man… or what's left of him. Frankly, I'm told, he looked like a dog's breakfast and they had to use dental records and DNA.'

'In that case, you do not have all of them,' Gillian concludes.

'What do you mean?'

'If he wasn't on that train, then there is another one.'

'Yes, the trainee driver… what's his name?' Jon presses a few buttons on his keyboard with his curry-infected fingers. 'Malik Sadat, that's him!'

'No, one more!' Gillian leans over the computer screen. 'Have you got the names of all the people on that train?'

'We do, yes, but why do you say there was another bomber?'

'Charlie!'

'The bomber's name is Charlie? It doesn't have the right ring to it,' Jon scrutinises Gillian's face with concern. 'What are you on about, Gillian?'

'No! Charlie, my son-in-law to be… He was on the train. He saw two men – two men of Middle Eastern or Asian background – they were pushing to the front of the train. There were two of them, do you understand? Two of them on the train!'

'P'raps he saw the trainee driver and the one who got away – that would make two,' Riley attempts to introduce reason and method to the conversation.

'No. The old man, the one I came face to face with…' An imperceptible but chilly shudder travels through Gillian's spine at the memory of the encounter. 'He was at the rear of the train. He alighted from the last carriage. He was nowhere near the driver's cab.'

'So there is a third one…'

'Charlie saw two of them going for the driver. He recognised them when he was shown photos of all the passengers. One of them is -'

Erin is hurrying towards them in a state of agitation. Her pony tail bounces from side to side. 'Gillian!'

'Not now, Erin,' Gillian squints at her, none too pleased to be so rudely interrupted. 'What are you still doing here? I thought I asked you to deal with Weston-Jones.'

'I am! This is it: Weston-Jones. A dog walker found a body near Sexton's Wood. It looks like it's Weston-Jones.'

'Shit!' Gillian curses. The man has impeccable timing – just as she was in the middle of something! 'We'd better be on our way.' She briefly fixes Riley with a commanding forefinger, 'You Jon, you'd better talk to Charlie Outhwaite. He's still in hospital. The Western National.'

# XXIX

PC Miller is at the scene and is briefing Gillian as she marches purposefully towards the taped off area, 'It's a shallow grave. Dug out in a hurry, just a couple of feet deep. A lucky find, if you can call it that, ma'am. The dog went after a ball and found a hand. 'Twas licking it. Mrs Moss over there,' he points to a middle-aged, corpulent woman, wrapped in a shiny thermal blanket and drinking from a polystyrene cup in the back of an ambulance. 'She's pretty shaken if you ask me... She found the dog licking the hand and couldn't bring herself to pull the wretched creature away from the corpse. So she called 999 and watched the dog dig. By the time we got here, the dog had successfully excavated most of the body.'

'So the grave's been disturbed?'

'Unfortunately. By the dog. Nothing we could do about it.'

Gillian ducks under the police tape, followed by Erin and Miller. She spies out Michael Almond, discernible by his huge moustache, busy at work as he points out areas of interest to the police photographer. It is indeed a very shallow, makeshift grave, a bit of upturned soil, some leaves and moss. An opportunistic crime. She leans over to take a close look at the corpse. It is discoloured and covered in muck, but there is no doubt – this is the once fresh-faced Joshua Weston-Jones.

'How long has he been here?'

Almond looks up at her from behind his moustache, and nods a curt hello, 'DI Marsh. How long? Can't tell you in greater detail than a few days: five to eight days.'

'He's been missing for a week,' Erin says.

'It'd fit.'

An unexpected feature of the scene is the fact that the victim is naked from his waist down. Gillian comments on this fact.

'We've bagged the clothes,' Almond says. 'They'll go for forensic analysis. They'll let you know what they make of it. I'm more interested in what the state of the body tells me.' He turns away and continues with his examination, making an occasional remark into his Dictaphone.

'So how did he die?' Gillian can't sit through every anal detail pertaining to the content of the victim's every orifice.

'My bet is a blow to the head. Several blows, in fact. His head was pretty much smashed in. Look here,' he points to the bloodied mass of tissue around the man's left temple, then runs his gloved finger down, 'I can feel the left cheekbone's been fractured in several places. I'll have the body on the slab as soon as they're finished at the scene. I'll give you more detail then.'

'We'd better inform the family,' Gillian says grimly. She half-expects to be crucified by the Weston-Joneses.

'Do you have an appointment?' the snotty butler – Gerard – inquires at the doorstep.

'It's about the young master, Gerard,' Gillian tries to be

tactful, though she feels like telling the old git to get the hell out of her way.

His already very pale face pales in comparison to what it was when he hears that. 'Yes, yes, that's good… We've news of Master Joshua. Follow me.' He leads Gillian and Erin to the same reception room as before, and within seconds, returns with both the lord and lady of the manor. They look composed, clearly not expecting the worst. Both of them look ordinary: just two average-looking people interrupted in the middle of their Saturday morning pottering around the house. She is wearing gardening gloves and in one hand is still holding a pair of secateurs. Her hair is greying, untouched by dyes, cut in a little bob with a thick fringe, in the fashion of the twenties. She has a voluptuous figure, full lips and a round face – Joshua inherited her appearance. The father is lean and stooped, and there is just a touch of anxiety in his eyes, something he tries to cover up with an upfront manner. He stretches his hand to Gillian, 'Sir Philip Weston-Jones. I believe you have found Joshua? Where has he been hiding?'

'DI Marsh,' Gillian shakes his hand, and points to Erin, 'DC Macfadyen.'

'How do you do,' he says, perfectly controlled.

'Would both of you like to sit down,' Gillian suggests, knowing what effect the news will have on their composure.

'Is it bad?' the lady asks nervously. 'Is he hurt?' Her husband ushers her to the sofa and sits next to her.

'Is it bad?' he repeats her question.

'I'm very sorry… We believe we've found your son's body. In Sexton's Wood.'

'What do you mean by his *body*? Is he dead? Is that what

it is you're telling us?'

'We would need a formal identification… we need you to come and identify the body, but yes, we believe your son is dead.'

'Phil?' Lady Weston-Jones gazes at her husband, her question quivering in mid-air, unanswered. Gerard groans from the corner of the room, which he has never left, keen to hear *the good news about Master Joshua.*

'This may be a misunderstanding,' Philip Weston-Jones says with a surprising lightness to his tone. 'What do you mean he's dead? Was there an accident? What? Talk to us, woman!'

'We don't know yet exactly how he died, but we have reason to believe he was murdered.'

The secateurs from Lady Weston-Jones's hand tumble to the floor with a clank. She jumps at that, startled. 'Phil… Phil…'she chants, searching for the comfort of her husband's hand. He offers it to her and takes her in his arms.

'To be sure. We need you to identify the body. Are you able to -'

'Yes,' the old man stands up. 'Let's be done with. I'm sure it's a terrible misunderstanding.'

There is no unseeing what he just saw. Philip Weston-Jones sobs by his dead son's side. 'Leave me alone with him,' he demands. 'Leave me alone with my son…' The shame of tears, the shame of his naked grief on display, for all to see, makes him shout. 'Get out! Stop staring!'

Gillian nods to Dr Almond and to Erin, and they walk out, leaving the door slightly ajar. It isn't quite the protocol to leave a civilian with a body before the full autopsy has been carried out, but Gillian has never followed protocol. Why break the habit of a lifetime? She gives the grieving father a moment alone with his child.

But only a moment. The investigation must move on swiftly. She returns and faces Weston-Jones from the opposite side of the slab. He is composed now. It didn't take him long to regain control of his emotions. The stiff upper lip at its best.

'Can you confirm, sir, that this is your son, Joshua Weston-Jones?' she has to ask the question.

'Oh yes, this is my son – my boy... Find me his killer,' he speaks through his teeth, his jaw taut and his speech stilted. 'Bring me his killer. It's one of those fucking squatters in the wood. One of them. Get him and bring him to me.'

'We'll find your son's killer,' Gillian assures him. She means it. It doesn't matter whether she liked the stuck-up toff or not – she will bring his killer to justice. Of course, *bringing to justice* isn't the same as delivering the killer into the hands of the father, who is raging with hate. 'Thank you for coming, sir. DC Macfadyen will drive you home.'

Within an hour, Dr Almond is ready to carry out the autopsy. Gillian isn't interested in every minute detail – she will have that in the post-mortem report, if she needs it. But she listens intently when the pathologist describes the wounds to the skull. 'A single blow to the back of the head. It didn't kill him, but it rendered him unconscious. The weapon was a blunt, cylindrical object with a ragged surface, going by the shape of the indentation.' He squints and picks up a pair of tweezers and pokes them gently into the wound to retrieve some microscopic object. He puts it under a microscope, adjusts the zoom, and delivers his verdict. 'Bark. Looks like bark. It was a tree branch that he was hit with.'

'Another confirmation that it wasn't premeditated: a random murder weapon.' Gillian observes.

'Looks like it. Plenty of tree branches in a wood. The murder weapon may still be there, blending in with the background.' Almond returns to the body. He resumes his examination of the skull. 'Now, the blows to the side of the face: those were much more violent. Repeated and frenzied, I'd say... The blow to the left temple finished him off, but there were several blows delivered post mortem. The skull is crushed in four places, the cheekbone fractured. Take a look at the X-ray.'

Gillian follows him and gazes, a bit distracted, at the X-ray whilst Dr Almond luxuriates in a detailed exposition. 'I'd say there were two assailants.' This statement captures her attention.

'Two?'

'You see, the blow to the back of the head was executed by a left-handed individual whilst the cluster of blows to the side of the face would indicate someone right-handed. Those blows were delivered from the front, by someone who was facing the victim. They're located in this area,' he circles his finger around the victim's left temple.

'So that'd be someone right handed. Even if they held the branch with both hands, they'd swing it this way,' Gillian demonstrates, holding an imaginary branch in her hands and taking a swing at the corpse.

'Yes, exactly. Whilst the blow to the back of the head caught the skull from this side,' Almond turns the head to show Gillian the wound.

'A left-hander,' Gillian concludes. 'Two different people... Same branch?'

'Probably. Though there could be two branches. Interestingly, though, the left-handed assailant hit the victim just once. It is the right-hander who went berserk.'

'OK. Thanks, Michael.' Gillian now has something to go on.

'Don't go away yet. There's something you need to know: about the victim's state of undress.'

'The missing trousers?'

'His trousers and shoes are missing, yes. I think the underpants were there, buried with him. Sort of – tangled around his ankles. The intriguing thing is that he was caught... hmm,' Almond smirks under his enormous moustache, 'In the act.'

'You mean he was having sex when he was attacked?'

'Right in the middle of it, I'd say.'

'Consensual?'

'On his part, yes. A decent erection by any man's standards.'

'Any defensive wounds to indicate -'

'A few scratches around the neck area. I've sent samples for DNA testing. We'll see what comes back.'

# XXX

Even though Gillian doesn't like being ordered around and told what to do, she has to agree with Philip Weston-Jones that the homeless people in Sexton's Wood are the most likely candidates for suspects. It looks like a group effort: at least two of them acted in cohort. There is a colourful assembly of misfits to choose from in the camp, so Gillian heads for the wood to carry out a reconnaissance. Erin comes along.

Reluctant to pay yet another visit at the Weston Estate, which is just a short distance walk from the wood, they park their car in a lay-by on the Sexton's Canning side, and go on foot, taking the much longer but pleasant footpath favoured by dog walkers and bird watchers. By a wooden bench dedicated to the memory of *Gloria Proust, beloved mother and wife*, they swerve off the path and head towards Sexton's Wood which looms before them forbidding and motionless a few hundred yards away. It is only four thirty, but this close to the winter solstice, the night has already begun its descent. The greyness of the landscape thickens with every minute.

'We'll have to tread carefully,' Gillian instructs Erin. 'We don't want to scare them off. You know how they are: here today, gone tomorrow. If any of them have something to hide, they'll up and go in a blink of an eye, and we won't track them down. They leave no traces behind, the homeless: no paper trail, no forwarding address -zilch.'

'How much should we tell them?'

'Only that we found a body, whose body it is, that it's been in the ground for a week or so… We'll ask if anyone saw anything, heard anything, came across any strangers in the wood. Treat them politely, Erin, and make them feel more like witnesses than potential suspects. That's all they are at the moment.'

'They won't be inclined to cooperate with the police in whatever capacity. Even if they saw something-'

'I know. Even if they know something, they won't be telling us in a hurry.'

'It's a bit of a wild goose chase, isn't it?'

'Not quite. I want to get the general vibe, you see what I mean?'

Erin frowns.

'Well, I'm relying on their… how should I put it? Their sense of community. If one of them has done the deed, then others would know. And they'd be in on it – you know, helping their mate. They would've helped bury the body. There'll be something in the air – a sense of something…'

'What?'

'I'll tell you when I find it.'

'If you find it.'

'It's perfectly possible this whole thing has nothing to do with them. We can't point fingers just because they're homeless, they smell, and have bad dress sense.'

'But they do have a motive. Weston-Jones was doing his best to get them evicted.'

'Yes, and we can't ignore facts. They have the motive, the means and the opportunity – the crime was committed right on their doorstep... But we don't yet have the evidence that any of them was involved.'

'Shouldn't we wait for it?'

'And let them all disperse into the night? They must know by now that we've found the body. This is why we must talk to them now – to get the vibe.'

Erin smiles under her breath at Gillian's strictly textbook detection methods. 'The vibe, yes.'

Gillian doesn't pick on the sarcasm in Erin's tone. 'We go in, we chat to them nicely and ask for witnesses... They'll tell us they saw and heard nothing. We'll go away, and that's when they may lower their guard. They'll be thinking: *the cops've been, sniffed around, found nothing, they got nothing on us – we're off the hook.* They're lulled into a false sense of security, and that's when we've got them where we want them.'

'Where does that lead us though?'

'Hopefully Forensics will come up with foreign DNA on the body. We'll go back and ask them for samples for elimination purposes, and all that. That's when they'll start panicking, but it'll be too late to run by then.'

The vibe isn't there. A jolly and carefree motley crew of familiar faces is going about their business of being idle and not giving a toss about the world at large. There isn't a welcoming committee on hand either – the police detectives' arrival is hardly noticed. The fire in the centre is crackling merrily, keeping the inhabitants' bones dry and warm. It is almost an idyllic scene. Six of them are there – it seems the whole lot of them are having a little get together – a veritable afternoon tea with scones, cream, and strawberry jam. If not a cream tea then at least beer cans are circulating, and for some a mug of steaming coffee, it appears. The stocky, happy woman is there, next to her scruffy companion who last time mocked Gillian about the livestock missing from the estate. The skin-and-bone bloke is puffing on a joint, and the short, wiry one in his fur-trimmed gilet, his hood over his head, is blowing steam off his tin mug; the lofty Izzie is there of course, as well as the man with his own vernacular, which is filled with words so convoluted in some obscure regional dialect that Gillian has no hope of interviewing him without an interpreter. When it comes to it. If it comes to it.

Gillian squats in front of the fire, next to Izzie. She has come to regard Izzie as almost a friend after their brief conversation on the hill two weeks ago. Erin wanders around the camp, unhindered and unchallenged. No-one cares. No-one has anything to hide. The vibe of guilt and reckoning isn't here at all.

'So what's the fuss all about?' Izzie asks.

'We found a body.'

'Told ya, Ron!' the stocky woman prods the skinny man with her beer can, 'Told ya it were a stiff in da! Ye owe me a fiver.'

The skinny man sniggers. 'Search me!'

'So who is it?' Izzie inquires.

'Joshua Weston-Jones. Your neighbour.' Gillian watches Izzie's reaction to that, but there isn't much to go on.

She shrugs. 'Can't say I'm sorry to hear it. He was a pig of a man.'

'Fuckin' bastard, he were!' the stocky woman concurs.

'Still, he was murdered, buried in a shallow grave, and we need to find out who did it,' Gillian points out, amiably.

'Search me!' the man called Ron repeats both the phrase and his toothless snigger.

The one with the indecipherable accent adds something, which makes them all laugh. Ron salutes with his beer can, 'Chin-chin!'

'What's yer friend sniffing for? She got a warrant, or some'in?' the stocky woman demands to know all of a sudden. Still, Gillian knows, the woman's unease does not amount to an admission of guilt.

'She's just looking around,' she says.

'Ye tell her not to touch anythin' what's not hers.'

'We're hoping you could help us with our inquiries. You know this wood inside out – you'd notice anything odd, any strangers wandering about…'

'Yes, we would, but haven't. You'd better ask them on the Estate. They've got many more visitors than we do,' Izzie says exactly what Gillian expected to hear.

'We will.'

'Good. Ye ain't hangin' this one on us!'

'I never said -'

'But ye was thinkin' just that!'

The fire is dying, but no one gets up to add any logs. The dark and the cold creep in to fill the vacuum. Gillian shivers. Erin is also back by the fire. She shakes her head – she's found nothing of interest.

'We'd better be going,' Gillian gets up.

'Good riddance!' Ron sniggers.

'If you think of anything…'

'We still have your number handy,' Izzie tells her. 'By the way, put your torch on – we've set up snares in the undergrowth. Rabbit traps, mainly. Better watch where you step.'

Gillian and Erin thank her for the tip, and take off, torches blazing.

They are halfway back to the car, the bench in memory of Gloria Proust within sight, when it hits Gillian: the man in the fur-trimmed gilet! Yes, he was familiar. Yes she knows him. She recognised the gilet, though perhaps without the oversized cargo trousers and the backpack, without seeing his face, which he hid behind the steaming mug, without looking into those narrow, hooded eyes – she didn't realise it was HIM.

Could it be?

She stops. Erin looks at her, baffled. 'What is it?'

Gillian can't be certain, but she can't take any chances. What if it is HIM? What if she has just let him slip away for the second time?

'That man, drinking coffee, with a hood on…'

'What about him?'

'He didn't say a word.'

'OK… so he didn't. Does that make him a suspect?'

'I think I know him. I think he's the bomber… I just need to look him in the eye. We need to go back, before he disappears into thin air…'

'Are you sure?'

'That's what I'm saying – I am not! But I must go back.'

Gillian has to think fast. He didn't expect to run into her – the only person alive who knows his face. The clever bastard, he hid in plain sight: amongst the homeless, sitting there by the fire, with not a twitch of a muscle. The bastard has nerves of steel. But now, she knows, he will be on his way. She knows he will take no chance of facing her by day. 'Call for backup. Call for Armed Response officers. Now, Erin! Back to the car... Get on the radio... no mobile signal here.'

'What are you doing?'

'Going back. I'm keeping an eye on him till they get here... I want to be sure it's him.'

'You can't go alone!'

'I'm not confronting him, for God's sake! Go and call for fucking backup, DC Macfadyen! Don't just stand there!'

Haji knows letting the woman go was a mistake. It was the gravest mistake he has made, and it may cost him his life. But she is so much like his beloved Svetlana! Fair and petite – one to take care of, to protect. He couldn't hurt a single hair on her head. He still can't.

She didn't recognise him, but she will come back, in broad daylight, and she will know him. She will come back because Haji has made another fatal mistake: saving Izzie from that man, the rapist. He should've known better. This is not Afghanistan where bodies rot away unclaimed and forgotten, where there is nobody to look for them, to bury them, to seek revenge – because everybody is dead, every father, every son, every relative. Whole villages are dead and no one is left to pursue justice. Here, it's a different world. Here, even a rapist and a scoundrel gets to be avenged, so the policewoman will come back and she will bring others with her.

Haji has to make a move before she does.

'I will be going,' he tells his companions.

'What? Goin' where?' Sally blinks at him, baffled.

'You don't want to know. Thank you for your hospitality. All of you.'

Ron salutes him with his beer can, 'Pity, man. Good knowin' ya.' Twitch shakes his head, but then, on second thoughts, he takes a puff of his joint and looks away, gazing blankly into space. Tomorrow, he will swear he's never known anyone called Sandman.

'You've got nowhere to go,' Izzie tells Haji. She already knows him too well. The more reason for Haji to leave now.

'I'm not going anywhere. I am just going away from here. It's better for you. The police – I don't like the police.'

'Who does! Pigs!' Ron chucks an empty can into the fire. The remnants of alcohol burst into a bright blue flame as they spill out of it.

'OK, you're right,' Izzie agrees. 'They'll be back. They won't give up. Let's go – I'll take you somewhere where you can lie low for a while, until the dust settles. We both need to go.'

She is right. He wouldn't want her to tag along with him, not ordinarily, but this is her turf – she knows her way around here. Haji is feeling in the dark like a blind man. He will let her lead him. If there is anyone he can trust, it is Izzie. She, too, has to run. They'll run together.

'We must go now,' he says. 'We get our things and go.' He gets up. His few precious belongings are in the den, buried under his sleeping mat.

'The police are on their way. You aren't going anywhere. It's over.' The voice of the policewoman comes from the darkness, outside the reach of the campfire light. Haji freezes, and waits. The policewoman enters the circle of light. She is talking slowly and softly, lulling him into resignation, and then surrender. He knows precisely what she is doing. She is buying time, enough time for her backup to arrive. But they are not here yet, and she is not armed. Not like the last time. She has nothing to bargain with. But Haji does.

Fast as a desert snake, he pulls out his knife, grabs Ron by the scruff of his neck and lifts his scrawny person up, like a shield. He presses the blade of his knife to Ron's throat. Ron curses and tries to wriggle out of Haji's grasp, only hurting himself in the process. 'Fuck! I'm bleeding,' he squeals. 'What ya doin', Sandman!'

'Stay still,' Haji tightens his grip on Ron and presses the blade harder against his skin. 'Come here slowly,' he instructs the policewoman, 'Lie down on the ground, face down. Or he dies, and I come for you.'

Ron squirms and whimpers, 'I don't wanna die!' He cries like a baby.

Twitch springs to his feet and charges at Haji across the smouldering fire – a raging bull. He hurtles towards him, shouting unintelligible insults, or threats. Haji has no choice. In fact, no conscious thought enters his mind. He simply removes the knife from Ron's throat, points it at Twitch and lets the man impale himself on it. Twitch's eyes bulge in disbelief as his face levels with Haji's and blood gurgles out of his mouth. Haji twists the knife for good measure, and pulls it out of Twitch's chest, letting the man slump to the ground. Twitch falls backwards, into the campfire, sending sparks and a firework of ashes into the air; the fire feeds on the newly received fuel.

Haji swiftly returns the blade of his knife to Ron's throat and nods to the policewoman to take no more chances. He means what he says – she should know that by now. He let her go once. He won't make that mistake again. He wants her to lie down, face to the ground so he won't have to look into her eyes when he is killing her – he won't have to look into her eyes and see Svetlana. 'Get down!'

The clink of the skewer being pulled out of the spit-roast right behind him doesn't have the time to penetrate his mind, but the skewer takes only a second to penetrate his back and travel through his heart, emerging on the other side – just the tip of it, the sharp end protruding out of his chest as he gapes at it without comprehension. He can feel Izzie's closeness behind him and can smell her scent briefly, before he drops to his knees. She catches him just in time and lowers him gently to the ground. Her hands are bathed in his blood. She is crying, saying something to him, something he can no longer hear, but he knows – she is saying sorry.

He shouldn't have killed Twitch. He shouldn't have put a knife to Ron's throat. Mistakes have piled up – he can't unravel them. Not enough time before he dies.

Haji smiles at Izzie. He feels like smiling. He is dying in the arms of a woman who cares for him. She is crying for him. What better ending could he wish for? 'I'm sorry, so sorry, Sandman…'

'Don't be,' he says, 'It's nothing,' but the words are only formed in his mind, not on his lips. So she can't hear him. No one can. He has always been a man of few words – those few last words won't make any difference. Haji has nothing else to add.

266

# XXXI

The abbey is packed to the brim: the regular parishioners have never seen such crowds, not even at Christmas. And though it is almost Christmas, this congregation has nothing to do with the new-born King. In fact, this has nothing to do with birth, and everything to do with death. It is the memorial service for the victims of the Sexton's bombing. The Nativity scene and the few festive touches of baubles and lights clash with the twelve coffins lined along the main aisle – memory capsules of twelve lives extinguished. Their names and ages are read out. No one mentions the three dead who are behind the massacre: Haji, Malik, and Ahmed. They are not to be remembered. They must be left outside the abbey – there is no admission for them. Though they will receive forgiveness, as thou shall forgive those who sinned against thou, their names will not be spoken. Not in the same breath as the names of the innocents.

Gillian is sitting next to her daughter, taking comfort from her closeness. Tara's fingers are entwined with Charlie's, resting in his lap. He has insisted on coming to the service – to see his friends off. Tears are rolling down his cheeks. He clings on to Tara's hands, both of them hijacked away from Gillian. She doesn't mind. His parents, Jerry and Theresa, are also excluded from this intimacy. At least, they have each other. And they have their son, alive. Unlike Rhys's family. Unlike Sasha.

Sasha is holding on to her mother's arm. Clinging onto it. Poor Grace tries her best to offer comfort and to steady the sobs that shake Sasha's body. The girl was to be a bride only a couple of days from now. It is not to be. How do you explain to her why that is? Nathaniel gazes at her, a helpless father who has no answers for his child. He could not protect her from this pain – he didn't see it coming.

A slight woman with a girl of six, maybe seven years old sits in the same row. Both the woman and the girl are dressed in black. The girl acts older than her years as she purses her lips tight, determined not to cry when her father's name is read out. Its pronunciation is distorted by the priest – it is foreign and difficult to say, but the girl knows that's her dad: 'Andrzej Sokolowski, thirty-five…'

Gillian thinks she recognises an elderly lady with copper red hair, wearing a red summer dress under her unbuttoned coat. She is sitting with a young man to her left. Gillian knows her from the hospital – she saw her on a few occasions when visiting Charlie. The young man, in his thirties, has his arm in a cast and a dressing on his part-shaven head – he must have been on that train, and survived. Someone else in that family did not.

As the congregation sings the last hymn, Gillian hears the lady say, 'Oh, Harry, why did you bring me here? You know how I hate funerals.' There is a disquiet in the woman's voice, which sounds fragile as it vibrates above the low notes of the hymn.

The young man gazes at the lady and smiles ruefully. 'It's Dad's funeral, Mum.'

'I don't like it, Harald. Let's go home.'

'William, Mum, not Harald… It's Will,' he sighs. 'It doesn't matter. Let's go home.' He has given in to her. He takes her arm and hooks it over his, patting her hand affably, and leads her towards the exit. She leans towards him, rests her head on his shoulder. They are the first ones to leave the church.

As soon as the hymn is sung and its last note fades away, everyone else follows suit. It is slow-going; reporters from various local and national TV stations are gathered outside, filming the event, catching mourners and asking for interviews. They have laid siege to the abbey. A traffic jam forms outside the churchyard.

Like many others, Gillian is in no hurry to leave. The last thing she wants is for her face to be plastered all over the newspapers. Isabella Butler feels the same way. Celebrated across the land for killing the infamous Sexton's Bomber, all she wants is privacy – with her family: her mother and her son. The vicar has approached them to suggest a back-door escape route, 'If you follow me, Miss Butler, I'll show you out through the vestry. When you're ready, of course… There's no rush.'

'Thank you, Father,' Izzie nods and smiles. She is so polished, so polite… Dressed immaculately in an elegant long coat, her hair trimmed and beautifully styled, she is only a faint echo of her former self. Alongside her homeless garb, she has also shed her blunt mannerisms and coarse language. The woman who had returned into the lap of her family after years of dead silence… Gillian watches her from the corner of her eye and ponders the miracle. She hears her reply to the vicar, 'That'd be great, Father. If you just give me a minute. I need to have a quick word with DI Marsh over there.'

That surprises Gillian. She was sure Izzie – Isabella Butler – was done talking to her and talking to the police, and in particular to Gillian altogether. She had made it clear that she wanted to put it all behind her as soon as all the paperwork was done, as soon as the CPS confirmed that she had acted out of necessity and had no case to answer in the court of law.

Gillian turns to Tara. 'You go ahead. I'll follow in a minute.'

'Work?' Tara can see Izzie approaching, with Tommy in tow.

'Not sure. I won't be long.'

'You always say that.' Tara manoeuvres Charlie in his wheelchair to face the door. 'We'll go with Jerry and Theresa. I'll see you at home. Remember Dad's coming for dinner.'

'Yes, I know.'

They join the now diminishing queue towards the exit.

Gillian smiles at Tommy, 'Fancy bumping into you again!'

'We came because of Oscar,' he tells her, his face tight and dead serious. 'That's his coffin over there – the first one, with all the medals,' he points out. 'Major Oscar Holt MC! Did you know Oscar was given a Military Cross?'

'No, I didn't. I know he was a soldier.'

'He was. To the end.'

'I'm sorry I couldn't… help him, in time…'

'Don't be stupid! He died a soldier's death, you know! He would've loved that. I knew Oscar well.'

'Go and sit with Nan, Tommy,' Izzie touches his shoulder. 'I want to have a private word with DI Marsh.'

'I can sit quietly with you,' Tommy tries to worm his way into the conversation.

'No. I want to talk to her alone.'

Tommy scowls, drops his shoulders theatrically, and stomps away.

'How are you getting on, Izzie?' Gillian tries to sound casual though she realises that Izzie has every reason to hate her. She probably blames Gillian for forcing her hand - for killing Sandman.

'I want you to take this,' Izzie hands her a plastic pouch. 'Sandman's things, papers... I found it buried under his bed when we cleared things away. You need to have it. His name was Haji Mahsud...'

'OK, thanks. I'll pass it on. It's not my case.'

'But the killing of Weston-Jones is, isn't it?'

'That's closed now. We found his – Haji's – DNA on the clothes discarded in the grave. He is our killer. One more body to the count of many on his conscience won't make much difference to him.' Gillian says that to warn Izzie away from confessing. She has realised a while back that Haji Mahsud had dealt only the first blow, that it was the woman whom Weston-Jones had been raping who had finished the job - Izzie. The ferocity of the blows to his face and head confirmed that in her mind. She just chose not to pursue this line of inquiry. What good would it do to bury Isabella Butler all over again? She has only just been returned to her child and her mother. After ten years of self-imposed exile. What good would it achieve to put her through a trial for manslaughter?

But Izzie clearly disagrees. 'Not quite. I've been battling with this for days... I need to tell you this...' she hesitates and steals a furtive glance at Tommy, who waves to her, beaming. She turns to Gillian, 'That man – Weston-Jones – he.... He was a... What he's done – he'd do it again... I had to stop him! I -'

She swallows a gasp and, at that, Gillian steps in – to stop her. 'Don't. Don't say another word. I'm not here to hear it. I cannot hear it. Do you understand?' She grabs her by her shoulders and forces her to look back at her family, 'You can't do this to them, not again. Go back to your son and your mother. You've nothing to say to me. The case is solved. Go!' she pushes her away, and Izzie starts walking. She picks up Tommy's hand when he extends it to her, his other hand firmly locked in his grandmother's. They are leaving the church accompanied by the vicar who leads them towards the vestry.

'Thanks for these!' Gillian shouts after them, waving the plastic pouch. She has no regrets about letting Izzie go, though letting her go amounts to a dereliction of duty. It is her duty to uphold the law, but the law and justice aren't one and the same thing. Sometimes, like in this case, they even clash. On this occasion, justice has prevailed over the letter of the law. Gillian will have to live with it.

She goes through the contents of the pouch in her car. There are documents, money. There is a letter written in a foreign language, but the writing doesn't look Arabic, as Gillian would expect it to look, but more like the Russian alphabet. Then again, she isn't a language expert. They will work it out when she hands it in.

The most unexpected are the drawings: images of buildings, bridges and canals – probably Venice; a couple of mountainous landscapes; and finally, the portraits. Gillian recognises the faces: Izzie, her gaze distant and haunted, her long dark hair coiled around her neck; the man Izzie has saved, Ron – his portrait unfinished, but despite that his character is captured by just the few basic strokes of the pencil. There is another face – the paper is old and yellowed, and the lines are faded. It must've been done many years ago. It is a face of a woman with fair hair, bright eyes and smiling lips. On some level, Gillian ponders the possibility briefly that the drawing reminds her of herself. The shape of her face, her nose... She glances into the rear-view mirror, finds herself frowning back, changes her mind and twists the mirror away from her face. No, she imagined it. It's not her. How could it be?

Gillian leans back in her seat, throws her arms over the headrest, and thinks. She will have to take the pouch and its content to the station and sign it in. This is as good an opportunity as any to return the handgun. After all, it too belonged to Haji Mahsud. At last she'll be able to get rid of it. It's been burning a hole in her conscience, sitting there, buried in her back garden, waiting for Corky to dig it up. By returning it alongside the pouch she won't have to explain how she came into its possession. The unspoken assumption will be that the gun was hidden in the pouch and both were handed in together.

Gillian starts the engine, her mind made up. This is the second time today that she will bend the letter of the law. She mustn't make a habit of it. She is an officer of the law! Though, having said that, she is not sure for how much longer. Right now, she can't be bothered with upholding the law. It isn't like her to give up, but the way she feels now she couldn't care less about trying to wrestle that Hornby case away from Grayson. She will let him get on with it. Fingers crossed, he will fail.

# XXXII

On Monday morning, Gillian finds the translation of the letter found in the Sexton's Bomber's pouch, courtesy of Jon Riley. Jon has also left an enigmatic post-it note stuck to the letter: *They found her in Moscow. She hasn't changed her mind. Doesn't want her son to know. You owe me – Jon xx*

Gillian scans the letter – a window into a mass killer's life. The letter reads:

*Haji,*

*I gave birth to a son. He was born on 28th October 1986, at 4:05 in the morning. I named him Igor. He has a mane of black hair on his head and a heart-warming smile. He is beautiful, and maybe he even has your eyes, but make no mistake - he is MINE.*

*I will bring him up to be a good Russian. He will be a patriot. He will never learn who and what his father is. One day, he may even come to Pandsher Valley to get you and your kind.*

*I have learned about the massacre of the Russian troops in the tunnel that night when you came home with the crack of dawn, bathed in their blood. They were young boys there, some as young as eighteen. They were only guarding a convoy, seeking no confrontation with you. But you trapped them with no way out from that tunnel of death, and blew them up to heavens high, and you cut the throats of those who survived so that they could not speak against you. But the truth has come out. The truth casts longer shadow than your lies. And now I know you. I know who you REALLY are. And I despise you.*

*Do not try to find me or my son. Do not come near us. You are dead to me and to Igor.*

*Svetlana Pavlova*

## THE END

# SWIMMING WITH SHARKS
## Anna Legat

Just when things seem to be going right for Nicola Eagles, she disappears without a trace. Was it a voluntary disappearance, or was she abducted – or murdered?

DI Gillian Marsh is a good detective but as she delves deeper into the case, she realises that she may be out of her depth, because Nicola's disappearance is just the beginning…

# NOTHING TO LOSE
## Anna Legat

After a head-on collision resulting in four deaths and a fifth person fighting for his life, DI Gillian Marsh is sent to investigate.

Nothing seems to add up. How did four capable drivers end up dead on a quiet, peaceful country road?

As Gillian unpicks the victims' stories, she edges closer to the truth. But will she be able to face her own truth and help her daughter before it's too late?

# THICKER THAN BLOOD
## Anna Legat

After a head-on collision resulting in four deaths and a fifth person fighting for his life, DI Gillian Marsh is sent to investigate.

Nothing seems to add up. How did four capable drivers end up dead on a quiet, peaceful country road?

As Gillian unpicks the victims' stories, she edges closer to the truth. But will she be able to face her own truth and help her daughter before it's too late?